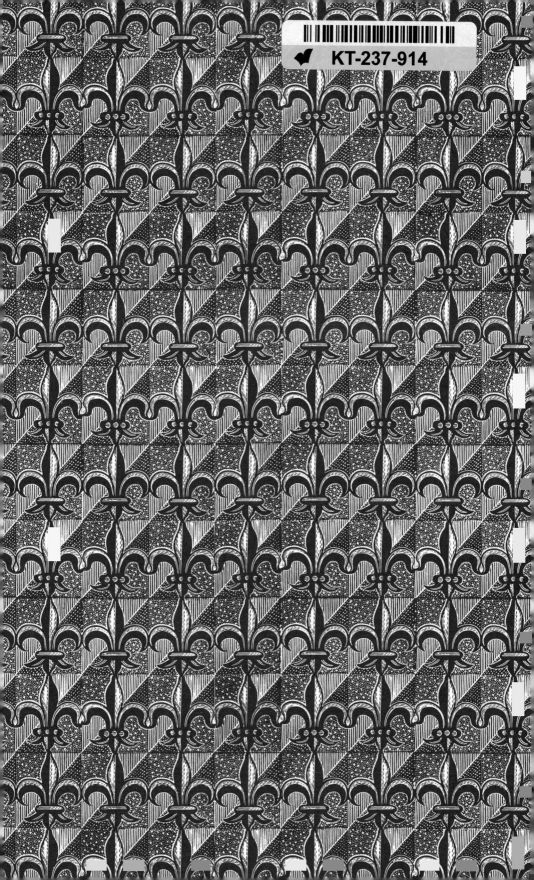

# A
# Solitary
# Grief

OTHER NOVELS BY BERNICE RUBENS:

*Birds of Passage*
*Brothers*
*The Elected Member* (Booker Prize winner)
*A Five Year Sentence* (Runner up for Booker Prize)
*Go Tell the Lemming*
*I Sent a Letter to my Love*
*Kingdom Come*
*Madame Sousatzka*
*Mate In Three*
*Mr Wakefield's Crusade*
*Our Father* (Winner of the Welsh Arts Council Prize)
*The Ponsonby Post*
*Set on Edge*
*Spring Sonata*
*Sunday Best*

# A
# SOLITARY
# GRIEF

## BERNICE RUBENS

SINCLAIR-STEVENSON

First published in Great Britain by
Sinclair-Stevenson Limited
7/8 Kendrick Mews
London SW7 3HG, England

British Library Cataloguing in Publication Data
A CIP catalogue record for this book is available from the British Library.
ISBN: 1 85619 057 9

Typeset by Selectmove Ltd, London
Printed and bound in Great Britain by
Clays Ltd

FOR
ROBERT LILLEY

'Cover her face; mine eyes dazzle:
    she died young.'

The Duchess of Malfi.

# One

ALISTAIR CROWN carried flowers *out* of the cemetery. He was that sort of person. He'd walked past it
on his way to the hospital. Why not? he thought. A small
detour amongst the graves would serve his purpose.
After all, it wasn't every day his wife gave birth to their
first child. Flowers were in order. He always did the
right thing, did Alistair, but never without being aware
of it. His 'right thing' was premeditated, performed and,
afterwards, smugly relished.

He carried the flowers furtively, as if embarrassed by
them. Not for their provenance – their source would
in no way disturb him – but for their untidiness and
lack of symmetry. For Alistair was a punctilious man
and needed order in all things. The lack of any kind
of wrapping disturbed him and he resolved, should
he have need for flowers at any other time, that he
would bring along his own paper. The bunch, though
irregular, was vibrant and varied. Alistair had chosen
his swag with care. He had given a wide berth to white
lilies, those sure indications of where he had been.
But the red roses could have come from anywhere,
as could the cornflowers. He'd been tempted by the
dahlias because of their bright colours, but, alas, they
were rooted around the graves and the clinging earth
about their stems would have been a right give-away.

As he walked, he shamelessly discarded the sundry
cards attached to the tributes. Behind him he left an
indifferent trail of black-framed *Ever in our hearts*,
*farewell*s. Alistair was not a superstitious man, else

1

he might have thought twice about looting a valley of death for the purposes of celebrating a new life. He tore off the last greeting card. *Bertie, we loved you. Mum and Dad*, he read. Well, Bertie would never have seen that, Alistair thought, and if Mum and Dad hadn't made their love clear in Bertie's lifetime, there was little point in showering it now on a deaf ear and a blind eye. Alistair thought in these terms because he was a psychiatrist and, as such, he knew a thing or two about family relationships. And now he was eager to put his ideas into practice. Because he himself was about to become a family man.

They'd phoned him from the hospital early that morning. His wife had borne him a girl, they'd said. He'd been gratified by their style of announcement. His wife had borne a girl for *him*. But he was none too happy about the gender. If his wife had indeed borne a child for him, she might at least have borne him what he wanted. Sometimes he disliked his wife a little. But I shall act like a gentleman, he said to himself as he walked. 'Gentleman' was what Alistair thought himself to be. It was a label to which he attached the utmost importance. Being a gentleman meant much more than mere courtesy. The label lay as much in what one didn't say as in what one did; in what actions one refrained from, as much as in what gesture was made. The quality of 'gentlemanness' was as much negative as positive. In this case, Alistair would refrain. He would hold his tongue. He would kiss his wife's forehead, hand over his flowers and request permission to view his daughter.

He realised then that no name had been envisaged for such an issue. As far as he had been concerned during his wife's pregnancy, the final choice lay between George and James. As a psychiatrist who knew everything about everything, he was aware that the correct appellation would give his son a good start in life. There were no sullied undertones in the names he had chosen. They were solidly English and undeniably regal. No hidden meanings could be read between their letters and their sounds were open to no variation, nor merited a nudge or a wink. A man with a name like George or James knew where he stood, and had known since his infancy. Alistair was convinced that identity problems in later life stemmed from the nature of baptism and that, if holy water had been sprinkled on the name of Peregrine or Fyodor, it would be downhill for the child all the way. He shuddered. Fyodor had been his wife's choice. During her pregnancy, she had become hooked on the Russian novel. He didn't object to that. That was all very well in its proper place. But he wasn't having it brought into his own home. After his outright rejection of Kyrillov, his wife had left the choice in his own capable hands, but those hands had never encompassed the possibility of a girl-child. Now he was reluctant to give it much thought, for in his heart he knew that, for a girl, any name would do.

He stopped at a tobacconist's. He needed to buy cigarettes. He anticipated a certain edginess in his initial encounter with his wife. Overnight she had assumed maternal status and she could not help but be changed by it. This would surely affect her attitude towards him. She would perhaps give off a hostile hint of superiority, but he would counter that with a reminder of how sorely she had disappointed him in the matter of the child's gender. He could do that and still remain the gentleman, as long as he did it in a whisper. Indeed, such a tone would underline his decency. Nevertheless, he would need some cigarettes. Smoking would give him something to do with his hands. He hoped that the baby would not be at her breast. What he had to say to his wife was private and whatever passed between them, either of loving or loathing, was

3

not for eavesdropping. He hoped she would have had the sense to put it away in time for his arrival.

He paid for the cigarettes and, on his way out of the shop, he picked up a copy of a give-away news sheet. With it, he wrapped the flowers and, holding them before him like an offering, he approached the hospital gates.

It was a National Health hospital, though the top floor was given over to private care. As the wife of a doctor, and of one who gave weekly service to the hospital's psychiatric department, Virginia was entitled to private care.

Alistair took the lift to the top floor. As the doors opened, he saw a nurse loitering in the reception area. He sensed that she was waiting for him. She smiled. 'Dr Crown?' she said, knowing it was he. Sister had adequately described him. 'Sister would like a word with you,' she said. She sounded nervous. Though not the bearer of bad news, she was about to lead him to its source, and the bearer of the bearer has an equally hard time.

At that moment, Sister Thomas appeared in reception, and the good nurse, her duty done, took to her sensible heels and fled.

'Could you come in a minute, Doctor?' Sister Thomas said. She led the way to her office.

Alistair wondered why she wished to waylay him. Perhaps she wanted to offer a vase for his flowers. He'd come across her from time to time and she was known to be pernickety about such things. He didn't like Sister Thomas very much. Occasionally he was called to her ward to attend a case of severe post-natal depression. Although he did not practise a pull-yourself-together therapy, he was often tempted by this method, especially where women were concerned. He had little support from Sister Thomas who knew that depression was real and no attention-getting device.

4

He sat in the chair she offered him.

'I don't know quite how to say this, Dr Crown,' she said.

Her Welsh accent grated on his ear. It was coarse, unladylike. Moreover, he sensed a trouble of sorts. Perhaps she wanted to move Virginia into a public ward.

'What is it, Sister?' he said with some irritation.

'Your wife is well,' she said, not looking at him. 'The baby is . . . er . . .'

'Is what, for God's sake?'

She raised her eyes to him. 'The baby has Down's Syndrome,' she said.

She saw the streak of rage light his cheek, and she knew that his bowels were melting.

'Rubbish,' he almost shouted. 'That's not possible.'

In her time, Sister had heard those words before, and all their sad sub-titlings. Especially in the old days when such a condition was unpredictable and therefore of more frequent occurrence. The terminology had changed too. In the old days, she would have said, 'The child is a Mongol.' But now they'd invented a more respectable term. But howsoever it was called, it always elicited the same response. Anger and abject disbelief.

'It's nobody fault, Dr Crown,' she added, for she knew the sparks of his fury. Blame, guilt, and a feverish shrinking of self-esteem.

'You've made a mistake,' Alistair said again. He gripped the corners of her desk. He could well have struck her, as any man would have countered such an assumed slight on his virility. He was trembling.

Sister Thomas put a hand on his arm. 'They're very affectionate children,' she said. 'She will bring you much joy.' As she had said many times before, omitting any reference to the heartache and the crying in the dark. Some fathers took it better than others. 'We'll try again,' was the most healthy response. But

5

she knew the likes of Dr Alistair Crown. He would need a lifetime to forgive what he was convinced must be his wife's diseased womb. He would not give her a second chance. Not the likes of Dr Crown. For that is how he read his calamity. He had to, else blame himself.

'Does my wife know?' he asked.

'We told her right away. She told me she was frightened of what you would say. No-one is to blame, Dr Crown,' Sister Thomas said again. If you had to say it even once, there was no point in saying it a hundred times. Scapegoating was part of some people's survival kit, and she knew that Dr Crown came into that category.

'Would you like to see the child?' she asked.

'No.' His response was immediate. 'I never want to see it,' he said. 'We must arrange for its adoption. Immediately.'

'I'm afraid that won't be . . . er . . . easy,' Sister Thomas said as gently as she could, though in her heart she had begun to dislike this man. 'Down's Syndrome children are . . .'

'Why don't you call a spade a spade?' he shouted at her. 'Spare me the fancy words. The thing's a Mongol. I want to be rid of it.'

'Adoption will be difficult.' Sister Thomas took her hand from his arm. 'Perhaps you should see your wife now,' she said.

His grip loosened on her desk and he covered his face with his hands. His shoulders heaved with sobbing. Sister Thomas put her arm round his back. At last the man had become human.

'I'll send for a cup of tea,' she said.

A cup of tea wouldn't cure Down's Syndrome but it would go a little way to making it acceptable. She held his hand while they waited. It was limp in her grasp. She shoved a tissue into his other hand, but, though he accepted it, he made no effort to wipe away

6

his tears. He was sobbing audibly now. And without shame. When Sister Thomas had taken his hand, he had allowed himself to become a child again. And as a child, he was freed of the need to impress. His sense of insecurity had taken root, but had not yet flowered. He felt comfortable inside himself. Sister Thomas's hand gave him a maternal licence for his weeping. Slowly his fingers closed onto hers. He deeply wanted to rest his head on her ample bosom. For in such a state he would be time-frozen, where no future sorrow threatened. As he responded to her hand-grasp, Sister Thomas took him in her arms and let him rinse her bib with his tears.

'What am I going to say to my wife?' Alistair mumbled.

'Hold her as I'm holding you,' she said.

The tea came and she disentangled herself. 'Drink it while it's hot,' she said. 'There's a good boy. I'll tell your wife you're here.'

Alistair's eyes slowly focused on the oak-grain of Sister's desk. He raised his head and followed with his eyes the spindly wood-sap as it spread, capillary-like, from the dark brown mother-vein. He traced its courses and its inevitability astonished him. He stroked it with reverence. Then, lifting the tea cup, he noticed how his hand trembled. He replaced it in the saucer. He viewed the cooling liquid as if from a great height, and it seemed to him to bear the face of Mars. The milk appeared to have separated, rising to the surface, and tiny globules of fat floated insolently to the rim of the cup. Quickly he gulped it down. He was frightened of where this sudden acute awareness would lead him. Frightened, above all, that it would lead to forgiveness. He willed his anger to return. He waited, stiffening. Then his fever returned, and he rose from his seat, grabbed the flowers, and fuelled his feet of fury to his wife's room.

He met Sister Thomas in the corridor.

7

'She's ready for you,' she said, touching his arm.

He wanted to ask her to stay with him. To protect him. He was not sure from what. Perhaps he needed someone to stay his hand from his wife's throat. Or someone who would seal his lips from kisses. But most of all, someone who would blind him to that thing that Virginia had borne. He hurried down the corridor. He would not hesitate at the door. He would give no time nor space for his heels to cool. He would make straightway for the bed, and there, panting, and with infinite relief, he would detonate.

Virginia was propped up against the pillows, her pale face suffused in the blackmail of frailty. And God help him, she was holding the thing in her arms.

He faltered. Outflanked on both sides, he didn't know where to attack first. Then he realised that the enemy was one. His knees were melting and the distance to the bed seemed a continent's width. Far enough, he feared, to drain his anger. Stiffening each limb, he goose-stepped towards her. He held the flowers as a shield, then raised the bunch to his eyes. Whatever it was that Virginia was holding to her breast would not be viewed in its totality. He had in mind an instalment plan. Starting with the feet. You couldn't see Down's Syndrome in the feet. Or legs, thighs, belly or shoulders. He would be safe with the torso. That terrain alone might inject him with a sense of paternity. But would it be enough to sustain him above shoulder-level? Dare he look into its undeniably illegal eyes, and feel the stirrings of fatherhood? His stomach heaved. He wanted to go away from there, from all that had brought him to this woman and this place. And, even as far back as those careless boyhood days, when he did not know that the sun could cast shadows.

Virginia was smiling at him. Sister Thomas had told her not to be afraid. Even so, her smile was detached from her fluttering heart. She was tempted to hold out

8

the baby as a token. But such a baby was no peace-offering. It was but a scoop of salt on his wound. So she held it close. Her shield against his wrath. For she knew his anger from the central swollen vein on his forehead that would only subside once that anger was spent. She held the baby close and she wondered whether she would have to use that same shield for the rest of her life.

Alistair reached the bed. He would have bent over to kiss her, but the thing was in the way and, in so doing, he could not help but catch sight of it. So he handed over his flowers instead. Unarmed, he looked at Virginia. He managed a smile but the vein on his forehead denied any pleasure. He would have given her words if he could have found them. But where was the language for horror, disbelief and, above all, blame? Even silence was unsafe for it spoke even louder of his paralysed tongue. Hence the smile, that had nothing to do with pleasure, but at least it was something. Thus he feared they would communicate for the rest of their days. Smiles between them but without sun, eclipsed now for ever by that dark shadow in her arms. She dared to hand it over. He took the bundle and its weight was lead. Still he would not look at it.

Virginia watched him.

'She's beautiful,' she managed to say. 'We shall have to decide on a name.'

'A name?' he said.

They were the first words he had spoken. She heard his voice breaking.

'Why?' he whispered. For to give the thing a name was to acknowledge it, was to confirm its being and identity. Without a name, it would perhaps cease to be, and as a first and last act of decency, perhaps, shrivel to nothing in its own anonymity.

'Look at her,' Virginia said. Her voice was suddenly strong. 'She's your daughter.'

9

Alistair turned his face away. Not only did his wife wish to name that which she had borne, she wanted to confirm kinship. No seed of mine, his heart told him, in that private language which he had understood since childhood. The heart-language that thundered his pleasures and soft-pedalled his pain. Now it spoke to him again. No seed of mine, it whispered. Yet he dared not look at it. At its face. Its full frontal. As a doctor he knew that, from its very first moment, there was no mistaking a Down's Syndrome child. An epileptic, an autistic, a defective, a spastic, all these can fool you for months, years even, and then turn round and declare themselves not whole. But a Down's Syndrome child lays its marked cards on the table at its birth. In its guarded look, if you can bear to view it, its message is clear. 'I have arrived to trouble you,' it says. 'I am the earthquake that you must piteously survive. If I'm lucky, I'll manage to break your heart, for under all those shattered pieces, there must be love. But if luck is not on my side, then you will forever pat my head, and, because you cannot hide my face, you will hide your own.'

And Alistair would not look.

He turned his face away and handed the bundle back to Virginia.

'What shall we call her?' Virginia tried again.

A name is only a name, his heart spoke to him. It confirms nothing.

'What d'you think?' he asked her, without tone or interest.

'We could call her Georgia,' she offered. It was near enough to the George he had wanted. 'Or maybe Gemma.' That was the closest she could get to James.

'No,' he said. 'Never.' He would not make do with half-measures. No George or James would have made such a sullied debut.

'What about Frances?' she said. She dared offer him only ambivalent gender.

10

He shrugged, He didn't care any more. 'Call it what you like,' he said. He felt unwell. His stomach heaved, and he rushed to her bathroom.

She heard him throwing his heart up. She held the baby close. She knew the child could not hope for a father. She looked at Alistair's flowers. She marvelled at their variety and was surprised and moved that he had taken such care with their choice. They were all her favourites. She laid the baby on her lap and, as she made a move to separate the bunches, she noticed a card, tied with crunched white ribbon to a bouquet. It was black-edged and crenellated. She read its message. *To darling Doris. Gone but not forgotten. From all at Number 12.*

She heard her husband heave in the bathroom, and in no way could she pity him.

'We'll call her Doris,' she shouted.

If her daughter could be nothing else, her life, at least, and perhaps at most, would be a commemoration.

# Two

TIME, GIVEN time, is a healer. A healer of grief. Grief is loss, and can eventually, somehow or another, be accommodated. But time does little for sorrow. Sorrow does not fade that reliably. It grows by what it feeds on. Doris was a sorrow. She could not help but get bigger. Even Alistair had to accept the fact that Doris would not go away. In the good old pre-antibiotic days, he thought, a Mongol child could be relied upon to die at least before adulthood. But they had to go and make progress in medicine. Now he knew that Doris was his lifelong albatross.

Virginia refused further children, and he did not press her. Both were wary of making another Doris, and this caution blunted appetite. Slowly their double bed became two. Not difficult to divide, because it had been two singles in the first place, with probably just this sort of contingency in mind, though in the furniture shop it had been promoted as a king-size double bed – the salesman had leeringly hinted at the allowance for togetherness and privacy, both of which needs that vast holding could accommodate. The split in the middle was masked by king-size sheets. So, after their wedding, they had gone like royalty to bed. Until the princess was born and the monarchy crumbled.

No, the bed was not difficult to divide. Over a succession of nights, the two sections could have been inched away from each other, while each partner pretended not to notice the growing gap between. No, it wasn't the bed. It was the headboard. That solid indivisible oneness, that throne-support, that innate board of judgement, clinging for its moral life to the constitution. That board could never be detached. Perhaps a simple screwdriver would have solved the problem. But that was too obvious, too noisy, and too crass a production. There would be no way of ignoring it, no way of excusing it, no rationale to offer, other than by acknowledging that which it truly was: the end of an affair.

So, one night, Alistair moved into the guest room, pleading pressure of work, and there he stayed, pressure or not, and the passing of time overcame the need for questioning. Shortly after his move, Virginia herself settled in Doris's room, and out of that bed that had turned so sour. Over the months, the master bedroom of the house turned into a lumber-room, a fitting epitaph on what it had become. A repository for those things too precious to be forgotten, but too guilt-riddled to be thrown away. A place for those things that would one day come in handy, but that never would, for their day had been, and now, in a different context, were as nothing. The limbo-lumber-room, that which had once been a palace.

Meanwhile, Doris grew.

Alistair kept his distance but sometimes, during the night, when no-one else was looking, not even Doris, he would look at her. But not at her face. Never at her face. He would view each other part of her and dwell on its normalcy. But never could he bring himself to raise his eyes to view that rash signature of hers. Not even as she slept, for Alistair knew that, in her unconscious state, she would only have emphasised the earthquake that she was.

Each day Alistair consulted in his consulting rooms, and listened to the endless recitals of pain, no less painful for being moneyed, and sometimes he nodded,

13

or occasionally he raised an eyebrow, the sum total of his communication. Only rarely did he open his mouth, not in summary or opinion, but simply to give access with one word to yet another avenue of despair. He wondered how people could live with such unhappiness, and with such untouchability, all that line of inconsolables who filtered daily through his doors. Often he thanked God he wasn't like them, and only occasionally was disturbed by the thought that, in the ratings of melancholy, there was very little difference between them and himself. But whether or not prompted by the similarity, he resolved, each evening on his way home from his rooms, that he would make a decision as to his future. This resolution comforted him and absolved him from taking it any further and he coasted on it for many months. In any case, a decision would have been far too difficult, for he had only two choices. His professional experience had taught him that, faced with limitless options, decision was facilitated, for it allowed for a change of heart. But in his case, he had the banal option of staying in his marriage or leaving it, and either choice seemed to him to be irreversible. For the Either/Or decision is terminal.

Then Doris, by the simple law of nature, even when that nature is perverse, reached her first birthday, and still Alistair had not been able to look his daughter in the eye. But lately he had taken to not looking at her more frequently and his concentration on every part of her, on each nocturnal visit, every part of her that is, but that which spelt out the earthquake, stirred in him an alien tremor which he could not understand. For want of any other explanation, he ascribed it to paternity.

He liked them, those tremors, he had to admit. They seemed to privilege him as if he, and only he in the whole world, had experienced them. Indeed he convinced himself that those tremors were his

14

invention, in the same way as, many years before, he had translated his first successful self-abuse; and, as with that invention, it was shame that prevented him sharing them with others. And greed, too. And meanness. For one does not easily share the key to the gate of ecstasy. So, on his nightly visits, eager and ashamed, Alistair caressed Doris's body. He started with the feet. An image from a Buñuel film seared his mind, dredged from his unmarried days and his film-buff nights. He would take Doris's little foot in his mouth and suck her big toe with relish. Then another image from the flickering projection room of his bachelorhood, that of Claire's knee, would stir a memory, as he fondled that infant cap, wrinkled with baby-fat and innocence. After the knee, he forswore other images, and fondled upward towards the neck, but with no erotica to prompt or to feed him. Sometimes he would gently cover her face with a sheet, lest his erring eye should light on her signature. This excursion around Doris's body was his nightly and secret worship, so that by the time his daughter reached her first birthday, he was deeply and uncontrollably in love with her. Yet he had never looked upon her face. His resolution to make a decision was no longer a comfort to him. It could no longer pay homage to his conscience, nagged as he was by that imperative love for the headless issue of his loins. He knew that one day he would have to look upon her face. Was his love strong enough to bear that confrontation? He feared that it might fail; but he feared, far more, that it might overcome.

Virginia had grown immune to his paternal indifference. She did not yet know of his nocturnal worship. Over the weeks and months of her first year, Doris had become a simple object of Virginia's loving and her handicap was an irrelevance. But Virginia's parents, who visited far more frequently than Alistair would

15

have wished, went even further with their first grand-child. Not only did they love her, they proclaimed her normal. They viewed any child unaffected by Down's Syndrome as faintly unnatural and they pitied parents who were not compelled to compassion. Alistair felt himself silently assailed on all sides. He felt their pity for him, and could not help but be diminished by it. He knew that no amount of knee-cuddling or toe-sucking, even if he could confess to them, would admit him to their adoring circle. He knew that, sooner or later, he would have to take Doris in his arms and look at her whole.

But, for that, he needed preparation. And in two stages. First his mother-in-law, from whom Virginia had inherited what she presumably had given to Doris. So on each of Priscilla Warner's visits, he sat and stared at her in dumb rehearsal. Perhaps her face was a logical preparation for Doris's, he thought, but in no way could he associate Priscilla with Claire's knee or Buñuel's delectable marble toe. He dared not make further comparison. After a while he switched his attention to Virginia, realising he had not looked at her directly for a very long time. He wondered if she revealed any clues. He was disappointed that she seemed to have inherited little of her mother's appearance, so perhaps that dress rehearsal of his was futile. He realised then that there was no valid preparation he could make for the final and terrifying step in his nightly exploration.

On the morning of Doris's first birthday, he noticed how he avoided his own face in the mirror and how, during the course of that day, he rushed past shop windows in fear of catching his reflection. In no way would he use his *own* face as rehearsal. The child's look took after its mother. Of that he had no doubt. Nevertheless, he removed the mirror from the wall of his

16

consulting rooms, and covered the stained square with an irrelevant map of the London Underground, which a paranoid patient had left behind, his personal guide through the labyrinth of escape routes. The Circle Line was shaded in blood-red. 'That's where they travelled,' his patient had declared. Those pursuers of his, hour after hour of giddying patience, waiting, waiting for him to step into their net. All other Lines were terminal, so he was safe as long as he rode them. And only then. Back and fore, back and fore. But he could be waylaid by sinister train drivers. They were the danger. In the pay of those giddy spiders on the Circle Line. In a suitably greased palm, the steering wheel could veer from a good and honest straight Northern Line onto the tracks of the Circle. No-one was to trusted. He had to be very careful.

'Surely it would be safer to avoid the Tube altogether,' Alistair had suggested in one of his very rare interruptions.

'But I have to live under the ground,' the patient had said. 'I cannot live for long above it.'

And here am I, Alistair thought, as he pinned the map to the wall, wandering in my daughter's netherhood, but to look on her face would entail suffocation.

He had promised Virginia that he would be home early. Such communication as they had was formal, polite and occasionally friendly. But it was a tenuous one and did not allow for the breaking of a promise. So he would make sure that he would home on time, even when that time meant attendance at his daughter's first birthday party. This was to be a public show, with friends, relatives and sundry children, all of them, in Alistair's eyes, spectators, witnesses of his daughter's outsiderness. And his mother-in-law, in her turn, a viewer of the others' aberration. His own parents lived in California where they had gone to settle shortly after Alistair's sister had married an American. They were

17

already grandparents when Doris was born. His sister had delivered twins, both of them viewable from top to toe. They knew that they had a third grandchild. Alistair had told them. He'd filled them in on her weight and her name, but no photograph had accompanied the announcement. And never would, despite their requests. They would visit one day, they told him, but Alistair dared not think about that.

What bothered him now was the party he was to come home early for. His daughter was to be put on show. How could he, so publicly, turn his face away. For in the past year, Virginia, knowing his aversion, had kept Doris out of his sight. How could he now ignore her in front of those friends of his? Especially Gerry Williams. Although Gerry was a close friend, Alistair didn't like him very much. At times he even loathed him. He loathed him for his clients. For in his consulting rooms, one floor below Alistair's in Harley Street, he sorted out the problems of Royalty, minor and discreet it's true, but purple nonetheless. Film stars, and recognisable celebrities, none of whom would dream of making the extra flight of stairs. He hated Gerry because he didn't deserve such clientèle. His psychiatric skills were mediocre, far inferior to his own. But worst of all, he had a little daughter whom he could happily look squarely in the face. Chrissie, they called her, compensation for the Christopher they had wanted. And little Chrissie would be at the party that afternoon.

As he waited for his last patient of the day, Alistair wandered to the window. Below, he caught sight of Gerry, as he folded himself into the passenger seat of his chauffeur-driven car. He was leaving in good time for the party. Alistair hated him. For the first time that day, the thought crossed his mind that he would not go home. At least not until the evening, when his daughter would be in bed and available for his painless exploration. He heard his bell, and he was grateful for a patient to take his mind off his problem for a while. And, moreover, that patient was his lone Tube-traveller.

He greeted him like a lost friend. For fifty minutes, no more, no less, he listened to his traveller's tales, and, though he had heard them all before, and all were the same, for one Tube is very like another, he listened as if hearing them for the first time. He interrupted only very occasionally, hoping that his patient would linger for a while at a station, that he would still himself and experience his stillness, more for his sake than by professional prompting, for although one Line was like another, stations were different and boasted their own character according to their regions. To linger awhile on the graffiti alone would have given some clue as to its provenance. But his client had no time to take in his station surroundings, since he used them only as tunnels for escape and bolt-holes from the terrifying Circle doors.

Thus his patient travelled until his fare-time was exhausted, but, that day, Alistair gave him extra time, loath to be left alone and to face the fulfillment of his promise. At length the patient was exhausted and requested permission to leave, to park himself somewhere, even if it meant above ground. Alistair smiled. He felt that in those last few extra moments, his traveller had made his first tentative and painful steps into what people called the normal world.

He saw him out.

'Happy travelling,' he said, and for a moment, despite the man's perilous journey, he might have changed places with him.

He locked his consulting-room doors and slowly he made his way down the stairs. It was almost 3.30. He'd have to get a cab. He'd promised to be there on time. He dawdled outside the front door. Fearful. He knew he'd have no trouble in finding a taxi. All through the day cabbies dropped their health-seeking fares along

19

the street and pick-up at any moment was guaranteed. As the first cab crawled by with its yellow light of availability, Alistair turned to the front door, checking that it was firmly shut. He lingered there long enough for the taxi to pass by. Then he hurried down the street, his eyes on the pavement.

'Alistair!'

A woman's voice. Familiar, yet heard long ago. He stopped and looked at her.

'Mary!'

'How long is it?' she said. 'Eight . . . ten years?'

'You haven't changed a bit,' Alistair said. Neither did he think so. The shining copper of her hair had not faded. Her curls had seemed to thicken with the years. He gazed at the unnatural green of her eyes that age had in no way legitimised. He stared into them and was stung once again by the pain of losing her so many years ago.

'Have you time for a coffee?' she said. 'We've a lot of catching up to do.'

'Of course,' he said. 'But there's nothing around here. Let's take a cab. I know somewhere near the park. We can sit outside.'

A taxi idled at the lights. He grabbed her hand and they ran for it, and settled, panting and falling together onto the seat.

Then he smelt her, that very distinctive red smell, as special and as tribal as the black, the white and the yellow, and the smell shipped him back into his early manhood and the passion of their long nights and days together. And how they were cut short. And again, the pain of loss. This time I shall never let her go, he thought. They looked at each other. Both knew that their parting must be forgotten. It had to be. And they kissed each other as if it had never been. Neither of them spoke. Alistair broke the silence only to signal directions to the driver and by the time they alighted

20

on the fringe of the park, no words had passed between them.

They settled at a table underneath the awning. They were the only customers.

'A perfect choice,' Mary said after the waitress had brought their order. She looked at him. 'You first,' she said.

'Did you marry Clifford?' he asked. He had to know. It was Clifford who had lured her away.

She nodded.

'Are you still married?'

'Not very much,' she said. 'And you?'

'I'm married,' he reminded himself.

'Children?'

Alistair shook his head without hesitation.

He would have denied offspring even if he had been able to look at his daughter's face. He wanted no extra encumbrances. He caught the time on her wrist. It was after four. They would have lit his daughter's candles. Perhaps even at this moment she was poised to blow them out. Then he saw that face that he had so often in nightmare imagined. He turned away from the puffed-out cheeks, from the eyes that wandered over the bridgeless nose. He shuddered.

'Is anything the matter?' Mary said.

'No. Nothing.'

'Then why are you shivering?'

'I shiver for the loss. For the loss of years together.'

She put her hand on his, but he was unaware of it. He swallowed the pain in his throat, that pain of his monstrous lie, his terrible denial of that faceless child blowing out the light of her first year. Until that moment, his blindness towards his daughter was a private sorrow. Now he had begun to exploit it, to use that invisible face as a veil for his lies. He knew it to be immoral in the extreme. He catalogued his transgressions that afternoon. First, he had absented

21

himself from the party. He had resolved, with little scruple, on adultery, and perhaps even more than that. But, worse than all of these, he had denied his daughter's being. He wanted to go home. He wanted to hold her in his arms and to say without looking at her, 'I'm sorry that I have used you for my deceit.'

'Shall we just . . . well . . . leave it?' Mary said. 'Our meeting disturbs you so.'

'No,' he said quickly. 'Not again. I won't let you go again.'

'Clifford's in Hong Kong,' she said. And that was all. He paid the bill while Mary flagged down a taxi. She gave an address in Kensington. In the cab they were silent, but it was not the easy silence of their earlier ride. Both knew that there was nothing to say, but both felt the need for words to cover words' redundancy. Alistair had no idea of what he was about but only words could have proved exactly what he was doing.

In the taxi, Mary prepared her keys. She too wanted no interval for words, words which might bring either of them to their senses. She led him through to the bedroom and quickly closed the curtains, for only the dark could orchestrate their uneasy silence.

Virginia's watch showed an offensive six o'clock.

All Doris's guests had gone home. Most of them had noticed the paternal absence. All but Doris herself, who had never associated her father with daylight. He was the accepted ghost of her nights. Virginia's parents insisted on staying. They used clearing up as an excuse, but in truth they were waiting for Alistair to come home so that they could give him what-for. They were surprised at their daughter's indifference.

At seven o'clock, Virginia put Doris to bed, and dawdled over it, wishing to avoid her parents' reproach. They stayed on, nevertheless. At ten o'clock, 'Oughtn't

22

we to ring the police?' her mother said. And at ten-thirty, 'We really ought to do something,' was her father's suggestion. They had by now withdrawn their accusations of negligence and, instead, were genuinely concerned for his safety. At midnight Virginia told them, 'Please go home. I'm quite sure there's some reason he's been delayed.' She insisted on their leaving and saw them to their car.

'Does he make a habit of this?' Mrs Warner could not help asking, wondering at her daughter's apparent lack of concern.

'He's done it before,' Virginia lied. 'He has some difficult patients.'

Why am I covering for him, she thought with a creeping feeling of self-disgust. She returned to the house and locked the door. She knew he would not come back that night. It was now too late for apology, for excuse. No patient story would be adequate. There were telephones. Wherever he was, and whatever he was doing, he was ashamed of it, ashamed of his fear. The fear of coming home and facing a face he had never seen. She clenched her teeth. She would not give way to tears. Tears were reserved for unhappiness and she wasn't sure of her feelings. Or indeed, of what she ought to be feeling. Since Doris's birth she and Alistair had slowly measured between them a stranger's distance. Sometimes she wondered whether she had ceased to love him and, in so wondering, came to the conclusion that her passion for him must be spent. Yet if he left her, she would crumble. Of that she had no doubt, and it was that breakdown that she could understand least of all. She would not miss his loving for he gave her none. Neither would she miss a battle, for between them was truce. And certainly she would not miss his parenting, for it had never existed. So why should she crumble? Among her women friends were some whose marriages were broken, loveless marriages

23

like hers, and battle-free, yet rejection had left them bereaved. Were they mourning mere history, regretting a negation of the past? And did they ever get over that? Death was cleaner, more legal, she thought. Widows were eventually consolable.

She went to bed but could not sleep. She tried not to think about where he was or what he was doing. The thought of another woman inevitably crossed her mind, and again she didn't know what she ought to be feeling.

Doris stirred in her sleep and gave a little moan. Perhaps she, too, was wondering about the where-abouts of her nocturnal ghost. The day broke slowly and the light filtered in slices through the Venetian blinds. The windows need cleaning, Virginia thought and was glad of a domestic issue on which to concentrate. She decided she would get up there and then and start cleaning. As she rose, she heard the key in the front door. She looked at her watch. Seven-thirty. A serious absence, she thought and perhaps a prelude to a total departure. She got back into bed. She did not want to confront him. Not without some clue as to how she should feel.

She lay back on the pillow pretending to herself that she was asleep. But she could not help but hear the gushing of the bathroom tap, and the unmuffled sounds of his stripping. She shivered with assault. It was the deepest offence. She tore out of bed and darted to the bathroom. He hadn't even bothered to shut the door. He was standing naked in the bath. The taps were still running, and she had to shout to overcome their gushing noise, but she would have shouted anyway and, as he bent to turn them off, her voice rang like thunder.

'Why can't you use *her* bloody bathroom?'

It was a relief of sorts. So too, was the sight of his crass vulnerability, standing there naked, pathetically

24

shielding that give-away member that had so clearly been elsewhere.

'I want you out,' she said, not thinking of what she was saying, but at least no longer wondering what she ought to feel. That too was a relief. To feel rage, to feel pain, and without questioning. For a moment she was glad he had chosen to cleanse himself on her territory and within her earshot, for that act was open to no other interpretation than an outright gesture of his cruelty and contempt.

'I want you out. And now,' she said again.

She returned to the bedroom. Doris was awake, and crying. She picked her up and cuddled her, shielding her face with her chest. Then she returned to the bathroom. He was sitting now, his back towards her, sponging his arms as if it were an ordinary day in an ordinary household.

'Is not Doris damaged enough?' she said to him. Then left.

As she dressed the baby, she realised that, since his homecoming, Alistair had said not a word. No explanation, no excuse, and certainly no apology. Was it possible that she had wrongly accused him? Perhaps he had spent the whole night with a difficult patient and with no access to a telephone? She realised she was only finding excuses for him, excuses that would enable him to stay in their home. She was ashamed of her own weakness, for she knew that only another woman could have kept him a whole night. And the bath was confirmation. For Alistair did not like baths. He was a shower man. A bath was far more serious. It had nothing to do with ablution. That was shower's work. No, a bath was a deliberate setting for recall, for meditation, and, perhaps, for decision.

She took Doris downstairs and prepared breakfast. But she prepared nothing for Alistair. She decided that this morning was the first of her broken marriage. In

25

many ways, she'd had a long enough dress rehearsal. She had learned to live alone. She had known the silences and the distance. And they had saddened her because that was not what marriage was supposed to be. But now, with Alistair dismissed, her expectations would change, and the silences and the distance would assume normality. Nevertheless she could not help but cock an ear for his descent and, when she heard his footsteps on the stairs, she was horrified to hear them continue to the front door. Then a pause, presumably for his coat, followed by the slamming of the heavy door.

'I'm changing the locks,' she screamed after him, though there was no way he could have heard. She shuddered with frustration. That final silence of his had been a greater assault than his arrogant ablutions. She mixed Doris's cereal with fury and, as she fed her, she was overcome by a frightening sense of disconnection. For a moment she wondered who was the child she was nurturing and why she looked so strange. As did everything that surrounded her. The house was suddenly alien as if, like the child, it belonged to somebody else, and Virginia was sitting in her single days, in the Soho café where she had first met Alistair, had picked him up in fact, pitying him for his sad isolation at the corner table. And because she was a stranger, he had poured out his story of Mary's rejection. She recalled her name with ease, though for many years she had not given her any thought. Mary was married now, she'd heard, and Alistair hers. Or was, as she suddenly realised, recognising their union in the dining-room suite, a wedding present from her parents, and the child in the chair, undeniably hers.

When the phone rang, she knew it was her mother, and all her defences returned. She picked up the receiver.

'Is he back?' she heard.

'Yes,' she said. 'He came back about five minutes after you left. It's what I told you. A patient had a fit in his office and he had to get him to hospital. There was no-one in the building and he couldn't leave him. So he went with him to the hospital' – she could hear her voice galloping, gathering speed with each invention – 'so he had to contact his family, his wife. Two kids. Alistair's a very caring man, you know.' On she prattled like a desperate minstrel, while from the other end of the line buzzed an incredulous silence.

'Why didn't he phone?' her mother said at last. 'Hospitals have phones.'

'The man was *dying*, Mother,' Virginia threw in for good measure.

'Thirty-four-years old. A wife and two kids.' Surely a measure of pity might arouse her mother's belief in her story?

'Well,' a voice froze over the wires. 'I'm glad he came back.'

Someone had to put the phone down. One of them had to end the conversation. And whoever did so, either Virginia or her mother, would have relegated the story to fantasy. But Virginia would not let go.

'Don't you want to know what happened to him?' she almost shouted.

'What happened to him?' her mother said without interest.

'He died, that's what. Thirty-four-years old. A wife and two kids.'                .

'I'm sorry,' her mother said, without regret.

'There's the door-bell,' Virginia invented. It had to be a third person, even an imagined one, who could be blamed for cutting the conversation short.

'I'll ring you later,' her mother said.

Virginia put down the phone.

Poor man, she thought to herself, convinced now of the young widow and two little orphans at the hospital

27

bedside. It took her a little while to disentangle herself from her own fiction and, when she did, her anger returned. And not so much with Alistair as with herself, that she should defend him with such alacrity. She recalled now that she had told him to leave. She had even threatened to change the locks on the door. But that threat he had not heard, drowned in the thundering silence of his leave-taking. She was glad of that. She would not change the locks. There was an irreversible finality in such a gesture. It was like closing the lid on a coffin. No, she would leave the locks, but she would not withdraw her wish that he must leave. But neither would she repeat it. One should leave one's options open, she thought, even though one had no options at all. She wondered whether he would come home that night. She thought he might telephone her during the day. That would be his way. His coward's way. He was a face-avoider, was Alistair, and not only of his own daughter's.

She finished feeding Doris, staring at her all the time, hoping perhaps to compensate for her father's blindness. Doris gurgled and grinned. She seemed to be totally unaware of the havoc that rumbled about her. And if she were aware, she was unsurprised, as if the chaos that was gathering had been her expectation from the very beginning.

# Three

ALISTAIR TOOK a taxi to the office. He could not face the public of public transport, or its noise, and he crouched on the edge of the seat and wondered whether the silence between himself and Virginia would ever now be broken. He tried not to think about it. He concentrated on a new patient he was expecting that morning. The man had asked the receptionist for an appointment, but had refused to give his name. Alistair thought he must be a celebrity of a sort, wishing to conceal his neurotic identity. He hoped so, for it meant that he could begin to compete with Gerry downstairs. He tried to concentrate on this unknown, to envisage what problems he would bring to his consulting rooms. But it was a quickly exhaustible speculation and he was forced to turn his mind to thoughts of what he was going to do about Virginia, about Mary, and, above all, and in a different breath and dimension, what he was going to do about Doris.

Virginia and Mary were intrinsic parts of the same problem, and the Doris dilemma had nothing to do with either. He wondered if he were falling in love with Mary. Then concluded that he had never been out of love with her. From which he deduced, with little difficulty, that he had never loved Virginia. He was wary of where his thoughts would lead him, for he knew that they would beg for some form of self-analysis. And he had done all that. It was his profession. It was his living. It would do little to help his personal problems. He could no more analyse himself than he could mend a pair of shoes. This comparison crossed his mind only because he chanced to view the sole of his shoe as it crossed his knee. I must remember to tell Virginia to get them mended, he thought. Then realised that she no longer played that role. Yet the thought of giving them to Mary was ridiculous. It was a request far too domestic, far too familiar, but, above all, far too menial for a star like Mary. No, he would discreetly throw them away and buy another pair. He was angry with Virginia that she had driven him to such a waste of money.

The cab pulled into the kerb. He measured out the exact fare, thrust it into the driver's hand, and fled before he could count it and notice the absence of tip. He rushed up the stairs to his rooms, hoping that Gerry's door was not open. He was in no mood to give Gerry an explanation for his absence at his daughter's party. Mercifully it was closed. Gerry was talking to his secretary, Fiona. More than a secretary, Alistair had often thought.

He put his ear to Gerry's door. He heard Fiona giggling. 'Stop it, Gerry,' she said. 'It's much too early in the morning.' He swallowed his disgust and tiptoed the last staircase to his own rooms.

'Your patient has arrived,' his own receptionist said.

'Did he give you his name?'

'No. I didn't ask him. He'd already made it clear he didn't wish to leave his name.'

'You were right,' Alistair said. Then, hopefully, 'Did you recognise him?'

'No. His face meant nothing to me.'

Then he must be a nobody, Alistair thought. His receptionist was a star-struck addict, and often wished she worked for Gerry downstairs. If she didn't recognise a face, then that face was nothing.

'Give me a few minutes,' he said wearily, 'then send him in.'

He went into his rooms, hung his coat on the hanger, sat down, and inspected the sole of his shoe. Damn Virginia, he thought. As soon as he'd finished with this new patient, he would phone Mary.

There was a timid knock on the door. The timbre of a knock was often a patient's give-away. It could betray fear, anger or aggression, or it could be a mere gesture of politeness. But Alistair would rarely allow for anything so mundane as good manners. Everything had to mean something. By the quality of this new patient's knock, he was a shrinking man with little self-confidence. So Alistair was astonished when the door opened and he saw the frame filled to its posts with a huge body of a man – no shrinking violet he, and, if he was lacking in self-confidence, then he was certainly compensating with aggression.

He strode into the room.

'Call me Esau,' he bellowed.

Alistair quickly made the connection. But he noted the clean-shaven face – even the eyebrows had fallen to the scythe – and he guessed that the face was a part of the man's body that did not betray his disturbance. But he needn't have speculated. Esau was already undressing. Alistair made no move to stop him. The man needed to display his proof, and he let him get on with it, as he watched, fascinated.

The stripping was slow. Almost a tease. The shoes came first and were neatly aligned. Then the socks, folded meticulously inside them. The bare feet gave an indication of what was to follow. Little was visible of proper feet, for whatever it was that he stood on was covered with a mat of silky black hair. Even the toe-nails were indiscernible, shrouded as they were with simian overgrowth. That was proof enough of his name, and Alistair was tempted to call a halt but a certain curiosity, an inquisitiveness that was entirely unprofessional, silenced him. He watched as the strip proceeded. As the trousers came off, the legs were no surprise, though a soupçon of knee was visible. More than a soupçon as Alistair noted on a second glance. Indeed the whole knee was shamelessly exposed in its bright whiteness, obscenely naked in the midst of that jungle of fur. Esau touched his knees, looked up at Alistair and smiled. He was at pains to point out that one and only part of him that did not require treatment in his consulting rooms. Alistair smiled back at him though he could have wept. Esau folded his trousers and hung them softly over the chair. For a man of such vast girth, he was astonishingly gentle. His movements had the grace of a woman, a gender so seemingly at odds with his coating. Esau passed on his underpants. Modesty perhaps forbade their removal. He continued with the jacket which he hung on the back of the door. The tie was next, and the unbuttoning of the shirt. Alistair had a glimpse of black shag carpet. Enough, he thought. The man had more than proved his name. Now it was mere cabaret. Esau teased off his shirt like a stripper her last veil, slowly, as if to reveal the final proof of his apehood. He peeled the shirt from his body with something like relish, a relish reflected in Alistair's eye. Not a slither of flesh was visible and, as each sleeve bared each arm in turn, he looked for skin in vain.

When it was done, Esau sat himself in a chair and raised the soles of his feet and the palms of his hands, in promotion of his hairless trophies. The show was over.

'Call me Esau,' he said again, then slowly he dressed himself, in reverse order, starting with his shirt.

Alistair stared at him all the while, wondering how he could help him. Wondering indeed whether it was a psychiatric problem or whether the man would do better to go to an electrolysist. But such treatment was painful, and, with Esau, would take a lifetime. He watched and waited. Esau was relaxed and taking his time. It was as if, with his exhibition, he had passed his problem onto somebody else. It was now the doctor's move. Undeniably. He finished dressing, tied his shoelaces and swivelled his chair round so that he looked Alistair straight in the eye.

'Is this the first time you've been to a therapist?' Alistair asked.

He was playing for time.

'No,' Esau said.

'How old are you?' Again Alistair temporised.

'Forty-three.'

'Why now?' Alistair asked. 'Why do you seek help now? Did something happen to you that you could bear it no longer?'

'Bear what?' Esau asked. He was clearly bewildered.

'Your . . . your hirsute nature.' Alistair put it as politely as he was able. The man would have looked more at home in a zoo.

'You mean my hair,' Esau laughed. 'I love it. Do you not think it beautiful?'

'Why are you here then?' Alistair asked patiently.

'To show it to you, Doctor. It gives *me* so much pleasure, I thought you'd like to see it too.'

'But why me?'

'I'm showing it to everybody. Anybody and everybody. I make appointments all over the place. Doctors, chiropodists, osteopaths. How can I harbour such a thing of beauty without its occasional display? I make my appointments early. I'm usually the first, so that I can give people a good start to their day.' He leaned forward over the desk. 'Dr Crown,' he whispered, 'you have to admit that for you this day is different from all other days. How often do your days begin with beauty?'

'Thank you,' Alistair said. He desperately wanted the man to leave and the only way to speed his departure was to acknowledge his gift. 'I am grateful,' he said, deeply wishing to see the hairy back of him, for he was suddenly overcome by such a pall of depression that he needed urgently to be alone.

Esau rose suddenly. 'I have an appointment with your colleague downstairs,' he said. 'I go to bring him joy.'

He was like an evangelist, Alistair thought, bringing God to the people, not in words, but in pictures, for he was living proof that Darwin might well have been a Christian. 'I'm grateful to you,' Alistair said again, and shook his hand. He knew that, downstairs, the priggish Gerry would give him very short shrift and, to prepare him, he said, 'There are people, you know, who won't appreciate your beauty.'

'I know,' Esau said. 'I have been stoned in my time.' He smiled and tightened his grip on Alistair's hand. 'Thank you for your time,' he said.

Alistair watched him as he lumbered down the stairs, but he closed his door before he reached Gerry's room. He did not want to witness his reception.

He returned to his desk. When he had first laid eyes on Esau, he had thought of Doris, though initially he had made no connection. But as Esau's strip proceeded, the imagined face of his daughter persisted, thrusting itself on his retina with each discarded garment. Which is why he had longed for Esau to leave. But now, in his absence, the image persisted and, in the vain hope of some relief, he began to doodle Doris's image on his pad. Since he had never looked at her face, he experimented with varied ensembles. He gave her Virginia's nose and his own chin, sometimes his eyes or Virginia's forehead, whiling away the time with different permutations and, as he doodled, his anger drained out of him.

When his receptionist rang to announce his next patient, he was glad that he had no more doodling time, for he knew that it would inevitably lead to decision-making. And for that he was not ready. He gathered up his drawings and was about to screw them up for the wastepaper-basket. But quickly he refrained. Such a gesture would have been by way of a burial. So he straightened them out neatly and placed them in his lockable drawer. Then, for a few moments he familiarised himself with his next patient's file. He wondered how Esau was doing below stairs. By now, he would have stripped himself clean, if you could call it that, all but for his fig-leaf which housed God knows what measure of pain. He hoped that Gerry had received him with kindness though he suspected that the Esau story would be dropped with characteristic contempt and cynicism in Gerry's much-frequented celebrity drawing rooms. He rang the bell for his next patient.

The day passed, measured out in patients' fears, obsessions, miseries and downright terror, and, at the end of it, there was no longer an excuse to postpone decision, if only the very fundamental one of whether or not he should go home. He had promised to phone Mary, and had been aware of it all day. And tempted by it too. But he could not talk to her without seeing her, and seeing her would have further complicated his decision. In any case, Clifford was due back from Hong Kong. In a way he was glad of it, for the presence of the husband would put Mary on hold. That left Virginia who had, if he thought about it, been on hold all their married life, and would, if he had his selfish way, remain so. But there was Doris, undealable with, that multi-faced doodle in his drawer.

He picked up the phone and dialled his home number. He was irritated that it was not immediately answered and he was angry with Virginia for keeping him waiting. It did not occur to him that she might have gone out. He envisaged her sitting all day by the telephone waiting for his call. His anger brewed while he waited, and when finally Virginia picked up the phone he bellowed into the receiver.

'What kept you so long?'

He heard an angry click and the dialling tone purred spitefully in his ear.

He seethed with rage, and then with a sudden relief. For a decision had been taken. And he had played no part in it. Therefore he was not responsible for its effects. Virginia had quite positively cut him off, an even more positive action than her threat earlier in the day. 'I would never have left her,' he rehearsed to himself, in case he was ever called upon to give account. 'She threw me out. What else could I do but leave?' That left Mary to deal with. For the time being, Doris would have to stay in the drawer.

He dialled Mary's number. He had no notion of what he would say to her. He hoped perhaps that she would give him a clue. That she would release him from a decision on his part as obligingly as Virginia had freed him. Yet he did not want to be released from Mary for he feared that he loved her still. He feared, too, that he wanted to marry her, and then, with little scruple, to leave her, as she had left him so many years ago. I'm not a very nice man, Alistair thought, as he heard the lifting of the receiver on the other end.

It was a man's voice. Clifford, he assumed. He had not prepared himself for that and quickly he replaced the receiver. He hoped that Clifford was having disturbing thoughts, including the obvious one after his absence in Hong Kong. Let them sort it out between them. Now he was faced with the practical problem of where he should sleep that night. Then the phone rang. It must be Virginia, he thought. Now it's *her* time to wait. He let it ring, savouring her irritation, then when he felt she was at breaking-point, he picked up the receiver.

'Hello?' he said, with as much indifference as he could muster.

'Was it you who phoned just now?'

It was Mary and her voice was a whisper.

'Yes,' he said smiling. He whispered too, as a co-conspirator.

'I can't talk now,' she said. 'Can I phone you later?'

'No,' he said quickly. 'I don't know where I shall be.' It was the truth and she could make what she wanted of it.

'Don't you want to talk to me?'

He saw her pouted lip, and longed for her. 'Of course,' he said. 'But . . . ring me in the morning at the office.'

'Do you still . . .?'

She could have been on the point of asking anything. He blessed the telephone, that so-thoughtful licence for non-commitment.

'I'll talk to you tomorrow,' she whispered.

'Can I see you?' he said suddenly. 'Now. Tonight.'

'It's impossible. Oh my God,' she raised her voice a little, then quickly put down the phone, and Alistair could even smell Clifford through her panic. He wondered what he looked like, whether after all these years he was showing his age. He'd had the kind of good looks that do not age well, Alistair was happy to recall, with a beauty that sits well only on an unlined skin. He hoped he'd gone to fat. He was rich enough for that, so their way of living indicated. Now he recalled Mary and their night together. It was not until the morning, when he was aware of the strange bed, that he had any notion of adultery. Again he thought of what he should do. He could not book into an hotel without some small luggage so he decided to return home with the excuse to pick up some overnight clothes. But he would wait, as he usually did, until nightfall, when Doris would be in bed and he could lighten his heart with his nocturnal exploration.

He took a cab home and ordered it to drop him on the corner of the street. He didn't want Virginia to make a note of his extravagance. There would be the question of alimony. Another new word and, like

37

adultery, a word to do with other people. Like Down's Syndrome.

Once at his door, he wondered whether he should use his own key. To ring the bell would be an acceptance of the fact that he had been turned out. That would teach her. It would put the ball firmly in her court. He pressed gleefully on the bell. She kept him waiting. He pressed again, longer this time, but still there was no sign of movement behind the door. But he could play the waiting-game too. He leaned his back on the bell and it resounded down the street like a neglected car-alarm, so that it was out of sheer social embarrassment that Virginia had to answer the door.

'Haven't you a key?' she said coldly.

'I thought you'd changed the locks.'

'What do you want?'

'I need some overnight things.'

Thus decisions are taken. And with no-one's intent. Simply by a rush of nobbled words that come from nowhere, that pace each other with illogical speed and daring. And suddenly conclusions are reached, resolutions are made, fixed, inflexible and final.

Alistair wished for a second chance, he wished he was outside the door again, his own key sensibly in his hand. And likewise Virginia. For what had resolved between them was what neither of them had meant at all.

Alistair walked past her up the stairs. There was nothing else that he could do. He heard Doris gurgling from the bedroom, that year-and-a-day albatross. He found himself hurrying, taking the steps two at a time, but even that was not meant, for his speed was hurtful and he had done hurt enough. But his feet were like the words, propelled from an unknown and malignant source. He panted into his bedroom. Once there, he sat on the bed and wondered how he had come to all this. But it was pointless to wonder and much too late. He knew she was waiting for him in the hall. Waiting for words from him, words that he himself had formed and directed, words which were his responsibility and his alone. Words that came from the heart and could be spoken by no other. But how could he give her any kind of words while he held a suitcase in his hand which would give the lie to any soothing speech of his? Yet he would not appear without a suitcase, for that was what the words had ordered. So he packed it quickly, taking the minimum. He would make his point, but at the same time he would leave the door open for his return.

As he expected, Virginia was waiting for him at the bottom of the stairs. Her mouth was firmly shut, choking on vocabulary. Whatever the words were, she would trap them, not trusting where they would lead.

But some words slipped through the net, and she wept at their treacherous release.

'Please don't go,' she said.

Alistair put down his case. Silence was now his right, but only if an appropriate gesture were made. I must do the right thing, he thought. I must put my arms round her. She will take it for reconciliation. But this is not necessarily what I mean. For in truth, if I put my arms around her, I am thanking her for saving me money on a hotel, for giving me a breathing-space before I make up my mind. But she will not read that in my embrace. She cannot afford to. I shall embrace her. She can read it how she will. He put his arms round her and thought of Mary.

Virginia folded herself into his known falsehood. She knew she had lost the battle, that now she had more or less given him permission to remain silent on his last night's absence. She was colluding, simply because she could not accommodate the truth that she suspected. But one question she could ask, and one that had little to do with herself.

'What about Doris?' she said.

'What about her?' He shivered. He'd rather she had asked him where he had spent the night.

'When are you going to be a father to her?'

'Give me time,' he said. It was the biggest lie of all. 'Can you get a baby-sitter?' he said, suddenly inspired. 'I'll take you out to dinner.' Anything but stay in that sultry domestic environment, orchestrated by Doris's gurgling, in which each silence would threaten eruption. Better a backdrop of clattering dishes and music, and other people on whom to speculate.

'I'll arrange it,' Virginia said.

He took his hold-all upstairs. But not into his bedroom. He took it into his study, and, without unpacking it, stowed it in a cupboard. Then he shut his door and dialled Mary's number. When Clifford answered he replaced the receiver. And he was glad. Now Clifford would really have something to worry about. One wrong number could have been an error. But two pointed dangerously towards adultery. He fiddled with the papers on his desk, and found himself, once again, doodling. Doris's face. He knew that this pursuit was an alternative to looking at his daughter's countenance. And that, in time, if he doodled diligently away, he would not even feel the guilt of avoiding her. 'I am drawing her,' he would say to himself. 'I look at her every day.'

He took a shower and changed. He heard Virginia in her bedroom. 'Where would you like to eat?' he shouted having decided on the exact restaurant. A noisy busy one, and one with a band.

'I'll leave it to you,' she said, as he expected her to say, as she had left most things to him since the day that they had met.

As soon as the baby-sitter arrived, Alistair left the house to wait in the car, leaving Virginia to make the domestic arrangements. He was glad to be alone, to indulge in a moment-by-moment recap of his Mary encounter. Recall in no way diluted his pleasure, and to test it, he went over it again and again, so that by the time Virginia approached the car, he was in a state of high ecstasy, which Virginia had to misread as his pleasure in her.

'Where are we going?' she asked.

'I thought we'd try the Cavern,' he said.

She said nothing.

She envisioned, with the beginnings of a headache, an evening of endless noise, so persistent that it would drown any conversation. Then she realised that that was exactly why he had chosen it.

'That's fine,' she said. 'Did you book?'

'No,' he said. 'Mid-week there's always room.'

There was still hope, she thought and prayed for a full house. But when they reached the restaurant it was, as Alistair had surmised, half-empty. But the noise was still deafening. They were shown to a corner-table, the waiter shouting directions in their ears. They settled themselves and Alistair was satisfied. Conversation, even if it were on the agenda, would have been impossible. They studied the menu. Virginia looked at Alistair and he mouthed something towards her. She shook her head indicating that he was inaudible. Alistair was satisfied. He had mouthed what he was choosing to eat, but he'd used it as a ploy for a test-run. Now assured, he touched her arm.

'I slept with Mary last night,' he mouthed.

She could not hear him.

'I love Mary. I'm going to leave you.'

Virginia smiled and shrugged again.

Alistair felt an enormous relief. At last it was out, even though unheard.

But it was a game, and two can play it, and Virginia had equal need for relief. She stared across at him and, as the band bellowed its babel, she mouthed, 'Where

41

were you last night?' Alas, the band cut out suddenly with not even a drum-roll to herald its exit, and the question quivered in the air between them, loud, clear, and demanding response.

Alistair trembled. There was no time to fabricate a lie. Neither could he hesitate, for hesitation would belie whatever followed it. So he told the truth, for that was all that was available to him. He noticed that the band had not only stopped playing, but had withdrawn from the platform, so he could expect no help from that quarter. The silence screamed his cue.

'I ran into Mary,' he said. 'On my way home from work.'

'Mary Chivers?' Virginia whispered. That name on which hers had been a rebound.

'Yes,' he said. 'I hadn't seen her for eight years.' It was the only clean thing he had to say, and he repeated it to underline his erstwhile fidelity. 'She's married,' he went on and he saw a glimmer of hope in Virginia's eye. But he dashed it quickly. 'Her husband was away,' he said. 'I spent the night with her.'

The band were making their way back to the platform. Virginia watched them, and waited for their sound, because she had no words to give him. That he had committed adultery hurt her enough, but what hurt her more was the fact that he had chosen to tell her, for, armed with that knowledge, it was incumbent on her to react in some way, whereas her ignorance would have sanctioned her inertia. The band struck up its din. She looked at Alistair.

'I want to go home,' she mouthed.

He could not hear her, but when she stood up, he understood what she had said. He followed her out of the restaurant, mouthing to a waiter an excuse for their departure. The waiter couldn't understand but it didn't seem to matter. He gave a shrug of his shoulders, a gesture which seemed to be the restaurant's password.

Outside Alistair opened the car door for her. It was the least he could do. And probably the most, he thought.

Virginia waited until the car was cruising, and on a road free of traffic-lights or necessity for gear-change, making a monotonous unchanging sound which would not interfere with conversation.

'What are you going to do?' Virginia said. 'Do you want a divorce?'

'It hasn't come to that,' Alistair said. Then added, with a touch of anger, 'Don't rush me.'

It was his anger that broke her. What right had *he* to anger? To table-turn so neatly?

'Stop the car!' she shouted.

He took his time. By the look of him, anger had given way to contempt. Slowly he pulled into a side-turning and turned off the engine with a prolongation that amounted to a talent. They sat for a while in silence. Neither knew how to begin. Both had learned that words can make decisions even before the need for a decision is considered.

At last Alistair broke the silence. 'It can happen,' he whispered. 'It can happen to anybody.'

For a moment she wanted to know what the 'it' was. Whether it referred to falling in love or leaving one's marriage. But it didn't matter. Either way, it was the end of things.

'What about Doris?' she said. 'Your daughter,' she reminded him, 'whose face you've never seen.'

'What's Doris got to do with it?'

Everything, she thought, then said it aloud, for there was no point in sparing him. 'If we'd had a normal child,' she said, 'this wouldn't have happened.'

'Perhaps you're right,' he said.

It put an end to the argument.

'Then what shall we do?' Virginia said.

'Just give me time.'

But Virginia knew the lie of that, and probably more acutely than he. She knew that in ten years hence she would still be giving him time and he would still be asking for it. Whatever move was to be made was positively hers. And she knew equally positively that she would make none.

'Let's go home,' she said. 'Whatever that means.'

He turned the ignition, and, all words spent between them, perhaps for now and forever, he drove home. As he pulled up in front of the house, 'Look,' he said. 'The roses are coming out. Aren't they a bit early?'

'Fuck the roses,' Virginia said.

# *Four*

A ND SO Virginia gave Alistair time, which she knew was a euphemism for licence. And the roses flowered, died and flowered again, and Doris blew out two birthday candles while her father was elsewhere. And then three. And, with greater temerity, four. And still Alistair had not looked on his daughter's face.

Yet the portfolio in his desk-drawer grew fatter. Every day, he Doris-doodled with increasing frenzy. For his wife's easy accomodation was driving him mad. In the last year, she had hired a nanny and had gone back to her old teaching job. She had made a life for herself that, though not exactly excluding Alistair, did not welcome him either. Often she entertained her new circle of friends, and all the while, even until late, she kept Doris by her side, as a safeguard against his entry. Even when she was alone, she kept Doris for company, so that she saw even less of him. Moreover she seemed perfectly happy, as if she was prepared to tolerate their arrangement for the rest of her life. Often she went out in the evenings, and only on these nights could Alistair venture out of his study. His nocturnal visits to Doris were constant, whatever time she was put to bed. Prior to each exploration, he was careful, without looking, to cover the face gently with a sheet. Once, in a panic, Doris struck him as a corpse that he, as a gentle doctor, had, with his sheet gesture, declared dead. Then he bent over and, repenting, kissed her body on every single part of her.

Then he would go back to his own room, and in his

45

loneliness he would telephone Mary. Clifford would answer, as Alistair expected, and Alistair would replace the receiver, knowing that Mary would know that he had phoned. Nowadays he saw less and less of Mary, even when Clifford was on business in Hong Kong. Like Virginia, she too had accommodated. She had settled for her marriage to Clifford, as little a marriage as Virginia's to Alistair, and, like Virginia, she had gone back to work. Clifford too had accommodated. His frequent visits to Hong Kong catered for all those needs that Mary couldn't satisfy, and his work gave him much pleasure. So that of all the participants in the drama, that Alistair himself had initiated, only Alistair could not accommodate. It was as if he had written a play but paid scant attention to the star role. The extras had taken over and re-written the script.

He was deeply unhappy. He felt, and justifiably so, unloved. He had lost none of his passion for Mary, but it found less and less to feed upon, for Mary seemed to avoid him, and it was only when Clifford was home, and a rendezvous was impossible, that she rang Alistair and confessed her unbounded love for him. He suspected she might have found another lover, and so jealous was he that he cancelled his patients for one whole day and shadowed her. He dogged her out of her driveway and followed her to an office, and he dawdled outside, scuffing his shoes on the kerb-stone until her lunch hour. While waiting he considered that he was going mad, and whether it was a moment to lose faith in his profession. He risked taking a mid-morning cup of coffee at a café directly opposite her office-building. From his window-seat he would miss nothing. While he sat there, he thought people were staring at him. A man sitting at a table alongside actually moved his seat, and Alistair was convinced it was to get a better view of him. The waitress, too, seemed to find him an object of some interest, for she kept passing by his table without the excuse of service. He ordered coffee after coffee. He picked up a paper-serviette and, with his pen, he began to Doris-doodle. Without any conscious manoeuvring, the face took on the shape of Mary's, and he realised with a kind of professional detachment that he was truly in a bad way and perhaps he ought to go and get himself seen to. But he didn't equate that person with himself. Suddenly he rose and paid for his coffees. He did not leave a tip. He felt that, in return for her service, he had given the waitress a show. He brushed past her on his way out and, as he crossed the street, he realised that he'd left his Doris-doodle on the table. He rushed back but only in time to see the waitress screw his albatross into a ball and dunk it into what remained of his coffee. His cheeks were suddenly wet. I'm falling to pieces, he thought. Again, the 'I' had nothing to do with himself, but could be any one of his patients whose pieces he picked up daily in his consulting rooms.

He paced the front of the building until a trickle of employees started to emerge. Then he crossed the road, for he did not want to be seen, and he stood in an open phone-booth, the receiver in his hand to off-set suspicion, for by now he was convinced that he was being watched, while he stared through the window at Mary's building. A passer-by looked at him, and he started to mouth into the receiver. 'Hello, hello,' he heard himself saying. 'This is me and I have a daughter. Her name is Doris. She's four years old. Almost five. But I've never seen her. Her face, that is. But I've seen the rest. Every single part of her, and I have to tell you that she is beautiful. What? What?' he said, for the man was still staring at him. He gave his voice a rest for a while and nodded his head from time to time, with the occasional 'Yes' or 'No'. He wished the man would go away. Then the man came towards him, threateningly it seemed. Alistair trembled. 'Yes, yes,' he shouted into the receiver. 'If you don't believe me, you can ask my wife. Her name's Mary.'

The man approached him. 'How long are you going to be?' he said crossly. 'I need to use the phone urgently.'

'I'm almost finished,' Alistair said with relief. Then, into the phone, 'Goodbye. I'll ring you later.'

He replaced the receiver and stepped outside, while the man entered the booth. Alistair noticed how he wiped the mouthpiece with the sleeve of his coat, as if he would disinfect it of Alistair's deceptions. Then he dialled urgently.

Alistair moved away, his eye on the building. He was not surprised to see Mary emerge. She was not alone. Around her waist was the arm of her companion. Alistair noticed that first. The white-cuffed wrist creeping beneath the jacket-sleeve and the tanned hand that rested so at home on the white linen of Mary's jacket. He raised his eyes to view that which was attached to the hand. Not Clifford. Even though he was in London, Alistair knew, for only that morning Mary had phoned him with a declaration of her love. No, not Clifford. Nothing like him. A much younger man, and therefore much younger than Alistair. It can't last, he consoled himself, and watched how Mary nestled her head against the man's shirt. Disgusting, he thought and felt sick inside. Then he turned away and rushed out of their sight, flagging down a cab as he ran, and directing it to his consulting rooms.

Once there, he closeted himself, and lay on his couch, that space reserved for everybody in the world except himself. It was the first time that he'd sampled it and, as he lay down, he felt himself trapped in the echo of all the terrified words that it had sprouted in its time. And all the alarming sounds. The clanging of the doors of Underground trains, as his subterranean traveller so desperately dodged the Circle Line. And Esau, though he had not lain on the couch, had left his words there, buried deep in the uncut moquette. 'Am I not a thing of beauty?' he had said, displaying himself for all to share. Or the whispered words of his evening patient, that man who would never risk the sunlight in fear of attack, not on himself, but on his shadow. 'They will stab my shadow,' he would whisper, 'and I shall succumb.' Alistair shivered in their echo. These were the whisperings of other people, he told himself. The language of rage, despair and pain was someone else's tongue. That nightmare couch was a guest-bed on which he had never slept.

He rose quickly. He wished he had not cancelled his patients. He needed one now to confirm his own outsiderness. 'I am well,' he said to himself. 'I tend the sick, and all of them are other people.'

He went to his desk and took out his Doris-portfolio. He took a clean sheet of paper and, as was his wont, he drew a circle as his starting-point. Doris's head. Usually he would doodle the chin before any other feature. He knew that, in a Down's Syndrome child, the taint would dwell on the upper part of the face and that, by the time it reached the chin, its appetite for eruption had waned, so that the chin was a chin like any other. Alistair would doodle a while on the chin, shading it, shaping it, relishing its normalcy. But today his hand refused. It would not even yield a chin outline. So, with great courage, he plunged into the deep end and started to doodle the eyes, those features he always left until last, because in no way could they be disguised. He'd always had difficulties with the upper parts of the face and his attempts were always painful. But this time, his hand moved freely, and even with a hint of pleasure. He sketched eyes with exaggerated freakiness and centred them with a bridgeless nose. As long as he was drawing, he felt no distaste, but when the nose was finished and the earthquake confirmed once and for all, irrevocable and inconsolable, his hand refrained and he could not

49

bear to look at his work. Yet in that drawing he felt that he had come closer than ever to Doris's resemblance, and, though it brought him no nearer to looking at her straight in the face, he felt he had moved a little way towards her accommodation.

He put the portfolio back in his drawer and he began to look forward to his night's exploration. But Mary's clear infidelity still needled him and, though in the course of his drawing it had slipped his mind, now it returned with renewed strength and bitterness. He picked up his telephone and dialled her number. He did not expect a reply. Both Mary and Clifford would be at work, but any communication, even one so negative as a ringing tone, would be a relief of sorts. He was astonished to hear Mary's very sleepy voice murmur a 'Hello' into the receiver. He knew that voice. That tired sated whisper of hers with its post-coital smile. He hung up, hatred in his heart. Quickly he sought out Clifford's number. He needed revenge. Swift and brutal. When a secretary answered, he asked with confidence and authority for her employer. She asked for his name. He told her it was a personal call and the assertion in his voice dissuaded her from questioning him further. She put him through.

'Clifford Wainwright here,' he heard, and he saw that pompous face of so many years ago with its chinless wealth and connections, and it gave Alistair the utmost pleasure to give him what-for.

'Who is speaking?' Clifford said with some disdain.

But Alistair ignored that request. Instead he came straight to the point. 'Mr Wainwright,' he said. 'If you care to go home at this moment, you will find your wife in bed with a younger man.' He'd thrown in the age for good measure. He waited for Clifford's spluttering, 'Who's . . . who's that?' to subside. Then he replaced the receiver.

He knew that, even if his affair with Mary was not

50

quite over, it had now very positively come to an end, for she would suspect that it was he who had shopped her. Well, at least, he thought, one decision had been made, even though he hadn't made it himself. But it would have to do. That left Virginia and Doris. Or rather, that left Doris.

His phone rang. He had given his secretary the day off, so he had to answer it himself. He hesitated. He feared it might be Mary. Or Clifford. He let it ring. Its insistence irritated him. It sounded urgent and suddenly he thought something might have happened to Doris. He snatched the receiver from its cradle.

'Hello?' he said.

The phone clicked. Clifford. Alistair knew. Poor old Clifford, checking on the identity of his cuckold. He smiled. He was glad he'd answered the phone. It put him squarely in the clear. He imagined Clifford rushing to his car and belting through the city, hoping to catch Mary in flagrante. And why shouldn't *he*, Alistair thought, why shouldn't *he* be in on the kill as well? It was, after all, his mise en scène. He locked his rooms, darted downstairs, took a cab, and made for Mary's Kensington address. Once there, he concealed himself behind a tree in the driveway, and he waited. He sincerely hoped that Mary was still entertaining and that poor Clifford's journey would not be in vain. He suddenly felt very well-disposed towards Clifford, on the basis of what he assumed was their common mistrust of women. That included Virginia, too, Alistair decided. But not Doris. Never Doris. Doris was of a different species entirely and gender had nothing to do with it. He thought of his last doodle, that supposed likeness, and he trembled.

He heard a car. From its sound it was a taxi. Clifford had clearly not trusted himself to drive. He heard the ping of a meter and he crouched behind the tree. Shortly he was rewarded by the sight of Clifford, tiptoeing up the path with as much speed as silence would allow. Alistair peeped from behind the tree and watched as Clifford stealthily slipped his key into the lock and slowly opened the front door. He left it open, probably not wishing to make any noise. He saw him slip off his shoes. Then he disappeared, presumably up the stairs.

Alistair waited. He wished he could get closer so that he might actually *hear* the discovery, but he daren't go any nearer the house. He waited, crouched behind the tree. From where he squatted, the house looked silent and peaceful enough. The spotlessly white net curtains, the neatly potted plants that filled the window-sills, the shining brass carriage-lamps that framed the doorway, all indicated a severe and absolute decorum within, so that the figure which came sprawling suddenly out of the front door, gathering its pieces on the gravel, seemed ill-bred and an insult to propriety. Alistair viewed him with relish. He watched as the man straightened himself, hitched up his trousers which had sagged to his thighs. His upper torso was bare and he clearly had nothing with which to cover it, except for a crumpled jacket which some unseen hand, no doubt Clifford's trembling paw, had thrown after him. He put it on and folded it over his chest. Then he limped along the path. His gait had no post-coital lilt.

He hobbled into the street and, after a short interval, Alistair followed him. He watched him hail an empty taxi, but it sailed past him, its driver clearly unwilling to pick up such an unsavoury fare. The same taxi slowed down for a respectable-looking Alistair. He gave the cabbie his home address, and settled smugly on the back seat, vibrating with a sense of poetic justice. Once in his study, he dialled Mary's number and, as he expected, Clifford answered.

His 'Hello' was disappointingly cheerful.

As Alistair replaced the receiver, he felt the onset of a depression. There was no longer any pleasure in giving

Clifford a bad time, nor even any purpose. He had lost Mary. Of that he was sure. But surer, too, that he had lost Virginia and, for some reason that he couldn't understand, that loss pained him far more. He was angry that she was not at home. Angry that she was at work. Angry that she had made a life of her own. And so had Mary, in her own way. Only he, the engineer of all that chaos, had come adrift.

He heard the front door open. Virginia. She would go straight to Doris, wherever she was. She would not know that Alistair was in the house and, if she did, she would take her time to acknowledge it. So he would show himself, he decided. He would confront her in the hall. He stationed himself outside the study door. He heard her footsteps, and others', too, and he feared that she might have Doris with her. He made to go back into his study, but Virginia was upon him and the shadow of Doris behind her.

Quickly Virginia turned, gathered Doris in her arms, and shielded her face with her cardigan. She wondered why she did so. Why she still felt it her duty to protect Alistair from his daughter.

'What are you doing at home?' she said.

'I had cancellations.' He smiled at her. 'May we talk?' he asked. He did not like the pleading he heard in his voice. Even less did he relish her response.

'I'm busy. I have things to do with Doris,' she said.

She started to lift the cardigan from Doris's face. It was a threatening gesture, and forced his withdrawal. He slammed the study door after him. His anger with himself was sublime. For the first time in many years, he felt that he had lost the upper hand, that suddenly, other people, women to boot, had him in their power and there was little he could do about it. He wondered why he had asked Virginia for conversation, when there was very little he had to say to her. Perhaps he hoped it would give her an opportunity to entreat him once

53

again to leave Mary, in which case, although he had already lost her, he might reluctantly agree, claiming it as an enormous sacrifice. And thus he would regain the upper hand. But Virginia was clearly indifferent, both to himself and to Mary, and it was this that disturbed him most of all. For he knew that there could be no improvement on indifference. It could lead nowhere except to the very worst form of tolerance. In other words, he would become an object of contempt.

He got out his pad and began to Doris-doodle. But the likeness he had erstwhile achieved now escaped him and, instead of features on Doris's circle, he found himself drawing houses for eyes, a phallus for the nose and a spoon for the mouth. But again, these were fantasies that belonged to other people, to people like his own patients, and each and every one of those symbols was open to his clever Freudian interpretation. But none of those aberrations had anything at all to do with him. Yet, in one corner of his mind, he acknowledged that these ravings had come from his own pen and he worried that perhaps he was becoming unhinged. I need a holiday, he thought. Two or three weeks in the sun. A lot of swimming and walking. Get my mind off my mind, he decided.

He was pleased that at last he had come to a decision, even a tangential one. He would start making arrangements that very moment. He opened his diary to search out a spare three weeks. On one page he noticed an entry that was not in his handwriting. It was unmistakably Virginia's and it marked Doris's fifth birthday. He bristled. He viewed the entry as a double affront. First, that she had had the temerity to invade the privacy of his diary, and, secondly, that she had felt she had to remind him. Doris's birthday was notched in his mind like a wound, forever green. From year to year, that day clung to him like a burr and with such tenacity that he knew that, even if Doris died, it would never relinquish its hold. Moreover a fifth birthday was a landmark. A legal age. Schooling unavoidable. Doris would have to be assessed. Her physical abilities and her mental age would be subject to examination prior to placing her in a suitable school. The whole process spelt out parental involvement. Once again he would be called upon to do his duties as a father, and once again he would have to run, as he had done on each of Doris's birthdays. As he had done when Virginia had first placed Doris in a special nursery school. She had asked for his co-operation, but he had refused to discuss it. He was not going to collude in any plans for Doris's future. He would not accept that such a future existed. Yet sometimes he would pass by the school on his way to work and he would idle at the railings and watch the children at play. Perhaps Doris was amongst them, but never having seen her face, and not being familiar with her wardrobe, he was unlikely to pick her out. There were a number of Down's Syndrome children in the playground and, unless you were a parent of one of them, they tended all to look the same. And, in Alistair's non-parent eye, but for gender they were indistinguishable the one from the other. There were others, too, of varying handicaps. There was much laughter and shouting, but the overall cheer had nothing to do with the heartbreak left at home. Two minders moved amongst the children. Both women. No job for a man, Alistair thought, and certainly not for a father. Then he would turn away and go to his rooms and deal with men with *real* problems, terrorised by feelings to which they were *not* entitled.

He looked again at his diary. He was tempted to cross out Doris's birthday reminder but that was too close to annihilation. Moreover her birthday fell in the only three weeks of the year he could clear for himself as holiday. He studied the entry with fury. He could not cross it out, but he had to make some gesture of protest. So he put a very positive question-mark after the entry. It needn't have meant the worst, for it could have meant anything. It would not stop him making his holiday plans, he decided. There was no harm in making preparations for escape. Now he had to decide where he should go. With some excitement he reached for his atlas, grateful for something to occupy his time. He had first to make the choice of continent. Once that was decided upon, the rest was easy. He was not a beach man. He did not worship the sun. He wanted lakes and mountains. That narrowed the field. He opened the atlas at random and landed in Chile. From the map's contours and colours he noticed an abundance of all that he wanted. The Andes range was in fact the country's cradle. That will do, he thought, and considered that his random choice augured well. He would take it further. Shutting his eyes, he circled his finger around the whole page, around and around and in contrary directions in order to disorientate himself, until finally he came to rest on what he thought was the middle. But it was Valparaiso. He was a little disappointed at the proximity of the coastline, but the place was at least accessible, a short drive or a train ride perhaps from Santiago. He felt a warm glow inside him that he had actually made a decision. He took his pad and made a list of preparations for his South American escape. He headed the list with a visit to a travel agent and, while thinking about his next requirement, he found himself doodling, first in squares and oblongs and then in circles, and then with the shocking inevitability to which circles led. Again Doris. And forever Doris. As he drew, he trembled. He knew that no holiday would cure his obsession and that, in any and every part of the world, he would be found doodling. He despaired now that he would ever stop, that perhaps even if he were, in desperate crisis, to look upon her face, even then he would not believe what he saw, and his doodling would still persist in his fantasies. He would go to his grave doodling, whether he had looked on Doris or not. He wondered whether he would outlive her, and who would weep at whose graveside. But such thoughts were not good for his doodle fantasies. They would render them grotesque. He stuffed the paper into his drawer.

He resolved never, never to doodle again for, that way, madness lay. But he knew that addictions were not so easily put aside, and that the pains of withdrawal might be unbearable. But he would try. No more Doris-doodling. But what would replace it? There was no question of the thing itself. Of actually viewing the flesh and blood of his model. 'I cannot do it. Ever. Ever,' he said to himself. Then wondered why. In his life, during his training as a doctor, he had been called upon to view the ugliest and most blood-curdling spectacles. The after-mess of road accidents, the putrefaction of gangrene, the grin of gaping wounds. Yet none of these had fazed him. He had looked upon them all with an initial shudder, and then with an indifference that allowed for efficient treatment. An indifference that he was able to achieve because, in all that outrage, there was no hint of personal offence. But Doris's face, whatever it looked like, was a personal affront, and it was that exclusive insult that forbade his Doris-viewing. For it was as if he himself had been maimed and carried the parent wound and Doris was a mere osmosis. But where did *his* wound come from, and of whom was he a percolation? He thought of his father, or perhaps it was his mother, but he knew that this was an endless pursuit and would never pin-point a target for blame. He wished he believed in God, God as the father of all living things, that father, the original, who was himself the primal wound that had affected the whole of mankind. Belief in God could be a convenience at times, but such belief could be an impediment to psychiatry. He thought of Esau, that transient patient

57

of his who, because he blamed nobody, had turned that unsightliness of his into a thing of beauty and was flaunting it with the zeal of a tub-thumping hot-gospeller. As the evangelist wished to share with others his love of Jesus and his joy, so Esau wanted to share his beauty. Life is so simple for some, Alistair thought. He wondered by what stretch of the imagination a Down's Syndrome child could be found beautiful and he knew it had nothing to do with the imagination. It had nothing to do with anything but loving, and for that, he had to admit to himself, he had little talent. Which thought brought Mary to his mind. He wanted her still but he knew that he could do well enough without her and this fact offended him, that he was able to live so blandly without passion. He'd had a patient once, he remembered, who'd come to see him with exactly that incapacity. It was a common enough complaint but he had never until now believed that he was subject to it. To everything unpalatable, including the siring of a Down's Syndrome child, he was immune. He recalled that patient again and wondered how he had treated her. He remembered that one day she had simply telephoned and cancelled her appointment, and he hadn't seen her again. She was either cured or disenchanted, and he suspected the latter. Sometimes, in moments of clarity, he had little faith in his profession, and regarded it as rather a dishonest way of making a living. In such moments, which were mercifully rare, he considered returning to medicine proper. He thought he might perhaps take a refresher course and work as a General Practitioner. At least that way he could see the results of his treatment. He could see them getting well or he could tend them at their dying. He could even deliver a Down's Syndrome child and look it squarely in the face. He warmed to this idea. If he could rid himself of that ragged stream of lunatics who filed daily into his consulting rooms, perhaps he would be less affected by their frenzy. Perhaps he would reach less often for his doodle, as an addict reaches for his fix. He was excited by this possibility of change. But he would think about it tomorrow. As he would about his holiday.

He heard a child's footsteps outside his door.

Quickly he shot towards it and turned the key.

The footsteps stopped outside and his heart pounded.

'Daddy?' Doris called.

He remembered the first time he'd heard that word. It was like a slap in the face. No doubt Virginia had been practising with her. As his key had turned in the lock shortly after her Daddy-less second birthday, he heard it singing from the kitchen. He hadn't answered. Since then, she had called it every time his key had turned and always the call was greeted by silence. Over the months and years that followed, the call of 'Daddy' gradually lost its interrogative tone and became simply a statement, a Pavlovian response to the turning of a key. Doris learned quicker than Virginia, he thought. She was happy enough to settle for his silent nocturnal visits.

'Daddy?' she called again.

This time Alistair heard the question-mark and he put it down to malicious Virginia-coaching.

'What is it, dear?' he said. The words curdled in his throat.

It was the first time, in the four-and-a-half years of her daughterhood that he had ever spoken to her, albeit through a wooden door. He suspected that Virginia was standing by Doris's side, monitoring what she thought was progress.

'Can I show you my new dress, Daddy?' Doris said. 'It's for the school concert.'

In four-and-a-half years, Alistair thought, she must have collected a wardrobe of new dresses, yet this was the first time she'd been prompted to request his approval.

'I'm busy now,' he said. 'I'm sure it's lovely.'

He waited for her footsteps.

'Daddy,' she said.

No question-mark. Just a simple statement of fact that, sub-titled, meant, 'Whether you like it or not, I am your daughter, and you are my father.'

He heard her moving away from the door, in the unsurprising echo of Virginia's tread. He was suddenly frightened. He suspected that this might mark the onset of a blackmailing campaign, disguised perhaps as a game of hide-and-seek, and that one day Doris might not even wait for the door-key, but would present her full frontal at the door. He started to panic. He had to get out. And quickly. If he stayed in his house a moment longer, he would only be colluding in a trap.

He took his suitcase out of the cupboard. He was glad that he had never unpacked it. He had no idea where he would go, but he would not pause to think about it. An immediate escape was imperative. But he could not leave until nightfall, until he was absolutely sure that the bait was well and truly asleep, and its angler too. He would leave Virginia a note, he decided. Just a few words saying he would come back at a convenient time for his belongings. She was entitled to no further information. He was not leaving his marriage. He was being driven out of it. He was not obliged to excuse himself in any way. He scribbled the note in a panic laced with his anger. He didn't even bother to sign it, not so much out of his rage with Virginia, but out of his own lack of self-esteem. For to pen one's signature is a small but undeniable token of celebration and, of that, he felt nothing.

He waited until midnight. Then, encouraged by the silence in the house, he crept out of his room.

He wondered why the landing-light was still burning. And he suspected a trap.

He crept towards the stairway and, there, hanging on the landing, lit by the overhead lamp, was a small pink gingham dress, its sleeves puffed out, and its skirt billowing over a white silk petticoat. There was nothing for arms or legs, those normal appendages but the metal question-mark of the hanger stood in for Doris's face.

Virginia had hung it there as his marching orders. Alistair had the feeling that he had lost everything.

# Five

THAT NIGHT he slept in his consulting rooms. On his nightmare couch. He was used to sleeping alone, but couch-sleeping was not solitary and all night he had his restless patients for company.

He was surprised by a knock on his door. He thought perhaps it might be Virginia, with Doris in tow. Or, more probably, the other way round. He hoped it was the cleaning lady.

'Who is it?' he called.

'Gerry.'

Alistair was not in the mood for visitors. He looked at his watch. Six o'clock. He wondered what Gerry was doing in his rooms at this hour. No patient, however desperate, could persuade Gerry to get to work at the crack of dawn.

'Come in,' he said.

Gerry put his head round the door. He was dishevelled and pyjama'd.

'I wondered whether it was you,' he said. 'I heard noises in the night.'

'What are you doing here?' Alistair asked.

Gerry poured his full bulk into the room. 'Same as you, I suppose.'

He grinned sheepishly and sat down in Alistair's chair. 'Janet threw me out.'

Alistair leapt in, on the defensive. '*Not* quite the same,' he said, with as much dignity as his unkempt state would allow. 'I left. I just didn't seem to fit in any more.'

'Has Doris taken your place,' Gerry asked. Or rather said.

'Do you have to shrink so early in the morning?' Alistair asked. 'It's not like that at all. And you? Why has Janet chucked you? And please. No analysis.'

'She found out about Fiona.'

'Your secretary?'

'It's been about a year now,' Gerry said. 'Thought I was getting away with it. Then her friend told her. Her best friend, I may add.'

'What are you going to do?'

'Think about it. If it weren't for my daughter, I think I'd leave England.'

'With Fiona?'

Gerry laughed. 'I don't think she would travel very well. You know,' he confided, 'Fiona's just an affair. Fine as long as Janet's in the background. But once Janet backs out, it's over. It's like a three-hander play. One pulls out of the cast, and it's not a play any more. What about you? If it isn't Doris, and it's not an affair, and I presume it isn't, what are you doing here?'

Alistair resented his presumption. 'What makes you think it's not another woman?' he asked.

'You're not the type,' Gerry said. 'I'm not suggesting you don't have the appetite. Or indeed the opportunity. But having a child like Doris for a daughter, puts a different complexion on things.'

'It's got nothing to do with Doris.' Alistair's voice rose.

Gerry knew best to let it lie. 'If you say so,' he said.

'I'll find a flat, I think. Give myself some space on my own. Think about it. Like you. All I know is that I cannot sleep on that couch another night.' He wondered how many shrinks in Harley and Wimpole Street, in that whole square mile of swindle, were usurping their patients' terrain, trespassing on their dreams and visions. 'Are there others like us?' Alistair asked.

'It's a risk of the profession,' Gerry said. 'Let's go out and get some breakfast.'

They went to an hotel near by, and ordered lavishly.

'I must say,' Gerry mumbled through a mouthful of toast, I rather like this kind of living.'

'You'd get tired of it,' Alistair said.

Gerry was not a pleasant sight. He ate with his mouth open, and one look would account for every ingredient of an English breakfast. No wonder Janet had thrown him out. Even without Fiona.

Alistair forced himself to stare into Gerry's face. And open mouth too. It was repulsive. Yet he kept his eyes on it. He thought about Doris's face and considered it could in no way be as repulsive as this one. Yet he was looking at this full frontal. He wondered about the notions of ugliness and beauty, and deduced that both were in the eye of the beholder. If Esau could view himself as a thing of beauty, and to the point of sheer Narcissism, then perhaps Fiona, or even Janet, could see beauty in Gerry. As Virginia could see it in Doris. Then why was *his* eye so blind? His profession told him it was parenthood, but his heart amended it to pride. He wished he were alone and that he had his pad so that he could Doris-doodle his pain away. His fingers itched for her eyes, her nose, her chin, all those untouchables and unviewables. I must look at her, he decided. I must force myself to look at her face, to examine it minutely, to touch it even, as I touch every whole part of her body. But, in that moment of decision, he caught sight of Gerry's mouthful of kipper, and he knew that nothing in the world could remove that paternal cataract from his eye.

He wanted to get back to his rooms. He had patients all morning, but the afternoon was relatively free.

He would spend that time looking for an apartment. Around his professional area and all the off-shoots of Baker Street, there was an abundance of flats for short-term rental. They were for tourist families who wanted to save on hotels. It was now the off-season and he did not expect to have any difficulty in finding a place to live. He would phone the agents as soon as he got back to his office.

When the waitress brought the bill, Gerry fumbled in his pockets. And so did Alistair. Both were mean men, and neither was ashamed of it. The fumbling went on for a while, for both men fumbled seriously and earnestly. Their faces were solemn, for meanness precludes a sense of humour. The waitress hovered and her presence gave more urgency to their search. They fumbled, both of them, frantically. One of them would have to give, and each one was going to make damn sure it was the other. The waitress sighed, but her impatience fazed neither man. They fumbled away and always in the same pocket, for to look elsewhere would have been a clear indication of avoidance.

'There are people waiting for your table,' the waitress said.

'We are not yet ready to leave,' Gerry told her, on his dignity, and took his hand out of his pocket once and for all.

Alistair followed suit.

'Would you pay at the desk?' the waitress said. Defeated, she walked away, and left them a breathing space, both with their hands on the table.

'Shall we go Dutch?' Alistair said at last, wishing to get back to his consulting rooms.

'That's fine by me,' Gerry said in a tone of profound generosity. He looked at the bill and made a quick division. Then, without any fumbling, he quickly drew some change from his pocket and meticulously counted out his half-share. Alistair did likewise.

'No tip, I don't think,' Gerry said. 'The service was abominable.'

They ambled out of the restaurant without the speed of guilt and, as they walked up Harley Street, Alistair asked Gerry where he was going to sleep that night.

'I'll ring Janet,' he said. 'Take her out to dinner. Sweeten her up a bit.'

Alistair wished him better luck than he had had with such a manoeuvre.

'I shall find a noisy one,' Gerry was saying, 'to drown the conversation that we don't have.'

As they reached their street door, they saw Esau coming towards them. Esau on his early morning rounds.

'Here comes the fucking gorilla,' Gerry said. 'Has he called on you yet?'

'Yes,' Alistair said. 'I found him rather pleasant company.'

'Off his rocker,' Gerry said. 'I gave him very short shrift. God help us, but he's going to stop and talk.'

Esau did, and with a large smile.

Gerry quickly excused himself and ran up the front steps.

'Why are people in such a rush?' Esau said.

'He has a patient.' Alistair considered why he was so anxious to cover for Gerry. It wasn't loyalty to a fraternity; it was to protect Esau from insult.

'How are you, Esau?' Alistair asked.

'You remember my name,' Esau smiled.

'Your name, yourself, very clearly,' Alistair said. He felt suddenly very affectionate towards this man.

'Where do you live, Esau?' he asked.

'Not far,' Esau said. 'Just round the corner. I have a whole house. It was my father's. He worked as a doctor there. He left it to me when he died. Would you like to see it?' Esau asked with a child's eagerness. 'You could come for lunch.'

'I'd love to,' Alistair said. He felt their meeting was fortuitous, that it might open an avenue of friendship and exploration that he had never experienced before.

He wrote down Esau's address, and arranged to be there at one o'clock.

'I shall go shopping,' Esau said. Then, looking straight at Alistair, he put his hand on his arm. 'You *do* find me beautiful, don't you?'

'Of course,' Alistair said, and somehow regretted his acceptance of lunch. He was not frightened of assault. Esau was too gentle for that. Perhaps it was fear of the man's expectations. He decided to leave Esau's address with his secretary. Someone would know where he could be found.

Once in his rooms, he called the house agents, and made appointments to see three flats that afternoon. He did not expect Virginia to phone during the day. He considered himself well and truly expelled from the marriage. Neither would Mary call. She too had tired of him. He realised then that he had no personal friends. All his acquaintances were bound up with Virginia and his marriage. He felt isolated and alone. He thought suddenly of his parents, and all the news of which they had been deprived. Doris's face. And now the end of his marriage. He felt a depression coming upon him and he was glad when his first patient arrived.

Miss Wetherby was now in her ninth year of therapy and this morning, for the first time, Alistair wondered whether she was making any progress. He thought that he might come clean with her and tell her that he could do no more. He was aware that he'd made a small fortune out of her distress, but, if he should now ask her to desist from therapy, her withdrawal pains would only add to her despair. Her three-times-weekly visits to his rooms were probably her only reason for going out at all, and to be deprived of this facility was tantamount to sentencing her to a life's imprisonment. Miss Wetherby bore her suffering with what looked suspiciously like enjoyment.

She was not a likable woman and, today, Alistair began to loathe her.

'How are you today, Miss Wetherby?' he said.

'The same.'

For nine whole years, three times a week, this had been their opening exchange. Sometimes he thought that Miss Wetherby would have been better off had she been poor. That with her money, and she had a great deal of it, she had indulged her pain, no worse and no better than any other patient's, except that she nourished it with her wealth. He decided that this would be her last session. It seemed the day for giving people the boot, and Miss Wetherby might as well fit into the pattern.

'This will be our last session,' Alistair said.

Her face fell.

'Are you going away?' she whispered.

'No. But I do not think I can do anything more for you.'

'But where shall I go?' The tears obliged. Money can produce anything.

'You don't need to go anywhere. Or to anybody else. After nine years, it must be up to you.'

'But I can't,' she said. The tears were falling now, adequately paid for. 'What shall I do with my time?'

That was the question he feared. And he responded with the phrase that he had buried in the back of his mouth ever since he'd put up his psychiatrist's plate. It was a monumental relief to set it free.

'You must pull yourself together, Miss Wetherby,' he said.

She gaped at him.

She had heard that phrase often enough. From her parents, when they were alive, her sisters and brother and her dwindling circle of friends. But she had never expected it from this quarter. Indeed, one of her main reasons for opting for therapy in the first place was the positive assurance that she would never hear that phrase.

It was a breach of the etiquette of analysis and she had it in mind to sue him.

'What kind of therapy talk is that?' she said.

Money can buy courage, too.

It was the first time in nine years that Alistair had heard the faintest tone of resistance from her. Perhaps at last he was making headway. He would bait her, he thought, another unethical pursuit, but perhaps it would arouse in her a rage that might for a while offset her pain. It was worth a try.

'Miss Wetherby,' he started, 'let us spend this last session of ours recapping on your situation. I want you to lie on the couch and tell me exactly how you see yourself at this moment. I want you to start with your feelings about my termination of your therapy. The withdrawal of your crutches. The brutal push into the outside world.' He set the stage for her rage.

Miss Wetherby did not go meekly to the couch, as was her wont. She strode towards it, made to kick off her shoes, then changed her mind. Why should she not soil his bloody couch? So she lay on it, dirty shoes and all, digging their dirt into the uncut moquette.

'D'you really want me to tell you the truth?' she threatened him.

'Say whatever you want to say,' Alistair said.

She plunged in at the deep end.

'I've been making enquiries,' she said. 'You've got a very ugly daughter.'

Alistair's heart turned over.

In his professional capacity he knew that such a statement was part-projection and part-revenge. Possibly more of the latter. A sudden realisation of nine

69

years of three-weekly payments, and their offensive calculated total, was more than enough to set the pot a-simmering. Money down the drain. Irretrievable. Patients have killed their analysts for less. But Miss Wetherby didn't have the strength, or the legality, and of the latter she was acutely aware, for, in her daily humdrum life, she was an upright citizen, obedient, dutiful and law-abiding. So she would kill him with words, and words were free. No price to be paid for words. So she let Alistair have it, digging in her dirty heels, and out of her polite mouth came a stream of vocabulary that, even laundered, might have shamed a dockside. Alistair listened and desperately tried to remain professional. Not an easy task, since the target of all Miss Wetherby's abuse seemed to be poor Doris. She was intelligent enough to know that Doris was Alistair's Achilles heel, and this she prodded with relentless and hammering obscenities. In his work, Alistair was acquainted with the obscenity syndrome. More commonly it was manifest in senility, when women, and occasionally men, of erstwhile impeccable refinement, whose limit of blasphemy was a whispered 'Damn' or 'Damnation', would suddenly and unaccountably season their conversation with cascades of incontinent smut. In times of crises, they would reach into the very sewers of language, as poor Miss Wetherby was doing now. In those labyrinthal drains, her despair sprouted words like 'fuck', words which had nothing to do with fornication, but were simple sub-titles for her life of restraint, frustration and loss. The word 'shit' perhaps afforded some measure of relief; but all those words which relate to women's shame were a gross and crude apology for being a woman in the first place.

Poor Miss Wetherby. Alistair tried to concentrate on her pain, to be moved by it even. He longed for his doodle-pad and some Doris-release. He let Miss

Wetherby hold forth, but he ceased to listen. But the 'daughter' stung him. It had become an obscenity like all the others. But more frequent. And each time she re-sharpened the word with her tongue so that it landed like a honed arrow in Alistair's heart. Gradually her speech decelerated, and the obscenities drowned themselves in their sewers. All but 'daughter' which floated like scum for a while, and then it too gave up its wretched ghost, as poor Miss Wetherby reverted to the lady she had been nine years and thousands of pounds ago.

She sat up and saw her shoes. 'Oh dear,' she said, and her distress was clear. 'I'm so absolutely sorry, Dr Crown. Look what I've done to your couch. It will need cleaning and perhaps a re-upholster. But of course I shall pay for it. Such shocking vandalism. I am indeed deeply sorry.'

Her apologetic mien was infinitely worse than her rudeness and he heartily wished she would go.

'Please send me the bill,' she insisted. 'I really don't know what came over me.'

I hope, Alistair thought, she has forgotten, for how could poor Miss Wetherby learn to live with such recalled embarrassment?

'Goodbye, Dr Crown,' she said, holding out a gloved hand, now in complete and ruinous control. 'It's been a pleasure.'

'Goodbye,' he said, and sadly watched her go.

Nothing, nothing at all had been achieved. She would return to that same polite routine, her daily round of bitter decorum, of enraged courtesy, and thwarted breeding. In the fullness of time, and full of manners, she would die of well-bred anger, that they would probably diagnose as cancer of the womb. Poor Miss Wetherby.

When she had gone, Alistair reached into his desk for his doodle-pad. But at the last moment he refrained.

Miss Wetherby had given him a punishing dose of Doris and to doodle her now would risk her annihilation. He was glad when his next patient arrived.

Mr Kaye was relatively new on Alistair's couch. He was in his mid-fifties and Alistair was his first sortie into therapy. He had been married four times, and it was only when his fourth wife had left him that the thought crossed his mind that there might be something wrong, not with the women, whom he had always blamed, but with himself. There might be. Just a very slim possibility. And it was this thought that had brought him to Alistair's door. What had quickened his steps was the fact that he had met another woman with whom he had fallen deeply in love, and he desperately wanted that relationship to flower and to flourish and, most of all, to last.

On first meeting him, almost a year ago, Alistair had viewed him with despair. The man's arrogance was sublime. He could be told nothing. For everything, he knew. But he was an ignorant man, with an ignorance that was encyclopaedic. For he knew absolutely nothing about absolutely everything. Alistair disliked him. He knew that the arrogance alone would take months if not years to break down and that what, if anything, would be found in its place might be equally repugnant.

But Mr Kaye had responded well, and only occasionally a hint of the old swagger returned. Indeed sometimes he was as courteous and as well-mannered as poor Miss Wetherby, and at such times Alistair wondered whether such a change could be termed improvement. Nevertheless, over the months that they had worked together, Mr Kaye had become acquainted with his own failings and was in the process of repairing himself.

But this morning he arrived in a mood of abject depression. The inevitable had happened. His new, or now, not-so-new love had left him.

'Women,' he spat out with contempt, and in that moment Alistair saw all their months' work crumble into dust.

'Sit down, Mr Kaye,' Alistair said, for Mr Kaye had been standing while blurting out his catastrophe into air polluted still with poor Miss Wetherby's filth.

'I'm not going on that couch,' he said. 'It's dirty.'

Belligerent, Alistair thought, even as he had been on his very first visit. 'You don't have to go on the couch,' he said. 'You can sit on the chair.'

'I'd rather stand,' Mr Kaye said.

It did not augur well.

'You won't mind if I sit?' Alistair said.

'Please yourself.'

Alistair settled himself down. 'Now tell me about it,' he said. He could not disguise the weariness in his voice and he made no attempt to cover it. He was perilously on the point of not listening at all, as Mr Kaye droned on with his complaints that life had treated him so shabbily. And it was all women's fault. Beginning with his mother.

But they had done all that bit, Alistair thought, in their first sessions together, and here was Mr Kaye again, dragging that wretched mother of his out of her grave once more to re-crucify her in death since it had failed to work in her lifetime. Alistair closed his eyes. If Mr Kaye were to look at him, he would take it, he hoped, for deep concentration.

Which Mr Kaye did, satisfied that his recital was having the desired effect. It was only when Alistair started to snore that the concentration verdict became faintly questionable. Mr Kaye was shocked. After having dealt vaguely with that, he was offended, and insult was harder to accommodate.

'Dr Crown,' he bellowed.

Alistair woke up with a start. 'I'm . . . I'm sorry,' he said.

Then Mr Kaye came into his arrogant own. 'I don't pay you good money three times a week to take your siesta,' he said.

Money again, Alistair thought. And what was *good* money? Was it the opposite of bad? And what was the difference? It all came down to money.

'I'm sorry,' he said again, though he wasn't sorry at all, as some of Mr Kaye's belligerence infected him. 'I'm tired,' he said in measured tones. 'I didn't sleep at all last night. Moreover, I'm depressed myself.' He raised his voice. 'And to tell you the truth, I'm bored. Please go away.'

Mr Kaye stared at him. Unbelievingly. 'But this is your fucking *job*,' he shouted. He too had sewers at his command.

'I know,' Alistair said, 'and I'm not very good at it.'

'I'm not paying.'

'Of course not. Forget it. Just don't come back.'

Mr Kaye made to button his coat, then realised that he hadn't unbuttoned. 'I don't understand anything any more,' he mumbled.

Then made for the door.

'It's you I'm sorry for,' Mr Kaye said.

Then he opened the door quietly and as quietly closed it after him.

Alistair sighed with enormous relief.

He had never before turned away a patient. It was an act, he knew, that withdrew his entitlement to practise. Perhaps that was exactly what he had had in mind. He was bored. Bored with people's problems, bored with their suffering. When Mr Kaye had embarked on his recital of his latest rejection, Alistair knew he had heard it all before. And not only from Mr Kaye. It was time that he changed direction, and not only in his job, but in his whole way of life. But for the moment he would sleep.

An unbearable fatigue overcame him and most of it was depression.

74

He rang his receptionist and told her he was not to be disturbed. He was not expecting another patient. But the disturbance he wished to be protected from, referred to phone-calls, one of which he fully expected to be from Virginia.

He took off his shoes and lay down on the couch, wishing Mr Kaye had done him the favour of dislodging Miss Wetherby's salacious imprint. It loitered underneath him, in cold comfort. Mercifully, he fell asleep almost at once, but was prey to nightmarish visions which, on waking, he dared not analyse. He looked at his watch. It was time for his lunch appointment with Esau. He wondered whether he should go. He feared the experience might thrust him into an even deeper depression. But he was curious. He wanted to see how Esau lived. He washed quickly and left his rooms, praying not to run into Gerry, whose dilemma was as boring as Mr Kaye's.

When he reached Esau's house, he was amazed at its size. It spread over the corner site of two streets, and by the look of its front door it was of single occupation. For it sported no brass plates as was the custom in that area, neither did it have names or numbers of apparent divisions. Esau must rattle about the place entirely alone. He rang the brass bell and waited. In time he heard footsteps, and so light was the gait that he thought it might be a child's. So he was surprised when Esau himself opened the door, and more than a little astonished to note that he was totally naked.

He was smiling.

'Come in and welcome,' he said.

Alistair followed him through the hall.

Esau led him to a living room. It was large and lugubrious. The walls were oak-panelled and to each section was attached a large animal head. Mainly antelope. On the floor was a scatter of tiger-skin rugs and a deer-skin half-covered the black grand piano.

75

Esau's family had clearly been into hair. It was the most depressing room Alistair had ever seen, and it did little to improve his temper. But Esau was very welcoming and after a while Alistair did not notice his nudity. In any case, he was hardly unclothed. His fur skin was coat enough.

He offered Alistair sherry, then sat him down on the sofa.

'Shall I play a little before lunch?' he said.

Alistair had no idea what he had in mind. He could not help feeling nervous. He risked a 'yes' feeling that a 'no' might denote a misunderstanding. Esau moved towards the piano and Alistair relaxed.

'A little Schubert is called for, I think,' Esau said. His fingers drifted into a phrase from a *Moment Musical*.

Alistair felt that his ring on the bell had interrupted Esau's playing. And now he would continue. Alistair watched him. On his face was a smile of such contentment, amounting almost to bliss, and such a peace within, that Alistair felt a small touch of envy. What has become of me, he thought? I have a daughter pushing five-years-old whose face I have never seen. I have a marriage which, to all intents and purposes, is broken. And I'm having lunch with a piano-playing ape.

He watched, rather than listened, for Esau's face was suffused with a compelling tranquillity and for a moment Alistair could see Esau as Esau saw himself. Simply as an object of intense beauty.

He walked over to the piano and, as the piece drew to a close, he put his hand on Esau's furred shoulder and squeezed it a little through its coating. It was a gesture of the most profound gratitude. He would tell Esau his story. All his working life he had listened, turned his ear to others' tales. And each one, though like any other, he tried hard to hear for the first time. Until today, when, in a costly moment of clarity, he had seen the alarming

76

futility of his work; when he had recalled each tale of suffering as only a slight variation of another; when he had concluded that pain was so boring it sent him to sleep. A costly moment indeed, for its clarity was so intense, that it had blinded him to the inviolate principle of his work: that pain, whether merited or not, was still pain; that suffering, however boring, was somebody's cry of despair. Today Alistair had become blind to his vocation and deafened by the sound of his own voice calling for help.

Yes, he would tell Esau his story. He would become a patient as he had been in his training, and Esau, in his peace, would guide him.

They moved into the grand dining room. Esau had taken great pains with the preparations. The family silver was much in evidence. Alistair had expected a vegetarian spread, for that cuisine seemed to be in keeping with Esau's nature. So he was surprised by the very red and rare meat that Esau served, together with wines and all the ingredients of delicious but unhealthy living.

Alistair waited until they were settled.

Then, 'I have problems, Esau,' he said.

There was a silence. Esau was clearly considering his response.

Then, 'Tell me,' he said.

And so Alistair poured out his story. He told him about Virginia and their unreliable union. He told him about Mary, too. He left Doris until last. He found it painful to speak about her, but less and less painful as he unfolded the story. As he talked he kept seeing the pink gingham dress with its metal question-mark that stood in for the face.

'I can't look at her, Esau,' he said. 'I think I would fall apart.'

Esau sipped at his wine. 'Let's first be practical,' he said. 'Where are you going to live?'

'I have appointments. This afternoon. There are many short-term lets around here.'

'Would you consider staying with me?' Esau asked. It was an invitation of warmth and without any pleading. 'This is a large house. You could have your own quarters. Think about it.'

But Alistair needed no time to consider. And not just for convenience. He wanted to *be* with Esau. He wanted to live within that man's terrain of peace. Where, for the first time in his life, there would be no judgement

'Thank you,' Alistair said. And again, 'Thank you.'

'Will Doris be at nursery-school this afternoon?' Esau knew the perils of hide-and-seek.

'She's there till four o'clock,' Alistair said.

'Then you've time to go home and pack your things.'

He walked with Alistair through the hall. 'Here's your key,' he said. 'This is your home now.' He opened the front door.

'Thank you,' Alistair said again.

Esau put his hand on Alistair's arm. 'There were many times,' he said, 'when my father couldn't bear to look at *me*.'

# *Six*

ALISTAIR RANG the bell before putting his key in the lock. He wanted to make sure that nobody was at home. He opened the door and checked once again. Then he went straight to his room and packed. He packed all his clothes, and most of his papers. He thought of leaving another note for Virginia but he could think of nothing to write. He had no intention of giving her his new address for one day he might find the pink gingham dress on his door-step and it would not be on a metal hanger. He rushed out of the house, loaded the car and drove away.

But he need not have feared Virginia's blackmail. For Virginia had written him off. The hanging gingham dress had been her signature, and signed, too, on behalf of her daughter. For she had found a replacement, both as husband and father.

Hugo was the administrator of Doris's school. In this capacity he worked as a parent-counsellor. One morning as Virginia settled Doris in her class, he called her into his office and remarked that he had never met Doris's father. A cover-up was ready on Virginia's tongue as it always was in defence of her husband's negligence.

'He's . . . he's away.'

Hugo smiled. 'You can tell me the truth, Mrs Crown,' he said.

After that it was easy and, with little sense of betrayal, she told him the whole story.

Thereafter he had taken a special interest in Doris, an interest which slowly spread to embrace her mother, too. Their relationship was an easy and a happy one, and gradually, in the course of it, all that Virginia could manage to feel for Alistair was pity. She envisaged that, in time, she and Hugo would marry and between them they would make a half-brother or sister for Doris. Doris had settled happily into the threesome. She looked upon Hugo as her day-Daddy, though she said nothing about the night specimen, fearing perhaps that, although she enjoyed his visits, they were illegal.

That morning, Virginia had read Alistair's note of separation. She was relieved. She hoped that, in time, he would ask for a divorce. They would come to an amicable arrangement. There would be no argument about custody. Alistair would not even claim visiting rights and it would all be over as if it had never been. She had not mentioned Alistair's departure to her mother, though she had phoned that morning. And certainly her mother had no idea of Hugo. After Alistair's absence from Doris's first birthday party, and all subsequent ones, her parents would understand. Both of them. They might even rejoice. Alistair's parents were a different matter. Virginia had no contact with them. They had never approved of her. It was Alistair who kept in touch. She wondered if he had told them about Doris's condition. Or even of Doris's existence. But that was Alistair's problem, as were so many others. She hoped he would find another woman. Then she could loosen up on her pity, for that pity was an impediment to her own happiness.

She left Doris in the playground with other children and she went to Hugo's study. Over the last few months it had become a daily routine that she would spend some time with Hugo before the bell rang for assembly.

She told him right away.

'Alistair's gone,' she said. 'This time it's for good.'

80

'How did it happen?' he asked.

She told him the story of the gingham dress. 'I'd bought it for the end-of-term concert,' Virginia said. 'She was so excited. She wanted to show it to him. 'What does he look like?' she asked. It broke my heart. But he wouldn't come out of his room. So I hung it on a hanger on the landing. That way, he'd see the dress, at least.'

'Poor man,' was the only comment Hugo made, and it served only to feed Virginia's already well-stocked fund of pity. 'Will he come back, d'you think?' Hugo asked.

'How can he?' Virginia said. 'He's frightened. I've protected him for so long from Doris's face. Now, after last night, he would not trust my protection any more. No. He won't come back,' she said.

'Perhaps it's for the best. For everybody,' Hugo said.

She looked at him. She knew what he had in mind and was glad of it. She knew, too, that he would give her time to adjust, but not long enough to get used to, and even hooked on, living alone.

'Would you like to go out tonight?' he asked. 'I think you need company. I'll pick you up at seven. Then Doris can show me her dress.'

'No, she won't do that,' Virginia said. Doris would not replace Alistair so quickly. But she did not want to hurt Hugo, so she offered some excuse. 'It's a surprise for the end-of-term concert,' she said. 'She wouldn't want you to see it till then.'

'Three whole weeks,' Hugo laughed. 'I wait with baited breath.'

The bell rang for assembly. Virginia settled Doris in the hall, and went off to work. During the course of the day she thought of phoning Alistair, but feared he might misinterpret her call. She didn't want him to come back. But she was concerned that he had somewhere to sleep. That his mood was not as low as it should have been.

*

81

But she need not have worried. Alistair was on something of a high. While driving back to Esau's, he had made the decision to quit his profession. He could not do it immediately. Some of his patients he could transfer to other therapists. But others, those who were close to the end of their treatment, he would not drop so easily. He reckoned that within three to six months he would be rid of them all. Rid of all that suffering, all that repetition, all that moneyed pain. He did not consider what he would do in its stead. Perhaps he would leave England altogether. He would miss nothing, he considered, except his nocturnal visits. At the thought of those, he knew that he would be tied to Doris all his life, wherever she might be, and that, as she grew older, he would tread more gently. He daren't think of her as a woman, for to explore her then would be another kind of expedition altogether. But, until that time, he would never leave her.

He let himself into his new home. He called from the hall to Esau. There was no answer, although he heard him moving upstairs.

'Esau?' he called again.

'I'll be down in a moment.'

The voice was dull. Something had happened to Esau since their lunch together. Perhaps he had changed his mind. Alistair left his cases by the door and waited at the foot of the stairs.

'Are you all right?' he called.

As Esau appeared at the turn of the stairway, it was clear that things were not right at all. His face was bleeding. The blood had matted into his hair. One eye was very swollen and his great naked body was trembling. He gripped the banister with one hand. Alistair's heart turned over and it astonished him that he could be so moved by another's distress.

'What happened?' he said.

Slowly Esau descended and, as he neared the bottom, his face broke into a painful smile. 'My father hated dentists,' he said. 'He used to say they were scum.'

Such injuries could not have been inflicted in a dentist's chair, and Alistair wondered what dentistry had to do with his wounds. But first he had to care for him.

'Have you put anything on that eye?' he asked.

'I've bathed it. And the mouth. It looks worse than it feels.'

Alistair took his arm. 'Come and sit down. You must be in shock.'

He led him into the living room and sat him down. Then, sitting by his side, he took his hand. 'Tell me about it,' he said. How often in his consulting room had he wished to take a patient's hand? To hold it, to squeeze it perhaps, with some measure of sympathy. A gesture that would have by-passed months and even years of therapy, that would have substituted for the silences, that would have released the restraints. He noticed tears gather on the rim of Esau's good eye, and Alistair had the feeling that no-one on earth had ever held the man's hand before.

'I don't know what it was that my father had against dentists. I think it must have been envy, because they managed to earn so much money. He had no reason for envy, because he was a very rich man. Anyway, he hated them and, whenever he came across a pleasant one, he found it very inconvenient. He was sort of racial in his hatred of them. It was blanket judgement. For some illogical reason, I inherited that hate. It was my way of pleasing him, I suppose. One of many, many ways. And I still hate them, and I suppose that's because I want to honour his memory. Why, I ask myself. Why?'

Alistair had misread Esau. He was far from being a man who blamed nobody. He hated his father with as much passion as Mr Kaye his mother. He simply put a good hairy face on it, and Alistair had been fooled. He'd wanted to be fooled, perhaps. He'd wanted an Esau who was not in pain. 'Go on,' he said. Tell me what happened.'

'Today I felt differently,' Esau said. 'It might have been something to do with you. I thought it would be a good day to try to break that particular chain of inheritance. I decided to parade my beauty before a dentist. After you'd left, I felt really excited, and I picked one at random. One quite near here. And I phoned for an appointment. I said it was an emergency. I was so excited, Alistair,' Esau said, leaning towards him. I felt I was talking to my father for the first time in my life. And not only talking to him but taking my own stand. Well, I went to his surgery, and I started on my routine. You're familiar with it. His nurse was in the room, but that didn't worry me. I have shown myself to women doctors in my time. They, too, are entitled to a sight of my beauty. I don't know what came over that dentist. Perhaps it was the presence of his nurse. But he didn't say one word to me. He didn't even tell me to go. He simply picked up one of his instruments from the table and threw it in my face. The nurse was appalled. I saw her face, but I think she was too frightened to help me. I dressed as quickly as I could. Then I left. He hadn't said one word to me. What makes me so sad Alistair,' Esau confided, 'is that, as I came home, I began to think that my father was right. And that's not what I had wanted at all. I wanted to prove that he was wrong, in order, in some way, to prove myself. All that's much worse than the cuts and bruises you must bring yourself to look at Doris you know.'

He said it all in one breath, with urgent continuity.

Alistair held onto Esau's hand. Here was a lesson for him, not one that was taught with any threat or judgement, but simply a lesson by example that one could take or leave at one's will. He could never hope for a better teacher, but Alistair was not ready. And he knew that, if he was not ready now, he never would be. Besides, he was angry, not only for himself but on Esau's behalf. He wanted that dentist sued for grievous bodily harm. He would take up the cudgels for Esau. It would be a way of excusing his own lethargy.

'What's the name of this dentist?' he asked.

'It's not important,' Esau said. 'He has his own problems and he must deal with them.'

'You have to sue him. He can't be allowed to get away with it.'

'Can you see it written in the tabloids? *Dentist sued by Naked Ape?*' Esau said.

It was clear that Esau had no illusions, so there was no point in Alistair having them on Esau's behalf.

Then Esau began to laugh. 'I'll get even with my father yet,' he said. 'There's no shortage of dentists in this part of the world.'

Alistair wanted to discourage him from further dental forays. Though not necessarily belligerent, dentists had an armoury of lethal weapons to hand. Even the most mild-mannered of them might feel provoked and threatened by Esau's self-proclaimed beauty. He explained the nature of his concern to Esau, but Esau brushed it aside. It was as if he were willing his own martyrdom. That the only way he could revenge himself on his father was to die, even though his father was no longer alive to repent or to mourn him. Alistair feared for Esau.

'Let me show you to your rooms,' Esau said.

He insisted on carrying Alistair's cases and led the way up the stairs.

'Did you grow up in this house?' Alistair asked.

'Yes,' Esau said. 'I was born here. My father delivered me. I grew up sheathed in oak-panelling.'

'Do you have brothers? Sisters?'

85

'No,' Esau said. 'I'm an only. My father took one look at me, one of his very infrequent looks, and decided that one of my kind was enough. I was born like this, you see. Covered in hair from top to toe.' There was no bitterness in his voice. Nor even anger. Life had played a mean trick on him and he simply wanted the last laugh. And that laugh would probably resound in a dentist's treatment room.

He opened the door of what looked like a study. 'These were my aunt's quarters,' he said. 'My mother's sister. She was a doctor too. Gynaecologist. Never married. She used to look at me a lot. I can't say that her looks were all that comfortable, but at least she had no problems looking at me. This was her bedroom. And bathroom,' he said, moving around the suite.

'Where is she now?' Alistair asked.

'Dead. They died. All of them in one year. Father, mother, aunt. And in that order. And they left me all this oak panelling.'

'Why d'you stay here?' Alistair asked.

'As soon as I've laid the ghosts, I'll move,' Esau said.

'Have you no other family?'

'A cousin. In Australia.'

'Do you ever think of marrying?' Alistair said.

Esau put his hand on Alistair's arm. 'Thank you,' he said. 'That's a question that could only come from one who thinks I am perfectly normal.'

'And so you are,' Alistair insisted. 'You're a beautiful man with a lot of hair.'

Alistair wondered at his words. He viewed his meeting with Esau as nothing short of a turning point, for the man had unleashed in him a dimension of feeling he had never known before. He realised how frozen he had been until now. Perhaps a frozen heart was a prerequisite for a good psychiatrist. Certainly he had managed on it well enough for so many years. To thaw such a heart would free a passage where compassion would run riot and that would never do for a therapist. More and more he felt driven out of his profession, more and more he felt unqualified. And more and more, he felt relieved. But Esau worried him. There were sundry ways of coming to terms with one's parents, whether they were dead or alive. Tortuous ways, self-flagellating, and, more often than not, ending in failure. But Esau's methods were something more. They were dangerous. They put himself at risk, at physical risk, to say nothing of the humiliation of his spirit. As a therapist, he could not ask him to desist from his routine, not without long-term guidance towards an alternative. But as a friend, he could counsel him, warn him, and care for his safety.

'How long have you been doing your rounds?' Alistair asked. It was a question that might have been posed to a commercial traveller. And it meant the same. For Esau was in the business of selling, of selling beauty, but, like a whore, what he sold he still had. No capital investment in such a venture. Only a sure but certain erosion of the spirit.

'Just over a year now,' Esau said. 'I started a few weeks after my father died. They were all gone by then, mother and aunt, and I could hurt nobody. It seemed the only thing that I could do once they were gone.'

'Why did you have to do anything at all?'

'I had unfinished business to attend to.'

That phrase. That unwieldy compulsion that drove so many desperate feet to the therapist's couch. Unfinished business. The hardest business on earth to settle.

'I started on doctors first,' Esau went on. 'That seemed to be the obvious choice. I've only just got round to therapists. I was going to leave dentists till last. They're my biggest hurdle. As you can see,' he laughed.

'I want you to stop it,' Alistair said. He spoke as a friend, a couchless pursuit.

'I can't,' Esau said.

'What d'you hope to achieve by it all?'

'I want to walk with my father.'

After that, there was nothing to say. His pain was so close to the surface, Alistair thought, so eruptible, yet so guarded by that smile of his, that was simply an alternative to a coiled scream. He feared for Esau's future.

'When my wounds are healed,' Esau laughed, 'I shall start again on dentists.'

'And when you find one who will look at you, and find you beautiful, what then?'

'Then I will find another. And another. For forty years my father hardly looked at me. I have many slights and mockeries to settle. Come, let me help you unpack,' he said.

'Will you promise me something?'

'What's that?'

'That you don't pay any more visits without telling me and telling me exactly where you will go.'

'I can't promise that,' Esau said. 'You go about your business as I shall go about mine. There are thresholds of intimacy, you know.' He put his hand on Alistair's arm to offset the hurt his remark might have caused. 'Don't worry about me,' he said. 'I don't know how to handle other people's concern. I've had little practice in that area.'

He knew about himself, Alistair thought. He knew the core of his distress. He knew himself with perilous clarity. He had to go his own way.

He began to empty his suitcases. Unpacking is a very private pursuit and only in certain circumstances can it be shared. A daughter can unpack her mother's case, or a son his father's, because parents' secrets tend to be sadly known. There is nothing to hide. But the reverse would be an intrusion. As for lovers, such a sharing would be impossible. For, however close, there are still areas of privacy that are crammed into

corners and pockets of suitcases. But between friends
unpacking can be a joy, without fear of revelation and
with a mutual respect. This man must be my friend,
Alistair thought as he handed his shirts and underwear
to Esau, who stowed them neatly in drawers. And
likewise with his suits into the wardrobe. No comment
was made on the colour, the cut or the cloth. It was
as if the two men had known each other all their
lives.

'We must come to some arrangement,' Alistair said,
and he stowed the cases under the bed.

'What kind of an arrangement?' Esau said.

'Well I can't stay here for nothing.'

'Why not? You're my guest.'

'A guest can stay for three or four days,' Alistair said,
'but after that he qualifies as a tenant.'

'He qualifies as a friend,' Esau said.

It was unanswerable. 'Thank you,' was all Alistair
could say.

'I shall now dress for dinner,' Esau said.

'Let's go out,' Alistair suggested. 'We must celebrate
our friendship. You choose where you would like to
go.'

'Chinese. Without a doubt,' Esau said. 'It was a
cuisine my father hated. Almost as much as dentists.'

Alistair was slowly discerning the pattern. In the
course of learning to know Esau, he would become
equally acquainted with his father.

Over the next few weeks, Alistair learned that Esau's
father had a xenophobic fear of anything that wasn't
entirely English. This fact he deduced from Esau's
confessed love of travelling abroad. His father, too, was
a man of brass bands, fanfares and military marches.
Which was why Esau played Schubert with triumph.
But every conversation between them finally turned
to dentistry, and it came as no surprise that Esau's

final break with his father was occasioned by his announcement that he wished to become a dentist.

'I didn't mean it,' Esau said. 'I said it to bait him. He told me that if I took such a step, he would never speak to me again. So I passed on that one and I grew a beard instead.' He laughed with that laugh of his that had nothing to do with mirth.

Over the weeks, Alistair grew familiar with that laugh. He would time its appearance, for it was as much an appearance as a sound, and it always made its entrance after a reference to his father. It was like a twitch sent to accommodate that legacy of pain.

'What did your father say to the beard?' Alistair asked.

'It was the last straw for him.' Again a funereal boom of laughter. '"Haven't you got hair enough?" he said. Then he turned to my mother and said, "Your son! The ape!"'

His laughter was a clap of thunder.

Alistair put his hand on Esau's arm. 'You were badly served,' he said. Both the gesture and the statement would have had no place at all in his consulting rooms. But he was done with all that, at least in his heart, and in his life too, as soon as it was practically possible.

They were an odd couple. Esau concerned himself with domestic matters and the charge of Margaret, the daily, who was a family retainer. And every day he did his rounds. Alistair, too, went about his business, and on his return, over supper, they would exchange their day's accounts. After his dental calamity, Esau had reverted to doctors and he would regale Alistair with stories of his visits. He would insist, however, that he had let dentists off the hook only temporarily and that, in his own time, he would deal with them.

They were, to all appearances, an old married couple. Together they would clear the table after supper, and do the washing-up. Then they would sometimes play chess together, or Esau would play the piano. Occasionally Alistair would go back to his home late at night, stealthily insert his key in the lock, and creep up the stairs to Doris's bedroom. There he would blindly cover her face, and begin his explorations. He was never tempted to look in on Virginia. Since his meeting with Esau, and their burgeoning friendship, he had begun to view Virginia as a stranger. The irrational bitterness he had felt towards her had evaporated and gave him a measure of relief. He no longer blamed her for Doris's abnormality. He had accepted that no-one was to blame, and that acceptance had brought him closer to the notion of parenthood. Yet he had not stopped doodling. And doodling with increasing frenzy. And always on the quiet. Between patients in his consulting rooms where his Doris portfolio thickened with each day. But he had not yet brought his doodles into Esau's house. Somehow they had no place there. His indifference to Virginia had spread to Mary, too, and possibly, he thought, to the whole of womenkind. He recalled their affair with an after-taste of disgust and with a certain shame at having shopped her to Clifford. His meeting with Esau he considered as a new beginning. He wanted to put all his past behind him. His marriage and eventually his profession. All that is, except for Doris, whose future was eternally linked with his.

Since leaving Virginia, he had sent her weekly cheques through the post. Enough money to cover her expenses. In return, Virginia would acknowledge the cheque and forward his letters to his consulting rooms. The postal service seemed adequate communication for both of them. So Alistair was surprised, on reaching his office one morning, to answer the phone to Virginia who requested an appointment to see him. Her formality might well have belonged to a new patient.

91

'I'll come alone,' she said.

'Would you like lunch?' he asked. There was no harm in a friendly gesture. In any case, he preferred to meet her in a public place.

'Not really,' she said. 'I'll come to your rooms. It won't take very long.'

'All right,' he said. 'If that's what you wish.'

He wondered what she wanted from him. Perhaps a permanent settlement of a kind. Perhaps even a divorce. He would acquiesce to both. But he would not relinquish Doris. He did not want custody. At least, not yet. As long as he could not look at his daughter, he knew there was no way he could care for her. All he wanted was nocturnal visiting rights. And whenever he so wished.

He had one patient to see before Virginia would arrive. His Tube-traveller. He would be a patient who would be difficult to transfer. He was nowhere near the end of his treatment, and Alistair despaired that he would ever again walk the streets freely. Yet he couldn't drop him, else the man would be sentenced to a lifetime of Outer Circle.

He arrived sweating. The overland journey from the Tube exit to Alistair's rooms must have been a thrice-weekly nightmare for him.

He went straight to the couch and lay down, shutting his eyes in the vain hope that he would be invisible.

'I am not here, Doctor,' he said.

He would often begin his session with that remark. It was his way of expressing his utter weariness with his treatment and his sheer loss of faith in any cure.

'Where are you, then?' Alistair asked.

'Anywhere but anywhere,' the man said.

'Then you are nowhere.'

'Nowhere and nothing. Leave me alone.'

'Would you like to sleep?'

'I'd like to die.'

Alistair was tempted to cross over to the couch and touch him, as he would a friend, for comfort. But that was not allowed in these rooms, and the sooner he got out of them, he realised, the better.

'I am better,' the man said suddenly, but his tone of melancholy persisted. Indeed it seemed to be intensified by his discovery. Alistair was slightly taken aback. This was something new. He recapped on his patient's previous opening remarks; his loss of faith, his craving for invisibility, his wish to die, all these he had expressed before. Now clearly, in the light of this recent statement, those remarks had other meanings. If he was cured, as he considered himself to be, then why the loss of hope, the death-wish, and the need to hide?

'Go on,' Alistair said. 'You said you are better.'

'I made a mistake,' the man said. 'I am cured, but I am not better.'

Alistair didn't know how to follow that one. 'Go on,' he said, putting the ball squarely in his patient's court.

'I've been riding the Tube all morning,' the man said.

But that was nothing new. His patient spent his life underground, dodging his pursuers.

'I've been riding on the *Inner Circle* Line,' he said.

He should have bruited it with a sense of triumph, for was not that Line the perilous trap, that snare that, all his underground life, he had avoided on pain of death?

'On the Inner Circle,' he repeated. 'Round and round.'

'Well done,' Alistair said. Now was not the time to interrupt. But a word of encouragement would not go amiss.

'I went round and round until I was giddy. I sat there and I waited for them. I changed seats a couple of times. At one point, between Bayswater and Barbican station, I was alone in the carriage. Absolutely alone. No protection whatsoever.' He paused. Here was the point of it all. 'And they weren't there,' he said. 'No-one. None of them followed me. No-one was after me.

93

They were gone. All of them. They were there. No doubt about that. But they couldn't see me. Because I am invisible.'

Finally Alistair cottoned on. The man's pursuers had indeed disappeared. In that sense, his patient was cured. But the man clearly could not live without them. They *had* to be there. They had to be shadowing his every move. And his only rationale to keep them there was to declare himself invisible. Alistair admired the man's reasoning and marvelled that man's survival instinct can be of such a desperate nature that, in its name, he will render himself unseen.

'But *I* can see you,' Alistair said.

'Of course you can. But you are not one of my demons. You can *afford* to see me.'

Alistair was at a loss as to how to deal with him. He longed for the erstwhile straightforward paranoia of his Tube-traveller. That was dealable with. That was text-book stuff. But invisibility? He could recall no chapter-heading that would cover that.

'I can't live without my demons,' the man was saying. 'I'm lonely. I want to die.'

Again Alistair was urged to touch him and to utter all the banalities of solace. Everything will come right in the end. You'll feel better in the morning. You just have to pull yourself together.

'I'm cured,' the man said again. 'But I am not better. So now what are you going to do?'

Alistair felt as if he were on trial, and that, perhaps, without any attempt at defence, he should plead guilty. That way he could be rid of him, and the man could take his invisibility elsewhere. But it would be a gross admission of failure, and, though Alistair wished to leave the profession, he was too good a psychiatrist to leave it simply because it had got the better of him. What he wanted most was to play for time. He wanted to discuss the case with Esau. For some reason he thought

Esau might have the answer. Esau, who cultivated the very opposite of invisibility. Perhaps it was the flip-side of the same coin. But, for now, he had to give the man some guidance.

'What does it feel like, not being followed?'

'Lonely,' the man said. 'Terribly terribly lonely. They might have been demons, but they were my companions. And now I have nobody.'

'They have freed you to find others,' Alistair said. 'Others who are not demons. How do you feel above ground?'

'Fresh air chokes me,' he said. 'I liked it underneath. All those polluted smells. The sweats of rush-hour. The sticky straps. The breaths of smokers who cannot smoke. The heat of women work-bound. It was like being back in my nursery.'

The key word. It rang liked a cracked and boring bell, that word that must be ringing up and down Harley Street a thousand times a day, in the echo of which countless therapists pounced in Pavlovian and jubilant response to that very clue from which all their subsequent treatment would stem. But the word gave Alistair no pleasure. For he knew it would lead to years of patient investigation which, if successful would end in a primal scream. Complete disintegration. And then what? More years of repair, of picking up the pieces, those that were not over-shattered, and trying to make the man whole again. So that he could walk the streets without fear, bait for muggers, so that he could get a job, make money, exploit others, find a wife, have children, in time, batter the wife and abuse the children. All those normal everyday things. All the pursuits of those who had never laid and would never lay themselves on a therapist's couch. His patient was much better off underground, Alistair thought.

But he was curious about that nursery word. More often than not, it was associated with recalled pleasure,

95

and if there were smells, they were of garden flowers through open windows or rose-scented talcum-powder and soaps. What hell of a nursery must his patient have recalled if it was so redolent of pollution? He wondered whether he should take up that oh-so-convenient clue. He was tempted.

'Pollution in your nursery?' he asked.

There was no answer. Alistair walked over to the couch. It seemed that his patient was fast asleep. Clearly that 'nursery' word had slipped from his lips when he wasn't looking, when he was off-guard, and its echo had so frightened him that he had to take refuge in sleep. But that way nightmares lay, especially if sleep had been induced by such terror, and Alistair considered that he had better wake him, for his conscious state, miserable as it was, was preferable to the horror he might encounter behind his closed eyes.

He shook him gently and the man woke in a fright. The sweat slowly poured from his forehead. He had clearly begun his journey into hell.

'Thank you,' he said. 'I am deeply grateful.'

'Would you like to go home?' Alistair said. 'I think you need a proper sleep. In your own bed. You've had an overwhelming day.'

The man sat up. His eyes were still closed. 'Where am I?' he said.

'You're in Dr Crown's consulting room,' Alistair said.

The eyes remained closed and the man began to grope his whereabouts.

Alistair's heart trembled. The man had assumed blindness, for that was the only way he could survive. Alistair took his arm. 'I'll call you a taxi,' he said. He rang his receptionist and arranged that she take care of seeing his patient home. Then he led him to the door.

'I shall expect you on Wednesday,' he said.

'Only if I can find my way,' the man said. Then he smiled. 'I like not seeing,' he said. I feel I'm not

96

responsible any more. Perhaps I shan't come to you again. Nothing is my fault any more.'

So many clues in one session, Alistair thought. So many key words. So much sudden understanding after his years of burrowing underground. The man was right. He was cured. But he was not better.

Alistair had scruples about letting him go. He wasn't sure how blind the man was. He wished he would open his eyes. He would risk asking him.

'Why don't you open your eyes?' he said.

'Are they not open?' the man asked.

'No.' Alistair was patient. 'They're shut. No-one can see with their eyes shut.'

'Then open them for me,' the man said.

Alistair went towards him. He made to touch the man's face. Then suddenly he thought of Doris and withdrew his hand. He realised how he himself affected blindness in order to avoid her face. And if he was entitled to that escape-route, what right had he to deny it to his patient?

'It doesn't matter,' he said. 'Your sight or otherwise is your own business.'

He led him to his receptionist's office, and left him in her bewildered hands.

Then he returned to his room and reached for his Doris-portfolio. He did not try to stop himself. He needed his fix, for without it he would have crumbled. He would doodle until Virginia arrived. He started on a new sheet of paper and, as was his wont, he began with a circle.

Then, without realising it, he shut his eyes and drew blind.

And, for the first time, he did not start with the 'manageables', the nose, the mouth and the chin. He plunged straightaway into the epicentre of the earthquake, into the heart of the crater itself. He began with the eyes. First one and then the other, and blindly joined them with an offensively concave bridge over the nose. A lump formed in his throat and he knew he must quickly sketch in the 'manageables', those features to which he could happily link his paternity. When it was done, or when he thought it was done, he opened his eyes and what he viewed melted the lump in his throat which thawed into tears. For Doris had overreached her circle, and, it seemed, with audacious deliberation. The nose, the mouth and the chin were obediently in their proper places, but the eyes had spilt over the circle-saucer, like shapeless slops. For some reason, Alistair was convinced that, at last, after all his doodlings, he had achieved a photographic image. He stared at it. This was his daughter. He put the sheet gently into the portfolio and shut the drawer. Then, his head in his hands, he waited for Virginia to arrive.

She was prompt. His receptionist announced her. Even so, she knocked on the door before entering. She clearly intended a formal visit.

'You look well, Virginia,' he said as she came in.

He found it an effort to be polite. The image he had drawn of Doris scarred his retina. He could not erase it and he knew that there would be little logic in doodling any more. For he had drawn the truth and guesswork was no longer permissable. If, in his urgent addiction, he would reach for that portfolio again, it would only result in a reprint from that appalling negative that his blindness had dictated.

He stood up and made to offer Virginia a chair, but she had already seated herself on his couch. It was strange seeing her seated there. She didn't look like a suitable case for treatment. Far from it. She looked healthy, happy and whole. Alistair guessed that she might have found a lover, and that thought did not particularly disturb him. As long as she kept the lover away from Doris. Doris was *his* territory, his nocturnal terrain.

'You look well,' he said again.

He suspected that a request for a divorce was on the tip of her tongue. And so it had been, on her way to him, but now she had decided to stifle it. A divorce was too final, and though she held out no hope of, nor even desire for, reconciliation, the matter of Doris could not be so easily negated. And it was really about Doris that she had come to to talk, though on that subject she hardly knew where to begin.

She reached into her handbag.

'I have some new photos of Doris,' she said. 'Would you like to see them?'

Alistair trembled.

'No,' he said. 'I'm not ready.'

She closed the bag.

'I heard you come home the other night. I heard you go into Doris's room. What did you do there?'

He decided to tell her the truth, for God knows what she might otherwise think.

'I go to her room often at night,' he said, by way of facilitating future visits, for he intended to make a habit of them. 'I go to get to know her. I have to tell you that I cover her face. I shut my eyes and I cover her face. Gently with a sheet. I cannot look at her face. But every other part of her body I know. I'm trying, Virginia,' he said. 'I love her as much as you.'

She felt deeply sorry for him. She marvelled, too, at how much he had changed, how, without any seeming effort, he managed to be so truthful. And somehow, so innocent. She could think of nothing to say. He was too vulnerable for attack, and too naive for argument.

'Why don't you . . . you try looking at her photographs? As a kind of first instalment.'

She opened her bag again.

99

'No,' he said quickly. He had his own photos, but he would make no mention of his portfolio. 'I'm not ready. When I'm ready, I won't need photographs,' he said.

'Are you all right?' she asked after a pause.

'Yes, of course.'

'Have you got somewhere to live? I don't want to know where.'

'Yes,' he said. 'I'm settled very comfortably.'

She looked at him for a while.

'I'll go then,' she said. 'There's some post for you.'

She opened her bag again.

'Don't worry,' she said. 'I'm only getting out the post. There's a letter here from your parents.' She handed it over. 'Do they know about Doris, by the way? About the Down's Syndrome?'

'No,' Alistair said with an honesty that gave him a measure of relief. 'I haven't mentioned it.'

'Perhaps you should,' Virginia said gently. 'They'll blame me, of course. But I don't mind. Because I know that no-one is to blame.' She leaned over his desk. 'Including you, Alistair,' she said.

He smiled at her. He realised how little he had valued her in the past and he realised, too, that it was through that very lack of respect that he had been able to love her in the first place. But now he admired her as a stranger. He was glad that she seemed well, but he wished that she would go. Her handbag threatened him.

'Goodbye, Alistair,' she said. 'You know you can come to the house whenever you like.'

'Thank you,' he said.

In the old days, he would have asked her to give him time. Now he knew that it wasn't time that he needed. It was courage and faith, and perhaps he could catch a little of those from Esau. He locked his consulting rooms and hurried to his new home.

# Seven

HE CALLED, 'Esau,' as soon as he put his key in the lock. There was no reply. Once in the hall, he called again. Again there was no answer. Esau was not at home.

Alistair surmised that he was still on his rounds and he prayed that he was giving dentists a wide berth. He was disappointed. He felt, as he had so often as a child, coming home from school and finding his mother out as she always seemed to be at teatime. He never got over that disappointment. It was more than just a feeling of let-down. It was a sense of having been betrayed. He called Esau's name once again, not for answer, but for some reassurance from the sound. Then he went into the living room and sifted through his post. There were two psychiatric journals. These he didn't even bother to open, but threw them straight into the waste-paper basket. There was an offer of a time-share on the Costa del Sol, and that went the same way as the journals. He kept the letter from his parents till last. He always had trouble with their correspondence, even before he had Doris-deceived them. Now his hesitation was compounded by that deceit. He knew the letter would contain more pleas for Doris's photograph and not-so-veiled criticisms of Virginia for her negligence. Their letters were getting more and more difficult to reply to. He looked around for something else to do, something to postpone the opening. He called Esau's name again as if the sound would give him courage. Then, unable to delay it any longer, he slit the envelope. He wanted to read it quickly, to get it over and done with. Which was just as well, for its contents could not bear a second reading. No 'perhaps'. No 'maybes', no loopholes for a change of mind. Just a simple statement. They were coming to England to celebrate Doris's fifth birthday.

They had the decency to add that they would be staying in an hotel. That would lighten the load a little, but would do nothing to soften the two blows he had to deliver: the breakdown of his marriage, and the news of their not-so-beautiful granddaughter. He had no doubt that they would blame Virginia for both, barely holding their tongues on 'I-told-you-sos'. But, for all their protests, they would not stop making him feel that he'd been a naughty boy, as they had made him feel so often in his childhood. He wondered whether he should write to them and break both pieces of news in fine and dishonest writing. Perhaps that would curb their travellers' itch. It could not be relied on. But he would do it anyway. It was three weeks to Doris's birthday. He could mention the school concert and the pink gingham dress. But that would bring their arrival a week forward. He decided not to mention it. But bigger than all those problems, of his broken marriage and his fractured child, was his inability to look at his daughter in the face. How could he explain that to his parents? His mother would force him to look at her, trick him into a full-frontal, and he knew that even his mother, that offensive tower of strength, could not bear the consequences of his screamings. He called, 'Esau,' again, for comfort. Then he tore the letter into many angry pieces and sprinkled them like seasoning over the bland and dishonest claims of psychiatry and time-share.

He poured himself a drink. He wished that Esau would come home. He had so much to share with him. His last patient's protective blindness, Virginia's visit, and the letter from his parents. He heard his key in the door, and he rushed into the hall to meet him. Esau was smiling as was his wont, and unscarred.

'No dentists today,' Alistair said.

'A couple of doctors. Pretty straightforward. And a masseur. My first masseur. A bit off-territory I'm afraid, but a whole new area to explore. I don't think my father knew any masseurs, but if he did, I'm sure he would have viewed them with the same contempt as he considered dentists.'

'Where was this masseur?' Alistair asked.

'In an alley off Tottenham Court Road.'

Alistair tried not to show his concern. There were masseurs and masseurs, and, in the quarter that Esau had visited, a masseur could have been anything. Some even claimed that they were osteopaths, but, whatever they said they were, their business had little to do with medicine.

'Did he massage you?' Alistair asked.

'Yes. He seemed very anxious to do that. He thought I was beautiful. Have you ever had a massage, Alistair? I can recommend it. It makes you feel very good all over. Fulfilled as it were.'

For some reason, Alistair was convinced that Esau was a virgin.

'Did you make another appointment?' he asked.

'No. He asked me to come again. But I won't. He has seen me once and given me his approval. I don't need to see him again.'

'But will you go to other masseurs?'

'Why not? They're an untapped audience.'

'There are masseurs in Harley Street,' Alistair tried. 'Outside the square mile, they tend not to be qualified.' He knew he was wrong, but he had to warn Esau. This new exploration of his was perilous. 'We could look in the directory,' Alistair went on. 'There must be a list.'

'I'll do that,' Esau said. 'But first let's have a drink.'

They returned to the living room. Alistair poured Esau's favourite and handed it to him. He felt safe with Esau around. He felt a sense of 'home' that he had never felt in his marriage or his childhood.

He told Esau about his parents' letter.

'What am I to do?' he said.

'You mustn't let them rush you,' Esau said. 'Their visit is an artificial pressure. You must look at Doris in your own good time, and then you will be able to look at her for ever. And with love.'

'But how can I avoid it? I shall have to spend time with them. And Doris too.'

'You must avoid them. You must leave London. Let's go on holiday together.'

Alistair touched Esau's arm. He warmed to his enthusiasm, and he was sorely tempted by his suggestion.

'I can't,' he said. 'I haven't seen them for eight years. It would be hurtful.'

'You're right,' Esau said.

'But we *will* go on holiday together,' Alistair said. 'I'd like that very much. When they've gone back to America. But there's nothing to stop us going away for a weekend. Next weekend, perhaps.

'Could we go to Paris?' Esau was like a child. 'In all my travels, I've never been to Paris. I want to see the gargoyles on Notre Dame. I think gargoyles must be good for you.'

'Why?'

'Because they're grotesque. *Really* grotesque. That's their nature. No-one could deny their ugliness. They are factual eyesores. We could feast on them for a while, and then we will understand beauty.'

'We'll go to Paris,' Alistair said. 'We'll take a late flight on Friday evening. But no doctors. No dentists, and certainly no masseurs. It's a holiday from routine for both of us.'

*

For the rest of the week, Alistair could hardly contain his excitement. Not once did he reach for his Doris-portfolio. He refused to dwell on his parents' visit. Neither did he bother to write to them. He would deal with it in his own time. He made one Doris-visit and, for the first time, he talked to her. In whispers because she was asleep. He told her he was going to Paris to see the gargoyles and that he would bring her a present. He told her what a gargoyle was. 'A factual eyesore,' he said, quoting Esau's words. That night he had hopes that soon he would be able to look at her. For a moment he had forgotten the last image he had made of her.

His last patient before the weekend was his Tube-traveller. He half-expected him to cancel his appointment and, when he was ten minutes past his appointed hour, Alistair was disturbed. So it was a relief to hear footsteps outside the door. He listened carefully, for there was something unrhythmical about the steps. There seemed to be three feet in operation instead of the usual two. Alistair went to open the door. The third foot revealed itself as a white stick. His heart turned over, both in pity and anger. The anger was mainly directed at himself. He felt responsible, for he had not understood the cause and effect of the man's condition. He did not know how to continue with the treatment. He could play it by the book – psychosomatic blindness was not all that rare – but that would mean years more of three-point tapping. Or he could counsel him as a friend. To hell with analysis, he thought.

He took the man's arm and guided him to the couch. Then he sat beside him, taking his hand. He scratched in his mind for the man's name. He excused himself quickly and went to his desk. He sought out the book in which he kept the basic data of his patients. They were in alphabetical order but, since he had no notion of the man's name, he was obliged to skim through the whole list. He did it furtively; then he was aware that there was no need for stealth since the man couldn't see anyway. Blind people, Alistair realised, were available to all manner of deception and he disliked himself a little for taking such advantage. He went through the notebook and reached poor Miss Wetherby. And after her, in the last but one entry, lay Mr Robert Wiles. Aged forty. Married. One son. Tube-traveller. Persecution mania.

He rushed back to the couch.

'I had to check on my notes, Mr Wiles.' It was a half-truth, though he didn't think that Mr Wiles was fooled by it. 'Can I call you Robert?' he said.

'Why Robert?' Mr Wiles asked. 'Robert is not my name.'

'It's the name you gave me,' Alistair said. It was not a good start.

'I gave you Robin. That's my name. You know, like the bird. Though it's just as well I'm not a bird. A blind robin wouldn't get very far.'

Alistair cursed his secretary and resolved to give her a piece of his mind, then realised that there had been a turnover of at least three secretaries since Mr Wiles had registered his underground complaint so many years ago.

'I'm sorry,' Alistair said. 'Then, may I call you Robin?'

'If it makes it easier for you,' Mr Wiles said.

If seeing through your psychiatrist represented progress, then Robin Wiles was certainly better, Alistair thought. He did not deny it. 'Yes,' he said, 'it does make things easier for me.'

'Then go ahead,' Mr Wiles said. 'And you don't have to hold my hand. Unless that makes things easier, too.'

Alistair loosened the hand. If he held on to it, he would weaken his position, and he himself would become the patient, and Mr Wiles the counsellor.

'You realise, Robin, that you're not blind,' he said.

'It's a phsycosomatic blindness that you have. It's self-induced to protect you from reality.'

'I don't care how you diagnose it,' Mr Wiles said. 'I'm not impressed by your fancy words. I am blind, really blind, because I *want* to be blind. I like it, you see. Besides, I don't have neck pains any more.'

Alistair was slowly sinking out of his depth. 'What neck pains?' he asked. 'You never mentioned neck pains.'

'They were part and parcel of my way of life,' Mr Wiles said. 'They were part of the package. When I lived underground, dodging the Circle Line, I kept looking behind me. Over the years, I developed a crick in my neck. I got used to it, but it was painful, and the only way to relieve it was to turn round again. So even when I knew it was safe, I was still looking for them. But since I'm blind, I'm not looking any more and my neck is not painful any more.'

'Well, that's one advantage, I suppose,' Alistair said.

'One of many,' came the reply. 'Blindness offers much freedom. I don't care any longer what people think of me, or how I look, of how I eat or talk. I am not responsible any more. Nothing is my fault. Nothing. I have recaptured the innocence of infancy. Do you not envy me, Dr Crown?'

'In that respect, yes,' Alistair said. 'But I can see many disadvantages. I would be distressed, for instance, if I could not look upon my wife or my daughter.' To all intents and purposes, he had no wife, and as far as Doris was concerned, he might as well have been struck blind at her birth. It occurred to him now, not for the first time, that he too, had induced blindness as far as Doris was concerned. He had much to learn from Mr Wiles. Perhaps they could cure each other.

'I know how my son looks,' Mr Wiles said. 'And my wife. Their images were imprinted on my sighted eyes. And now they have moved into my mind. I don't need to see them any more. Love has nothing to do with seeing. Sight is only a bonus, and one can live without it, for its loss does not preclude love.'

Alistair knew about that kind of loving. His nocturnal and unlit explorations were testimony to that. Perhaps he need never look at Doris and he could love her as well as did Virginia.

'What does your son say about it all?'

'He's angry,' Mr Wiles said. 'He tells me to pull myself together. So does my wife.'

'Doesn't that mean anything to you?' Alistair asked. 'They're hurt. They want to be seen.'

'I am not responsible,' Mr Wiles said.

And that seemed to be the end of the matter.

'Then what can I do for you?' Alistair asked. 'Why have you come?'

'Simply as a courtesy,' Mr Wiles said. 'I had an appointment and I'm keeping it. I apologise for being late, but blindness tends to hamper mobility.'

'Then there *is* a disadvantage,' Alistair said.

'Only if one wants to get somewhere in a hurry. And why should one want to do that?'

Stalemate again.

'I wanted to let you know in person that I shan't be coming any more. You did cure me, Dr Crown, and one day, perhaps, I shall be better.'

'If your sight ever comes back, Mr Wiles,' Alistair said – there seemed little point now in calling him Robin – 'would you come and see me? Not as a patient, but simply to let me know?'

'Of course,' Mr Wiles said. 'But I doubt and I sincerely hope that that will not happen. My sight might send me underground again.'

He got up to go and stretched out his hand.

Alistair took it. 'Goodbye Mr Wiles,' he said, 'I wish you well. Though he had no idea any longer of what 'well' meant. 'Can you find your way?'

'I know your stairs by heart,' Mr Wiles said. 'I can manage them blindfold,' he laughed.

When he had gone, Alistair had a sudden urge for his portfolio. But he refrained. He suddenly remembered Paris. During Mr Wiles's visit, his holiday weekend had entirely slipped his mind. Now he grew excited again. He would go home. Home to Esau. And they would pack together.

He crossed Gerry on the stairs.

'You're leaving early,' Gerry said.

'Off to Paris for the weekend,' Alistair said. Then regretted it, for the news would go back to Virginia who would grossly misinterpret it.

'I won't say a word,' Gerry winked.

Alistair let that pass. 'How are you and Janet?' he asked.

'We're back together.'

'And Fiona?'

'Have to be discreet, old boy,' Gerry said, and bounded up the stairs.

Alistair was not impressed. In the old days, his pre-Esau days, he would have admired and even envied Gerry's sang-froid. Now it just struck him as infantile and hurtful. He hurried out of the building. He had begun to hate his rooms and all that they stood for.

He called, 'Esau,' as he put his key in the lock and, by the time he opened the door, Esau was waiting for him in the hall.

'I was waiting for you to pack,' he said. 'We have an hour before we leave. But let's have a drink first.'

The coming-home drink was now part of their routine, followed sometimes by Esau at the piano. But now there was time only for a mutual exchange of their day's activities. Esau had taken the day off. He had made no calls. Alistair felt that this was good news. That perhaps Esau's appetite for exhibitionism was on the wane.

Alas, Esau had spent his day in a successful search for a one-piece track-suit with trainers to match. He explained to Alistair that, with such an outfit, stripping-time could be cut to a minimum. Thus he could bring pleasure to more people in his daily rounds.

'It will enable me to make a quicker exit from the dentists',' he added.

So he hadn't given up after all. Alistair hoped that perhaps the weekend in Paris would change his outlook, though he could think of no reason for it.

As they packed, they grew silent. Both seemed apprehensive of the excursion. Both feared that they expected too much.

At last Esau said, 'The Seine will be a change from the Thames.' That at least, was a fact, based on no wishful thinking. If nothing else, they would experience that difference.

They had booked a weekend package deal which included the hotel, a medium two-star affair close to the Bastille. Although it was quite late when they arrived, Esau insisted they take a cab to the cathedral to loiter in its floodlit beauty. The Square was almost deserted when they arrived, and they separated, each going to one side of the church as if they would share it between them. Despite its grandeur, it was not forbidding; and, though Alistair had toured Notre Dame before, he was seeing it now as if for the first time. Hitherto, he'd come to Paris for medical conferences and he had seen the cathedral as part of an official tour, at which times it had seemed to belong to everybody except himself. Now he felt a hint of personal connection. He could not define it. Neither did he try. He knew it had nothing to do with worship or belief. He looked across at Esau. His huge body was still, almost statue-like, and he was leaning at a deliberate angle, as if he himself were a gargoyle fallen from its nest. Alistair watched him and marvelled at his fixedness, that immutable leaning from toe to head. He wanted very much to join him but he feared disturbing his stillness. He would wait until he resumed his Esauness, then perhaps they would move towards each other. Until that time he would stay where he was. He looked back at the gargoyles and out of the corner of his eye, he saw Esau straighten and move towards him. Alistair moved, too, and they met centrally where Esau stopped and resumed his leaning pose.

'People say,' he said, 'that the gargoyles are evil spirits flying from the church, where the spirit of God threatens to overpower them. So they fly for their evil lives. But some were trapped in their flight, so they hang there, stuck to the walls, where they perform as reluctant gutters. You see,' Esau said, straightening himself once more, 'even if you're that ugly, you can still be functional.'

'You knew that before you came to Paris, didn't you, Esau?' Alistair said.

'Yes, but I needed confirmation. Shall we find ourselves a nightcap?' he said.

They walked towards the river. Backlit by the cathedral, their silhouettes could have been those of a honeymoon couple. They walked in silence for which each was grateful. The sense of well-being that they shared needed no comment or ornamentation. Even while drinking their cognac together, the silence prevailed, acknowledged now by both of them as a token of their intimacy. They bade each other good-night in the hotel foyer and, in its breaking, heard, for the first time, the long and shared silence that had gone before.

In the morning, Alistair found himself breakfasting alone. Esau had left him a note in the dining room. He'd gone to the cathedral, he wrote, and would be back shortly. *Don't wait for me,* he'd added. *I'll join you for coffee later.*

Alistair read the note over and over again. It could have been a love-letter. He folded it quickly and put it away. He recalled Esau's leaning figure of the night before and saw him now, leaning still, gargoyle-like, functional, reassuring himself that, if he was nothing else, he could be put to some small use. It was a thought that worried Alistair. Nagged at him, for he knew that, for all Esau's protestations of beauty, he found himself painfully unviewable. But he kept his mind fixed on that leaning image of him, trusting, benign, fortuitously starred. He would keep that image in his mind and hold on to it until Esau's return.

But Esau was about his business or, as he himself would have said, about his father's business. He had been to the cathedral, and had leaned there for a time, his lips moving the while and his look one of innocent pleasure. A passer-by might have thought he was intoning lines to himself, thus adding to his pleasure in the view. A poem perhaps, or even, from his inclined stance, a prayer. For Esau it was both, and he repeated it to himself over and over again, both in iambics and entreaty. It was the poem and prayer that he daily hawked around Harley Street. He had sought out its translation and now, leaning in his idolatrous worship, he murmured to himself. 'Est-ce-que vous ne me trouvez pas beau? Do you not find me beautiful?' Over and over again. The French translation somehow made the question more rhetorical, and it pleased him.

Then when he was ready and the words were etched into his tongue, he straightened himself and walked from the Square. He had meant to return to the hotel. He had really intended to do that. He did not think that the repetition of those words would urge his feet in another direction. But the words had turned him on, and he itched for his Harley Street fix. He did not know Paris, and had no idea where doctors plied their craft. But within minutes he had nosed out with a survivor's instinct a brass medical plate. *Louis Medec*, it read, *Medicin*. The door was open and he took it for an invitation. He walked up the stairs where the legend was repeated on a door at the top of the flight. He knocked and, without waiting for an answer, he opened the door.

Dr Medec looked up from his desk and raised an eyebrow.

'Vous avez un rendez-vous?' he asked.

'Do you speak English?' Esau said and began to unbutton.

'A little,' the man said. 'What is wrong with you?'

'Nothing wrong,' Esau said. By now he had divested himself of his shirt and offered the promise of his hirsute splendour. 'I want to show you something,' he said. He spoke slowly and stripped to the rhythm of his syllables, wishing all the while that he'd worn his track-suit, so that by the time the sentence was out, he was, apart from his socks, completely naked. He took a deep breath. 'Est-ce-que vous ne me trouvez pas beau?' he asked.

Despite the fact the Dr Medec claimed a little English, Esau was not going to waste his good rehearsal. And he repeated the question, and then, with respect to the doctor's linguistic talents, he translated it. 'Do you not find me beautiful?' he said.

Dr Medec's jaw fell open.

Esau took it for astonishment, and for relish, too.

But his dropped jaw expressed neither. It was simply a signal of his abject fear. He reached for his telephone and with trembling fingers dialled a number. He managed a smile in Esau's direction. Whoever it was that he was phoning answered immediately. The doctor spoke very quickly and in whispers, far too softly for Esau's understanding. But the doctor's continued smile reassured him, and when he put down the phone, Esau took the opportunity to ask the question once again.

'Mais oui,' the doctor said, his eye on the door and his fists clenched. 'Très beau. Très très beau. Magnifique.'

Esau made to put on his shirt.

'No,' the doctor almost shouted. 'Please. S'il vous plaît. I'd like to look more. Wait a little. I look. With pleasure.'

Esau stood still for a while, then turned round so that he faced the door, thus giving the two gendarmes who burst into the room, a full-frontal signature of his guilt. 'Caught red-handed,' one of them said, or words to that effect, so Esau presumed, as they grabbed each of his arms and turned him round.

One of them gave what sounded as an order.

'They ask you to dress,' the doctor said.

Esau was trembling. He felt the officers' hot breath breezing his beauty. He dared to look at their faces and noted, with little surprise, that they resembled his father. He dressed as quickly as his trembling hands would allow. He thought of Alistair and hoped that they could remain friends. This thought depressed him far more than his present condition. But worst of all was the feeling that he had been so grossly misunderstood. He did not blame the doctor but the frailty of human nature in general. He bent down to lace his shoes. He took his time, fascinated by the texture of the lace and the magnified grain of the fabric, sinewy, plaiting itself into resistance. He examined it closely, together with his fingertips as they manoeuvred the knot. His eye had achieved a clarity that he had never experienced before, and he knew that, were he to look into a face, he could, with terrifying accuracy, count every one of its million pores. He straightened himself slowly and, as he did

114

so, he felt his arms pulled behind him, quite gently, he thought. Perhaps they were helping him to his feet. Then he felt the metal on his wrists and he knew that he was captive. He opened his mouth to speak but he realised that even if he could make himself understood, he had absolutely nothing to say.

He walked between them. The staircase was narrow and they had to descend it in linked single file. Their steps were out of joint, and from below it might have looked like an unwieldly pas de trois of performers who were not on speaking terms.

Once in the street, the two gendarmes hustled Esau into a car. The engine had been left running, so take-off was swift. A crowd that had begun to gather dispersed quickly for want of spectacle. Withing seconds the police-hooter was blaring. The early morning rush-hour impeded its passage, and Esau was able to view a little of Paris in comfort if not in pride. He wondered what would become of him. He looked at his companions but their faces bore no expression. He presumed he would be taken to a police-station and there, charged, but with what, he could not imagine. The phrase 'indecent exposure' crossed his mind, but he couldn't equate it with his own nature.

Eventually the car pulled up at the police-station and, with little courtesy, he was man-handled inside. Then they led him to a small room and unlocked his handcuffs. The two policemen exchanged a few words, then one of them left the room. The other guided Esau to a chair and motioned him to sit down. He even smiled at him across the table. Esau returned the smile out of courtesy, though he couldn't imagine what either of them was pleased about. Esau thought again of Alistair. He would be awaiting his return to the hotel. He wished he spoke decent French. Then he could ask permission to make a phone-call. He felt frightened and powerless. He smiled again at his gaoler.

Then the door opened and the second policeman returned, this time with another officer and one of obviously higher rank.

'I speak English,' the newcomer said. 'I would like to ask you some questions. First, your name.'

'Esau.' Esau said it with relief. 'Just call me Esau.'

'Esau what?' The man was far from friendly.

'Waterson,' Esau said. The corseted tight-lipped label of his father.

'Where do you live?'

'In London.'

'What are you doing in Paris?'

'I'm on holiday. For the weekend.'

'Are you alone?'

'No. I'm with a friend.'

'Her name?'

'It's a man,' Esau said.

The officer sighed. It all figured. The world was an unseemly place.

'*His* name then.'

'Alistair Crown. Doctor Alistair Crown,' he emphasised, hoping it might make a favourable impression.

'Where are you staying?' the officer asked. 'You and this Dr Crown.'

Esau gave him the name of the hotel and asked if he could make a phone-call.

'I shall make it for you,' he said.

Then he left the room, accompanied by the second gaoler.

Esau looked across the table where the policeman sat, stony-faced. He tried a smile, but the man turned his face away in disgust. 'Est-ce-que vous ne . . .' Esau tried. But thought better of it. This man would not see beauty in a sunset.

At the hotel Alistair was growing restless. He'd long ago finished his breakfast and had drunk endless cups of coffee. He was growing anxious. Notre Dame was not very far away, and it was already mid-day.

When he was called to the phone, he sighed with relief and answered it, laughing.

'Esau?' he said.

'Dr Crown,' a voice answered and Alistair knew that that voice was in uniform. He trembled.

'Who is it?' he said.

'This is Police Officer Grasse of the Deuxième. We have your friend at the station. I think it is better you come to see him.'

'Is he all right?' Alistair asked. 'He's not hurt?'

'No. He's all right. Almost all right. Will you come immediately?'

'What is the address? I shall leave at once.'

The officer spelt out the address of the station.

Alistair put the phone down, trembling. Almost all right. The echo of that 'almost' nagged at him.

He ran out into the street and hailed a cab. He tried not to think about Esau's plight but 'almost' throbbed his mind like an ominous pulse. The station was not far from the hotel and he was glad when he arrived. But frightened too. Then suddenly he thought of Doris and realised that, since leaving London, she had slipped from his mind. Then he knew why Esau was at the station. He had simply found his Harley Street in Paris.

He darted inside and found the officer who had phoned him.

'I am Dr Crown,' he said. 'I have come to see my friend.'

'Perhaps we could talk a little first,' the officer said. He directed Alistair into his office, looking at him closely all the time. He found him totally nondescript. His features were all in the right place and appeared functional. He was neither tall, short, fat nor thin, ugly nor handsome. He simply passed as a man with no distinguishing marks. He scanned him closely for some

117

clue as to his friendship with that ape in the adjoining office.

'You're a doctor, Dr Crown,' he said.

'I'm a psychiatrist,' Alistair said.

A possible clue.

'Are you Mr Waterson's personal psychiatrist?'

'I am a friend. Why is he here?' Alistair asked. He felt himself scrutinised and he resented it deeply. He feared it too. He feared its implications. 'What has he done?' he asked again.

'He visited a doctor,' the officer said. 'Without an appointment.'

'There's no crime in that,' Alistair said. He was playing for time for now he knew exactly why Esau had landed in the arms of the Law.

'He stripped himself naked,' the officer said. 'His behaviour was threatening. The doctor feared for his life and he called us. We caught your friend red-handed, naked in the consulting room.'

Alistair laughed, then regretted it, fearing its misinterpretation.

'This is a serious matter,' the officer said.

'Of course it's serious,' Alistair agreed 'From a psychiatric point of view it is very serious indeed.' He had suddenly conceived a plan to get Esau off the hook. He would depict him as a lunatic who was not responsible for his actions. 'I am his psychiatrist,' he said. 'His friend, too. He does this sort of thing all the time in London. I thought perhaps a weekend in Paris might give him a break. I was mistaken.' He leaned over the desk. 'He has a very real problem, officer,' he said. 'He is deeply disturbed. But he is not dangerous. I assure you of that. I laughed just now because you said that his behaviour was threatening. He is the most gentle person on earth. He would not harm a fly.'

The officer twiddled his pen. He clearly did not know how to proceed. He wished he were not on duty.

'I'll take him home. Today,' Alistair said. 'We'll go back to London.'

The officer was tempted. To make a charge involved a long court procedure, and a plea of insanity even longer. He picked up his phone.

Alistair listened carefully. Out of all the words he could translate, London, aeroplane, today. He sighed with relief. After that assurance, he ceased listening. He thought of Esau and he feared for his reaction. A plea of insanity was clearly the only way to free him, but Esau might regard a plea of insanity as a betrayal, even though such a plea was forwarded in the name of friendship. The possibility of losing Esau as a friend was too painful to contemplate.

The officer put down the phone. 'There is a plane to London at six o'clock. You and your friend will be on it. I have made arrangements. A police-car will take you back to your hotel where you will pack, and then you will be escorted to the airport. Your patient will not be welcome in France again,' he said. 'Wait here. I shall bring him to you.'

Alistair waited. He feared that the officer would tell Esau the reason for his acquittal and that that great subdued temper of his would at last detonate in an explosive claim to sanity.

He listened, but there was silence all around him. He worried that he had to wait so long. Time enough, he thought, to appraise Esau of the cause of his release. But perhaps there was paper-work, Alistair consoled himself. Perhaps it was bureaucracy that was taking its time. He waited. He did not know what he would say to Esau. He would have to fashion two versions of the story, one on the assumption that Esau knew of the betrayal, and the other that he was unaware of it. But how was Alistair to know which version to offer him?

But he need not have wondered. The look on Esau's face as the door opened told him clearly that there was

119

no need for invention. The terrible Judas-truth would have to do. Esau stared at him, and slowly narrowed his eyes as he did so. It was a look of abject hatred, mingled with disbelief.

Alistair dreaded their journey home.

Two policemen accompanied them to the hotel, an escort each. Their entrance into the foyer caused some consternation. The concierge was clearly nervous for her reputation. One of the escorts offered an explanation. The horror was clear on her face and she looked at Esau with disgust, a look that seemed to embrace Alistair too, as the man who is known by the company he keeps. Those guests who were waiting for the lift, moved aside as if to avoid contamination. The four of them entered, and one pressed the button. They were silent. Not a word had been spoken between them since they had left the station. On the fifth floor, they separated. Esau's escort held him by the arm, but Alistair was simply followed, unaccused. He packed quickly and wondered how Esau was faring. Whether he was folding his clothes with his customary neatness or whether, like Alistair, his self-disgust was reflected in his negligence.

'I'm ready,' Alistair said not bothering with the French. If Esau couldn't come to France again, neither would he, so he wouldn't bother himself to be understood.

They left the room and went towards Esau's door. As they reached it, it opened. Esau had clearly packed like Alistair. Again there was silence in the lift, and silence in the car as they drove to the airport. Alistair dreaded the moment when they would be alone together and all the unspoken words would have to erupt between them.

They arrived at the airport an hour before the plane would leave. They were passed through customs and straight into the departure lounge. Alistair wondered when their guards would leave. But it was clear that they would see them onto the plane. And that they did, as soon as its readiness was announced. Esau's escort still held onto his arm, and their little group aroused the curiosity of the waiting passengers. Alistair felt humiliated and ashamed, but Esau was too concerned with what he saw as downright treachery to be aware of anything else. They were the first to board the plane. The escorts saw them settled in the very back row. Then 'Au revoir,' they said thus breaking the hours' long silence. Alistair would have wished them to stay, to travel with them even, anything to excuse those words that neither he nor Esau could utter.

Now they were alone in the plane. It would not be long before others embarked. Alistair knotted his seat-belt to give himself something to do. Then Esau did likewise. Alistair knew that one of them had to break the silence and, as he was scratching in his mind for something to say, Esau whispered, 'I have been misunderstood.'

Alistair shivered. The whispered tone in no way muted his plea. Indeed its echo was a scream. But what was worse was its languorous passivity. It was as if Esau was talking about somebody else, about an event to which he was, at most, a witness, viewing the unfairness of it all. Yet it lost none of its ring of accusation.

'Misunderstood,' he said again, hardly believing it.

'I had to say what I did,' Alistair said. 'It was the only way to get you out of there.'

'But you believed it, didn't you? You believe that I am mad.'

'No,' Alistair said quickly. 'I have never believed that. Never.'

He hoped he sounded convincing, for his heart doubted. A man traipses up and down Harley Street every day, in the business of striptease. They don't come much madder than that.

121

'I think you have problems,' Alistair said. 'So do we all. It doesn't make us lunatics. I know about madmen. Believe me. I see them in my consulting rooms every day.'

'I wish I could believe you,' Esau said.

'Look.' Alistair put his hand on Esau's arm. 'If I hadn't told them you were crazy, in need of treatment, you would be in a cell by now Awaiting trial, and God knows how long that would have taken. I *had* to do it, Esau. I would have missed you in London.'

This last seemed to placate him a little.

'But you misunderstood me,' he said. The passivity was diluted. No longer was he a witness. He accepted that he himself had played a role.

Alistair let it lie. Passengers were beginning to embark and there was something to view and to comment on. Nevertheless neither of them spoke, and the plane was airborne before they talked again.

'I'm not giving it up, you know,' Esau said.

'I haven't suggested that you do.'

'I can't. I have to do it. I can't stop myself. It's my whole raison d'être.'

Alistair had no intention of offering professional help. He preferred to support him as a friend. He said nothing.

'And what's more, next week I'm starting again on dentists.'

'And if you should succeed?' Alistair asked. 'If all the dentists in the whole of London were to find you beautiful, what then?'

Esau smiled. 'I would have won, wouldn't I?' he said.

'The past is past,' Alistair said. 'It's over. It's irreparable. Mistakes have been made, and, yes, you have been misunderstood. But this is *your* life, this in the here and now, and there is no point in wasting it on the punishment of others. Especially when they're dead. For it's only yourself you succeed in punishing.'

'Supposing I enjoy it?' Esau said.

'That I do not believe. And neither do you.' His voice was raised. 'I'm worried about you, Esau. What happened today could happen in London. Or you could be hurt. As you were before.'

'That's part of the deal,' Esau said.

They were about to land. For a long while there had been silence between them. Then, as the plane drawled to a halt, Esau said, 'I'm sorry I spoilt our weekend.'

'It doesn't matter,' Alistair said. 'We'll do it again. But next time, we'll go to Amsterdam.'

Alistair didn't know why, but he was aware of a gathering depression and, by the time they reached Esau's house, his mood was black with foreboding. He phoned Virginia immediately, anxious, for no reason on earth, about Doris. And it was Doris herself who answered the phone. His relief was sublime and only afterwards did he realise that this was the first time they had had conversation together. And the joy of it. The sheer invisible joy. There was, after all, another area of relationship he could have with his daughter. He need not confine himself to nocturnal visits. There was the phone. Through its invisible lines, paternity could not only be established, it could flourish. And daughterhood too.

'Darling,' he said. 'This is Daddy. Are you well?'

Oh, the relief of it. To call himself by that name that he had at such great pains denied himself.

'Where are you Daddy?' Doris said.

He saw her lips move and a swift sight of the tiny milk teeth. That mouth he had so often drawn with certainty and without fear. Her voice was smiling, but he did not dare to translate that smile into her eyes. He focused with trembling doggedness on her mouth. He dared not stray from that region, not even to the known and often-drawn nose, for that too might have been smiling and unrecognisable.

'Where are you Daddy?' she asked again.

'I'm at home,' he said and had never felt so homeless.

'But this is your house,' she said.

'Let me speak to Mummy.' She had exhausted him.

He heard Doris's Mummy call. 'It's Daddy. Tell him to come home.'

He heard Esau in the living room and the clinking of glass and decanter.

Esau was establishing 'home' for him. There was no point in going back.

'Alistair?' Virginia said into the phone. 'Are you all right?'

'Yes, I'm fine. I was away. Just a day in Paris. Had a meeting,' he lied, though he'd had meetings of a kind. 'Just wanted to know how you are.'

'We're well,' Virginia said. 'How was Paris. Did you have time to sight-see?'

'A little,' he lied again, though sights he had seen if not tourist ones. He wanted to end the conversation. He feared that Virginia might suggest a meeting. Suddenly he recalled his parents' impending visit. He had not yet told Virginia. They would *have* to meet. They would *have* to conspire.

'My parents are coming,' he said.

'When?'

'For Doris's birthday.'

'Where are they staying?' Virginia asked.

'In a hotel.'

'That's a relief. Have you told them about Doris yet? They should know before they arrive.'

'They will. They will. I'll write to them,' he said.

'D'you want to meet? We ought to . . . well . . . synchronise our stories. Or we could tell them the truth.'

'I'll think about it,' he said, knowing that he would never think about it. He dared not.

'I've poured your drink,' Esau called from the living room.

Esau was throwing him a lifeline. He realised that, in all the floating jetsam of his life, his unacknowledged daughter, his unnegotiable wife, his threatening parents, Esau and this house were his only anchorage. 'I'll ring you, Virginia,' he said, and he put the phone down. He went into the living room. Despite his conversation with Doris, or even perhaps because of it, his depression was in no way lightened. And, when he saw Esau holding his drink towards him, with that smile of ultimate forgiveness on his face, he knew that his sadness was centred, not around his family, but on the person of Esau, for whose being he was so very afraid.

'I'm sorry I spoilt our weekend,' Esau said again.

'It wasn't your fault. Don't ever think that. It's an experience and we can both learn from it. Now that it's all over, it even seems comical.'

'While it was happening,' Esau said, 'I wasn't afraid, but now, when I think about it, it fills me with terror.'

Alistair noticed how Esau's hand was trembling. He was in shock, and perhaps would remain so for a few days.

'You should spend a while in bed,' Alistair suggested, less for the rest than to keep him off the streets. 'Delayed shock can be serious.'

'Maybe tomorrow,' Esau said. 'Tomorrow's Sunday anyhow. But on Monday I must start again. Have to baptise my new track-suit.' He smiled, but Alistair noticed that the smile was jaded a little as if Esau himself was sick of it.

'In fact, I'm tired, and I think I'll go to bed right now. Now until Monday morning,' Esau said. 'Just to please you.'

But Alistair knew it was not fatigue that drove him to his bed, nor even delayed shock, but simply a deep and dragging depression.

*

125

Alistair let him sleep. In the evening he took him his supper on a tray. But Esau had no appetite. Neither did he eat for the whole of Sunday. He took tea occasionally, but he seemed to ache for sleep. Alistair became concerned, and began to regret his suggestion of sleep treatment. But on Monday morning, Esau came down to breakfast full of healthy appetite, wearing his new trainers and track-suit and raring to go. Alistair half wished him back in bed again.

'I've been practising,' Esau said. 'I timed myself. Twenty-six seconds is my record strip, trainers and all.'

'It's a very smart get-up,' Alistair said. 'Seems a pity to take it off.'

It was a pathetic try.

'Where are you going today?' he asked.

'I've got two doctors' appointments,' Esau said. 'Then I might try another masseur. Or maybe a dentist,' he laughed.

'You're teasing me,' Alistair said. 'Dentists are dangerous. You know that.'

'Yes,' Esau said, suddenly serious. 'But there's a kick in the danger. There's a kick in the risk. I felt that in Paris. That's why I wasn't afraid. In fact, I'm getting rather bored with doctors, who look at me and say I'm beautiful. I know what they're thinking. They think I'm crazy. Just like that French doctor. But he was frightened too. So he called the police. This lot here aren't frightened. They just want to get rid of me. So they pat my head and tell me I'm pretty. I'm not fooled, Alistair,' Esau said.

'Then why d'you do it? Why d'you go on doing it?'

'How else should I spend my life?' Esau said.

It was a phrase that struggled out of the very depths of despair.

'Please don't go out today,' Alistair begged. 'Play the piano, read, cook. Anything. But don't go stripping.'

'Don't worry about me,' Esau said. 'It's too late now for anyone to play my father.'

Alistair put his hand on Esau's arm. 'Take care,' he said.

# Eight

A LISTAIR was uneasy going to work that morning. He tried to ascribe his unease to the impending visit of his parents, to say nothing of Doris's fifth birthday. But he knew that greater than both these disturbances was his concern for Esau.

As soon as he reached his consulting rooms, he rang Esau's number. Margaret, the daily from Esau's childhood, answered the phone. 'Esau has just left,' she told him. 'Would you like to leave a message?'

But you couldn't leave concern, and certainly not through a third party. 'Did he say when he'll be back?' he asked.

'No. Perhaps you could try later.'

'I will,' Alistair said. 'But if you do see him, tell him that Alistair called.'

'I'll leave him a note, Dr Crown,' she said.

He had a morning full of patients and he was glad of it. He decided he would do his best to play the psychiatrist and offer friendship to none of them. At noon, in a break between patients, he phoned Esau again, but there was no reply. He would wait until lunchtime. If Esau had had a satisfactory morning, that is, a number of approvals, he would go home for lunch and call it a day. Otherwise he would strip to poor houses till teatime. Alistair wanted to slip home during the course of the day, but he had no interval long enough in between patients.

But he phoned often and each time there was no reply.

128

He tried to reason with himself. Esau was entitled to be out all day, especially on his first try-out of his new track-suit. But those two fasting days that he had spent in bed in the aftermath of his Paris arrest were legitimate cause for concern. Alistair was tempted to reach for his Doris-portfolio but he knew that that would only serve to heighten his anxiety. So for the rest of the day, he plodded through his patients with therapeutic apathy.

At five o'clock Virginia phoned. She thought they should meet and discuss his parents' visit. She suggested a new French restaurant near her house. 'You can come back for coffee after supper,' she said. 'Doris will be asleep.'

He noted her covert invitation to his nocturnal safari and he was grateful.

Before leaving his rooms, he tried Esau once more. This time the line was engaged. Alistair sighed with monumental relief. Esau was alive and chatting. He could enjoy his evening with Virginia and his night's wanderings, then later, over their nightcap, he would share his day with Esau.

He took a cab to the restaurant.

Esau's day had been eventful. Before leaving for Paris, he had lined up two appointments for the Monday morning. Two straightforward doctors. But his afternoon was free. His new track-suit itched for display. The thought of another dentist try-out crossed his mind but after his Paris experience, he was not yet ready for another risk. He pondered the possibility of another masseur, but decided to pass on that one since he was suspicious of the over-friendly welcome of his last call, and he sensed that that excessive bonhomie might extend through the whole profession. So he had decided to try a new tack altogether. He went through his father's directory of the medical square mile. Each time he picked up the book, and he often made reference to it, his fingers trembled as he scanned its pages. In his own fingers, he saw his father's. Hairless. Each one of them. Then he would clench his fist and snap the book closed as the target-name of his stripping revenge thundered off the page. But this time, he steadied his fingers and forced himself through the list. The directory was studded with sundry ticks marking the visits Esau had already made. Those that were successful were ticked in red, and those strippings that had fallen on indifferent eyes were ticked off in disappointed black. Overall, the reds were in the ascendant, a source of happy vindication to Esau whenever he looked at it. The directory was in alphabetical order, and the 'Consultant' section was the most thumbed. A few pages later bore the blackest mark of all, under the 'Dentists' column, and Esau quickly turned back. Then he saw, as if for the first time, that region that straddled the red and the black. The last of the 'Cs' before the perilous 'Ds' hoisted their impertinent flag. 'Cosmetic Surgeons'.

The column was pristine clean. Unthumbed on its untrodden path. It reeked of his father's contempt. Esau thrilled with a sense of arrival. An accolade of approval from a cosmetic surgeon was surely worth more than a hundred from the dental profession. It might well mark the end of his wanderings. The column was short. Unlike other pursuits in the directory, supply clearly fell short of demand, so it was not difficult to make a choice. The name 'Merryweather' took his fancy. Somehow it translated the worthiness of the profession. Honore Merryweather. Better and better. He dialled the number.

He desired a consultation, he said, and made an appointment for that afternoon. He was excited. He was about to call on somebody who was truly in the business of beauty, who actually made his living out of embellishment, so his findings, whatever they might be, should be considered definitive. In that sense, Esau knew how much of a risk he was taking and that it was even greater than that entailed by a visit to a dentist. For the latter represented only a physical threat, from which, if executed, one could recover. But the threat that the cosmetic surgeon might present was a moral one. Nothing less. And, whatever his verdict turned out to be, either of approval or outright condemnation, would oblige Esau to consider a very different way of life, the pattern of which could follow either simple forgiveness or rancorous revenge. He was acutely aware of the choice he would be called upon to make and that to keep such an appointment would be an act of heroism. He steeled himself as he rang the patients' bell.

He was slightly unnerved by the number of people already seated in the waiting room. All of them were women, and they regarded Esau with curiosity, scanning his face and body for some kind of prompting to his visit. But all looked in order, so between them they silently surmised that whatever he considered unsightly was well and truly hidden, which conclusion made them even more curious as to why he was there at all. Esau, for his part, viewed them with the same purpose. Most of them were clearly ante- or post-nose jobs, though one of them had a bosom which sat with utter contentment on her lap, though she clearly was not going to allow it that pleasure. On the whole they smiled at him, and he at them, in a natural conspiracy of those who go against nature.

The bell rang, and one of the women, the martyred bosom-bearer, left the room. There was a pointed silence after her departure. Esau sensed it was a silence of pity. Then the nose ladies started to whisper between them, and Esau sensed a threat of bonhomie that might, in time, include himself, so he reached for a magazine and busied himself with a range of country properties and interior design. But as he read, he eavesdropped.

131

As far as he could decipher, there was general acclaim for the good Dr Merryweather and his skills. Having made that general statement, each lady contributed her own personal experience of his talents. Only one of them contributed nothing. As yet she had had no experience. This was her first visit, and she was nervous. Her friend, clearly a post-nose job, had come to give her support. Out of the corner of his eye, Esau viewed both of them and found the one who was as yet untouched by Merryweather's knife far more attractive than the other. The bell rang again, and they both rose, the post-job urging the ante- to have courage. They were cheered on their way by the remaining women, and Esau quickly returned to his magazine.

There were three women left, two of them post-jobs, probably come for final clearance, so they were not likely to take very long. But longer, he feared, than he could maintain his interest in country estate. He reached for another magazine. This time it was a woman's journal and he oppened it at the agony column. *Dear Miss Linda,* he read, *I have an embarrassing problem. My upper lip is very hairy, and I'm beginning to grow hairs on my chin. My boyfriend is very decent about it. He says it doesn't matter. But I feel ashamed of it. What can I do?*

Esau was so engrossed in the poor girl's problem, and so eager to read Miss Linda's solution, that he hardly heard the bell that summoned the next patient. When he looked up from his magazine, only one lady remained. The threat of conversation was heightened, and he buried himself in Miss Linda's response.

*Dear Embarrassd,* she wrote. *This is a minor problem which is easily solved. There are many depilatories on the market nowadays, or you could even try electrolysis. But be sure that you choose a fully qualified practitioner. Best of luck.*

Esau closed the magazine in disgust. Depilation was anathema to him as was any other artificial form of

132

hair-removal. His hair was beautiful. Every strand of it. And it was incumbent on him to display it at every opportunity. He wished his turn would come.

Suddenly the one remaining lady rose, although no bell had rung. She walked towards the outside door then turned, as if she owed Esau some explanation.

'I'm going home,' she said. 'I've changed my mind.' Then she paused and stared at him. 'So should you,' she said. Then she was gone.

Her departure made Esau uneasy. Her words seemed to echo a warning. 'So should you,' she had said. Now he was alone and he dreaded the ringing of the bell. He tried another magazine but he couldn't concentrate. He undid the Velcro fastening of his track-suit, ripping it up and down in rehearsal. For the first time in his stripping career he was suffering an attack of nerves. He had half a mind to leave but he knew that a sense of failure would dog him for the rest of his days. For he knew that this consultation was the acid test. Beside it, all the approval or otherwise of doctors, psychiatrists, dentists, and even masseurs, counted for nothing. This visit threatened the irreversible truth.

When the bell rang, Esau rose and his legs were jelly.

He knocked on Dr Honore Merryweather's door, though it was not necessary for it was invitingly open. Esau was playing for time.

'Come in,' a voice said, and in its tone Esau recognised nothing merry nor honourable. It was flat, urgent, and clearly took no prisoners.

Esau stiffened his back and forced his feet inside.

Dr Merryweather was at his desk. 'Sit down,' he said without looking up. For a few minutes he went on writing, his eyes fixed on his papers. This hiatus robbed Esau of sudden display, his 'hey presto' revelation, and he was forced to spend the time scanning the pictures on Dr Merryweather's walls. Noses mainly, of various shapes and sizes. A few chins and a whole wall full of before and after breasts. Now, apart from his trembling, he was overcome by nausea and again he thought of leaving.

At last Dr Merryweather looked up from his papers and for the first time registered the gender of his new patient. He looked surprised. Males were rare in his surgery, and he thought perhaps the man had come on behalf of his wife.

'What can I do for you?' he said. There was no tone of caring in his question. Indeed it was not a question at all. It was simply part of his daily routine, his regular opener.

In the waiting and the sitting, the wind had been taken out of Esau's sails. Now he rose lethargically and in a weary gesture, and without appetite, he raised his hand to the Velcro fastening. He was aware that speed was of the essence and that it was in the name of that speed that he had bought the track-suit in the first place. So he willed his reluctant fingers into a ripping pace and in seconds he was as naked and as hair-wrapped as the day he was born. His track-suit had served him well, but he found no pleasure in its speed. Moreover his mouth was dry and he had forgotten his line. That line he had recited hundreds of times in consulting rooms up and down and across the medical square mile. It had gone. Gone to where it possibly belonged and from where perhaps it should never have left. Into black oblivion. Then a slither of memory returned.

'Est-ce-que vous ne me . . .?'

'You're a foreigner,' Dr Merryweather stated. It was his only comment. But his tone was one of accusation, as if only a foreigner could be capable of such a bizarre display. 'Put your clothes on,' he said with disgust.

At last Esau was roused, and his line, that time-honoured mantra of his that he had daily hawked in pursuit of his father's ungiving hand, those words now spilled to his lips' edge, and he delivered them with a

134

nobility that befitted their plea, sieving their glorious syllables into the astonished and deeply offended ear of Dr Honore Merryweather, who'd never heard their like before.

'Do you not find me beautiful?' Esau said, and wondered at it, as if hearing the words for the first time.

Dr Merryweather gaped at him. 'So you're *not* a foreigner,' he said. Now there was no excuse for such outrage. And he was angry, too. This man, whoever he was, had taken him for a ride. 'Dress and get out,' he shouted.

Esau stared at him and was stunned by his sudden resemblance to his father.

'No.' he said. He would not dress and he would not get out. And that was the end of the matter. He did a slow pirouette to underlie his refusal.

'I shall ask you once more to dress and get out,' Dr Merryweather said.

Esau stood still. 'Not until you have answered my question,' he said. 'Do you, or do you not, find me beautiful?'

'You want the truth?' Dr Merryweather said. 'You'll get it anyway whether you want it or not.'

Esau knew what was coming and he tried to ascribe the verdict to Dr Merryweather's anger. He wished he was shouting at him which would have confirmed his rage, but Dr Merryweather spoke in measured tones, slightly above a whisper. Esau began to dress. He knew it had to be his last performance. The show no longer had a raison d'être. As he dressed, he took no advantage of the track-suit's speed. For the time it took, it might have been a three-piece button suit. And all the while he listened to the drone of Dr Merryweather's verdict.

'You ask me if I think you are beautiful. You ask me because I am in the business of beauty and you think I ought to know. But what does it matter what I think?

135

The question is, do *you* find yourself beautiful? If you do, that is all that matters. But if you don't, there is nothing in this surgery that can help you.'

'I would still like you to answer my question,' Esau said.

'Sit down,' Dr Merryweather said. His voice was suddenly gentle, and Esau feared his kindness.

'I'd rather stand,' he said. He was less likely to crumble from an upright position.

'We don't understand the concept of beauty,' Dr Merryweather said, 'because very often it is in the eye of the beholder. Your wife, for instance, if she loved you, would certainly find you beautiful. And your mother. Without a doubt. That goes without saying.'

Esau sat down. He did not trust his feet for the next question. He looked into Dr Merryweather's face. It was solemn and concerned. If he wasn't exactly merry, he certainly was beginning to merit his forename.

'What about my father?' Esau asked.

'For your father it would not come so naturally,' Dr Merryweather said. 'He would have to work at it. A father very often has to *learn* to love his children.'

It was as if the man had known Esau all his life. His father, too. Else he was speculating.

But with remarkable insight or guesswork he said, 'There's a Portuguese proverb. The best revenge is to live well. Go home, and live with a vengeance.'

Esau rose. 'It's too late,' he said.

Dr Merryweather watched him go. 'Think about it,' he said helplessly. 'Please think about it.'

Esau shut the door behind him, lingered for a while, then opened it again as he had found it. As he walked through the hall he heard the tinkling of a bell. Dr Merryweather was back in the business of beauty.

Esau walked home like an automaton. All human motivation had drained out of him. He had achieved no peace. No ease. He put his key in the door of the house as if he had no alternative in the world. The familiarity of the hall and stairway appalled him. The house, a taxidermist's folly, smelt like a morgue. He took the telephone off the hook and let the cradle hang. He watched it oscillate for a while, and waited until it had found its own still centre. If Alistair phoned, he thought, he would assume that he was engaged in the business of living.

Virginia was already seated in the restaurant when Alistair arrived. There was an easiness between them, that unbending only achieved when there was nothing to hide. The incident of Mary was known, accommodated and forgotten, especially by Alistair who had consigned it to a deeper oblivion. The matter of Hugo was irrelevant. Even Alistair, had he known about him, would have agreed to that. Besides, Alistair and Virginia had something concrete to discuss, a matter that would take them through three courses without the threat of silences. Or frustrated argument. For Virginia had fully accepted and understood Alistair's problems both with his parents and Doris, and discussions could take place without acrimony.

'Well, at least they're staying in a hotel,' Virginia said. 'That way we don't need to tell them we live apart. They needn't know.'

'Won't they expect to be invited to the house?' Alistair asked.

'That shouldn't be difficult. They can come for lunch while Doris is in school. Or they can come during the day on the weekends. You can say you're out of London at a conference.' Virginia was very accommodating. 'How long are they going to stay?'

'They said nothing about that in their letter. Perhaps we can persuade them to go to Europe,' Alistair said.

'Let's talk about Doris,' Virginia said gently. 'They don't know she's Down's Syndrome. Are we going to say nothing and just land them with her? Won't that be a bit unfair. To Doris as well.'

'I'll write and tell them,' Alistair said. He harboured a faint hope that the news would put them off their journey. 'I'll write to them,' he said again. 'I'll write this evening.'

They had reached the dessert before they broached the question of Doris's fifth birthday.

'Will you come this year?' Virginia asked, 'My parents are used to your absences, but it will be difficult to explain them to yours.'

'I don't know,' Alistair said. 'I don't know whether I'll be ready . . .'

'Would you like to try a photograph now?' Virginia reached for her bag.

'No,' he said quickly. Somehow a photograph was more frightening than the real thing.

'I don't think you'll ever be ready, Alistair,' she said.

Perhaps she was right. That possibility terrified him.

'What about coming to the school concert next week?' she suggested. 'There are so many Down's Syndrome children. Perhaps you wouldn't even recognise her.'

'I know the pink gingham dress,' he said. 'Square by equal square.' He looked at her and winced at her sadness. 'D'you want a divorce?' he said. 'It really isn't fair on you.'

She didn't answer straight away. The question itself interested her far less than the fact that he had asked it.

'You've changed,' she said.

'In what way?'

'You're kinder. Much kinder.'

Alistair thought of Esau. Whatever change in him had been wrought by Esau. He was no longer worried about him. That engaged telephone-call had reassured him. He looked forward to going home.

'I don't want a divorce,' Virginia said. 'I hope we won't need one. Doris will bring us together again.'

She thought of Hugo and realised that her feelings for him were suddenly less profound. He could never match Alistair, because Alistair and she had history. And history is irreplaceable. 'Shall we go home for coffee?' she said.

Alistair looked at his watch. It was only nine o'clock but it was late enough for Doris to be in bed and well and truly asleep. 'That's a good idea,' he said.

He paid the bill and they left. He parked the car outside the house and idled there to give Virginia time to go inside and ascertain that the coast was clear.

After a while she came to the door and signalled him. She was aware of her continual collusion, but her alternative was to deny his access altogether. She never ceased to hope that in time he would confront his unwhole daughter, and, in acknowledging fatherhood, would accept, in a later breath, that he was a husband, too.

They went into the living room. He felt a stranger. The room was so different from Esau's where, on first entrance, he had felt at home. This room was a manufactured one, of instant growth, whereas Esau's had acknowledged the passing of time in its faded colours, its clutter, its remembrances. Here there was only the present, and what was history was no more than yesterday.

Virginia brought in the coffee and she poured their drinks. This part of their evening was a mere formality and both were aware of it. It was a simple decent prelude to Alistair's nocturnal visit. Without it, that visit would have seemed crude in the extreme. They talked little over their coffee. Alistair asked how Doris was doing in school. Virginia told him about the concert for which they were preparing. 'Only another three days. She's so excited,' she said. There would be singing and a play. Doris was going to be a fairy. 'Won't you come?' she said.

'No. I can't. The first time that I shall look at her will not be in a public place. It shall be where she can look at me with the same novelty as I shall look at her. It will come, Virginia,' he said. 'I'm trying.'

She raised her glass. 'Here's to your success,' she said.

She cleared the coffee away, giving him licence to go upstairs. From the kitchen she heard him open the door of Doris's room. She timed his steps to the bed, and then she turned furiously to the dishes, pinning herself to the kitchen, not wishing to linger elsewhere. If an outsider were to know of our situation, she thought, he would think us both mad, but he would sense in Alistair a little more than madness.

Alistair groped blindly to the bed. He felt where her face would lie, then covered that spot with a sheet. But this time he did not uncover her body. Shades of Esau's painful stripping forebade it. But he touched her body through the sheet, re-visiting those familiar curves and crevices. His hands told him that she had grown a little since his last visit. And, though he rejoiced in her healthy growth, he feared it too, for sooner or later these visits must, by nature, be denied him. He prayed that he could bring himself to look at her face before that time.

His visit was short, and he had to confess, less than fulfilling. It lacked the delight of his former explorations, and he realised that he was becoming aware of its poor substitute quality. In fact he was beginning to find it distasteful and, though he regretted this, he half-welcomed it too, for now he would be forced into confrontation, and the likelihood of that both thrilled and terrified him. He shut his eyes and uncovered her face. Then he tiptoed from the room.

It was not yet ten o'clock. Early enough to enjoy a nightcap with Esau and to exchange their doings of the day. As he was drawing into the kerb outside Esau's

140

house, a sudden anxiety assailed him. The house was in darkness. He tried to reason that Esau had gone out for the evening, but he had not mentioned it that morning and as far as he knew and had ascertained, Esau had virtually no social life. He was reluctant to get out of the car, but the longer he sat there, the further the fear invaded him. Then, angry with himself, he switched off his lights and got out of the car. He ran towards the front door, but there again he hesitated. It was the sheer blackness of the house that frightened him and warned of a grief within. With trembling fingers he turned the key. 'Esau?' he called as soon as the door opened. The name echoed through the dark house. He turned on the hall switch and the sudden light was an assault. Then he saw the telephone and its still and hanging cradle. His knees melted and he groped for the nearest chair. 'Esau,' he called again, and 'Esau,' over and over, hopeless for answer. He knew he had to search the house, if only to fill it with light, to dilute the fear that flooded him. He first lit the living room. There was no sign of recent habitation. No evidence of a pre- or post-prandial drink. Then the dining room and the kitchen, and the sundry offices on the ground floor. He lit them all, and all were as Margaret had left them. It occurred to him that Esau had been out all day and had not yet returned. And that it was Margaret who had accidentally left the phone off the hook. This thought cheered him a little and lightened his passage up the stairs. He went first to Esau's bedroom, flooding it with light. What he saw on the bed did not confirm his erstwhile hopes. Esau's new track-suit, neatly folded, one piece beside the other. So Esau had come home, had changed his clothes, and left again and it was Esau who had accidentally left the phone off its hook. He sat down on Esau's bed, trying to convince himself. But the sight of the track-suit was ominous and he didn't know why. He sat a little while, sensing he needed to gather strength,

141

then he went to the bathroom more for his own need than to search for further clues of Esau's whereabouts. But what he found turned his heart over. In the corner was a dust-pan and, beside it, a brush. The pan was bright yellow, a colour which amply highlighted the blackness of its contents. What struck Alistair most forcibly was the strict neatness of the ensemble. The pan was shining clean, and, though filled to the brim, there was no spillage. Beside it, the white brush, and on its bristles no hint of the carnage in which it had played an innocent role. Alistair inched towards the dust-pan and smelt Esau even before he reached it. Then, picking it up, he viewed the soft and silky tufts of black hair that had so painfully and cruelly clothed his friend. And he let out a scream of anger and grief and the gnawing pain of loss. Then he ran, calling Esau's name, from room to room, lighting them all. His own bedroom. Other bedrooms he had never seen. He panted at the foot of the second stairway and prayed for the courage to mount it. He had never set foot on that storey. Esau told him it had once been the nursery and the servants' quarters, but now the rooms were for lumber. The word was threatening. Almost obscene. But he had to view them. He had to ascertain that Esau was nowhere in the house, then he could even smile and fantasise that his friend was cured, and, now hairless and suited, he was celebrating his freedom. Why, Alistair thought, he might even be dancing in a disco. This thought cheered him for a while, at least long enough to see him to the top of the attic flight. He switched on a light. There was only one door and he hesitated before it. He could hear the frightened beating of his heart. Slowly he turned the handle, calling 'Esau,' to himself. It was black inside and silent, though he thought he heard the sighing of the wind. He felt along the wall for the light-switch, and, having found it, he rested his hand there a while. He knew with a sudden certainty that he need search no further. 'Dear God,' he said to himself. Then could think of no prayer, for he knew it was too late for favours. He pressed the switch. He tried to do it gently so that whatever news it was to shed light on could be broken slowly and in soft instalments. But the light was sudden and harsh. And monstrously cruel. Alistair screamed though he heard no sound, but his heart told him that he was screaming. And that he was crying, too. At first it was the symmetry that offended him as much as he had been displeased with the strict neatness of the dust-pan and brush downstairs. For of all the beams in that vast attic, Esau had chosen the very central one. Not for its height – there were others high enough for what he had in mind – but for its symmetry. He had possibly counted them out from one end to the other before fixing his friendly rope. And there he hung, central and almost still, like the cord on the telephone downstairs, both engaged in the business of dying.

Alistair went towards him. Esau hung there naked and innocent, more innocent perhaps than he had ever been. And certainly more naked. For he had shaved his whole body, including his great shock of hair. Alistair walked round him and noticed that his back was hairless too, all but for an area in the central region, where a clump of hair, clearly unreachable, proclaimed the Esau that he had known. He stretched out his hand to touch him, and then withdrew, fearing that a human touch might interrupt that journey of his into the unknown. That journey for which he had been at such pains to make ready. While he was shaving, had he sung a song? Alistair thought. Had he hummed a little Schubert, perhaps? Perhaps he had even been happy. For, as he de-coated himself, he became more and more fit to meet his father.

Alistair sat at his feet. He knew that he should do something, but he didn't know where to begin. He

143

should tell somebody perhaps. The police, or family, if he knew of their whereabouts. He wanted to cut him down and to cradle him in his arms but he would wait until his swinging body had found its still centre. Then he would know that Esau's journey was done. So all night he sat at his feet, weeping and sweeping the darkness away.

# Nine

H E WOKE, stiff and unbelieving, and what he had thought of as a dream now made itself abundantly clear. He knew that he must do something. He knew, too, that he must get out of that room. He kissed Esau's feet. 'I won't be long,' he said.

He rushed downstairs turning off the lights on the way. He felt offensively hungry and went into the kitchen to prepare himself some breakfast. He had to give himself time to think. In the hall he noticed the hanging telephone cord and a sudden rage against Esau seized him. A rope was an unkind legacy to leave to a true and loving friend. He replaced the receiver and went to make himself some coffee. He decided he would do nothing until Margaret came. He needed someone with whom to share his pain. He realised that he could share it with nobody else, that, apart from Gerry, who wouldn't in any case have cared, there was no-one whom he and Esau had known in common. They had always been pleasurably sufficient the one to the other.

He looked at his watch. It was eight o'clock. He would have to cancel his early appointments. His secretary would be there waiting. He turned on the coffee machine and phoned his office. He was ill, he said. He had to go to his doctor. He would be in at noon.

'What's the matter with you Dr Crown?' she asked.

'Gall-stones,' he said. It was the first thing that came to his mind.

'That's very painful,' she said.

He put the phone down.

145

He wished he could tell Virginia but how could she understand his pain if she had never known its cause? He still thought it was all a dream, and he called, 'Esau,' again, because he refused to believe what he had seen. He set out two coffee cups for their breakfast and poured Esau's favourite cereal into a bowl. He prepared toast for two and two glasses of juice. Occasionally the image of a hairless hanging swung across his eyes, but it was a dream, he kept telling himself, and wondered why he was crying. The coffee would make him better, he thought, and he gulped it, swilling his pain away. He heard the sudden drop of the paper in the hall, and he rushed to pick it up. He half-expected a hanging headline, and when all the paper had to report was a mere fifty dead in a terrorist's attack, he knew it must be a dream. Then why was Esau so late for his breakfast? He drank his coffee but now he had lost all appetite so he tried to read the paper, but the hanging shadow was like a cataract on his eye. He wished Margaret would come. He had told Esau he wouldn't be long. Perhaps he should go back upstairs. Perhaps Esau would like his breakfast in the attic. Like in the old days, perhaps, when it was a nursery. But, again, the swinging shadow. He wanted to shower but he couldn't face the bathroom. His own bathroom had no shower-cubicle. Esau's aunt had not believed in half-measures. He would have to make do with a bath which would take longer, but at least Margaret would have arrived by the time he had finished. He went upstairs, rushing past Esau's bathroom, and into his own. There he took time with his ablutions, his ear cocked for Margaret's key in the front door. He dressed slowly and went downstairs. He was no longer crying but it was no longer a dream.

Esau was dead and by his own hand. In a terrible moment Esau had wondered about his future, and in that same moment he had decided that life would be much easier without one. Alistair must respect him for that.

Now only grief was left, grief that time would offensively heal. He poured himself more coffee, then heard Margaret's key in the door. He rushed out to meet her.

'Whatever's the matter, Dr Crown?' She knew from his pallor and tear-stained face that something was radically amiss.

'Terrible, terrible,' he said. He almost dragged her into the kitchen. 'Terrible,' he kept saying.

'What is it? Tell me.' Though now she half-knew, for Esau was not there to greet her.

'Where's Esau?' she said.

'He's . . . he's . . .' He couldn't speak. Words would make it all too true.

'He's what?' she shouted at him.

'He's dead.' No preamble. No prologue. No 'almost dead', no 'a little bit dead'. Dead. Gone. Final.

'How?' she whispered. 'Why?'

He knew the 'how' of it, and she, having been with the family since Esau's childhood, she certainly knew the 'why'. But he could speak about neither.

'Upstairs,' was all he could say. 'In the attic.'

She rose, trembling.

'Don't go,' he said. 'It's terrible.'

'I was in this house when he was born,' she said going to the door. It was enough reason to mount the stairs. She was entitled.

Alistair felt he should go with her but he couldn't face that room again.

'Shall I come with you?' he asked.

'No. You've seen enough. I can tell,' she said.

She left the room and he listened to her going up the stairs. He heard how her gait faltered on the second landing, then stopped, her knees melting. After a while he heard the turning of the knob. He went to the foot of the stairs. She would need help in her descent.

147

He expected a scream but here was silence. It was as if Margaret was totally unsurprised. He waited. She would pray a little. Margaret was much given to prayer. Then he heard her keening lullaby and he sat on the stairs and felt the relief of sharing.

She came down shortly afterwards.

'We must tell the police,' she said.

'What about the family?'

'Only a cousin. Simon. In Australia. There's a telephone number. It will be in Esau's book.'

'Could you find it, Margaret?' Alistair said. 'I'm a stranger.' He felt his outsiderness acutely and it was painful, for he had thought of Esau as a brother.

'I'll do it,' Margaret said.

'Are there any friends?' he asked. 'People we should tell?'

'No. You were his only friend,' she said.

'He died all the same.'

'You are not to blame,' she said. 'All that started many years ago. I think you gave him the happiest weeks of his life.' She put her hand on his arm. 'Would you ring the police, Dr Crown?' she said. 'I'll look for Esau's book.' She could not deal with officialdom. She was easy only with family, and Alistair was glad to be spared that intimacy. Esau's address book would reveal secrets to which he did not feel entitled.

He went to the phone. He found it easier to inform the police than to break the news to Margaret. He would not have to accommodate their pain. It was a formal announcement and, as he stated it, he felt uninvolved, unconnected, as if he was reading an item of news. They would come straight away, they said. He joined Margaret in the kitchen. The address book lay on the table. It was painfully little, a few pages at most, and was testimony to the loneliness Esau had endured. Yet even in those few pages there must have been names, other than family. And who were they, those names?

Could they have been friends, or were they merely a catalogue of Esau's strip-audiences with comments of approval or otherwise alongside?

'This was his father's book,' Margaret said. 'Esau simply inherited it.'

So it was a lonely family, Alistair surmised, living in a loneliness that had shrouded them all.

'What was he like, his father?' Alistair asked.

'It doesn't matter what he was like any more, does it?' Margaret said. 'Not any more.'

She had thus told him all he needed to know.

'You know,' she went on, 'when you came, I thought things would change for him. He was happy. I'd never seen him happier. But the wounds were too deep. He's at peace now.' She started to cry. 'Such a gentle man,' she said.

They sat in silence until the police came. There were two of them and Alistair directed them upstairs. He took them as far as the second landing, then showed them the door. He waited outside. He could not bear to look at Esau's face again.

They had left the door open and he heard their breathless gasp.

'Poor bugger,' one of them said.

'Looks like a plucked turkey,' said the other.

Alistair went downstairs and left them to their indifferent business. Margaret was weeping in the kitchen. When he returned she straightened herself. 'I'd better phone Simon,' she said.

'What time is it now in Australia?' Alistair asked.

'It doesn't matter if it's the middle of the night. He has to be told.'

She went into the living room, taking the book with her.

Alistair waited in the kitchen. A policeman called 'Hello?' from the top landing. Alistair rushed up the stairs. Perhaps Esau had started breathing again.

149

'We've taken him down,' the policeman said. 'Where do you want us to put him?'

'In the bedroom,' Alistair said. 'I'll show you.'

Now he had to wait for them but he turned his face away. He heard them coming out of the room and he led the way downstairs. He thought of Doris. Doris was alive and well, yet he could not look at her. Now Esau was dead, and he would force himself to look at him. In some way, he thought, Esau's dead face might help him to confront his daughter.

He turned and looked.

Between them, the policeman carried Esau like a baby in a gentle cradle, their faces unofficially solemn and shocked. Their gentleness gave Alistair courage, and he walked with them to the bed. He pulled off the eiderdown so that Esau would have cover. They laid him down tenderly and Alistair covered him and looked into his face.

His eyes had been closed and a small smile had seemed to gather about his lips.

'Related, are you?' one of the policemen said.

'I was his brother,' Alistair said. Yes, that's what he had been. As loving, as irritated, and, now, as broken.

'We're sorry,' the other policeman said. 'You'd better call a doctor. Did he leave a note?'

'No. I don't think so,' Alistair said. 'He was just very depressed.'

'We'll report it,' one of them said. 'We have to, since we were called. But I don't think it will go any further. Just get a doctor. We're sorry,' he said, and they backed out of the door. 'We'll see ourselves out.'

Now Alistair and Esau were alone.

He sat on the bed beside him and took his cold hand in his. He could not help but wonder if he could have done anything to prevent his death, but he knew that the tying of that knot had begun many years ago, at Esau's birth perhaps, and that the umbilicus that had kept him reluctantly alive now served to put him at rest. He kissed his hairless head and left the room.

Margaret was in the kitchen. She had spoken to Simon, she said, and he was leaving on the earliest plane. He should be here by the morning, she told him. 'He will make all the arrangements.'

'D'you think I should leave, Margaret?' he asked.

'No. It would be better if you stay. Simon would not want to be alone. Now have some more coffee, Dr Crown,' she said. 'Then you must go to work. Take you mind off things. I shall see to the doctor and I shall telephone the rest of the family. There are some cousins in Yorkshire, apparently. So Simon says. I knew about them, but I thought they were all dead. They never had any contact with Esau, and, if I had my way, I wouldn't tell them. They didn't bother him in life. Why should they be interested in his death?' She started to cry again.

Alistair put his arm round her, but he could find nothing to say.

'I'll go and sit with him,' she said. 'It will calm me down.'

Alistair left for his consulting rooms. He had no appetite for work or indeed for anything at all. Since meeting him, he had always known that Esau would play a significant and beneficial role in his life. Now he realised what a chasm he had left. His only solace now lay in a Doris-doodle, that itch of his, which, in his mind and with no apparent logic, was intrinsically woven into Esau's person.

He hurried to his rooms. His patient was not due for half an hour and he spent the waiting time with his unviewable daughter.

But this time, in his doodle, she was faceless. No circle to frame that face he didn't know. No guesswork at nose, lips, mouth or chin. He shunned the face completely and started on the body, that region that

151

he knew by heart. He was reminded of the letter he should have written to his parents making it clear to them what kind of granddaughter he had on offer. Now, suddenly, it seemed unimportant. He had a sudden urge to talk to Doris. He phoned Virginia hoping that they had not yet left for school. But there was no reply. He felt rejected, isolated from the whole world, with a private sorrow he could share with nobody. He wished his patient would come. He looked at his appointments book. A Mrs Wallace was due. She was a relatively new patient and would clearly need many years of therapy. Her husband had left her after twenty years of marriage. She wanted to make a new life for herself. At least that's what she said, but she spent every waking moment re-living her past in a sheer orgy of hate and resentment. An orgy of 'if onlys', and complicated plans for revenge. Any sane man, Alistair thought, would have drowned her many years ago. But he was not in the business of judgement, he reminded himself. He would listen to her patiently, using her perhaps to take his mind off his bereavement, and at the end of the session he would donate his therapeutic comments.

She was punctual. He was tempted to ask how she was, simply as a formality, but refrained, because she was going to tell him anyway, whether he'd asked or not. She walked straight to the couch. Her gait was hostile, and her breath was fire. She kicked off her shoes and lay down.

'Well,' she said. 'I'm just the same. I've been here nine times and I'm not getting any better. You're the doctor. What are you going to do about it?'

'It depends on what *you* are going to do,' he said wearily.

'I'm doing my best,' she said.

'What, for instance have you done this week that is your best?'

'Well, I'll tell you,' she said. Her voice was aggressively threatening, and for his own protection Alistair turned a deaf ear. In any case, Esau kept intruding and, again and again, he wondered whether he could have done anything to prevent his suicide. He had no doubt that the Paris episode had triggered his final depression. But he was desperate to know how Esau had spent his last day and what was the nature of the encounter that had driven him over the edge. He could only speculate. He thought Esau might have risked another dentist, but in his guesswork he favoured a masseur, where the likelihood of misunderstanding, which Esau feared more than anything else, was most acute. He knew there was no way he could ever find out, and this factor added to his depression. It would have helped if he'd had someone to blame, although he knew that nobody was guilty, not even Esau's father, for he had had a father too.

'Well? Well?' Mrs Wallace was screaming from the couch. 'What do you think of that?'

'Go on,' Alistair said quickly, having no notion of what she had been talking about.

'Isn't that enough for you?' she said. 'Don't you think I did well?'

'What do *you* think?' The standard response of non-communication, the sub-title of 'I wasn't listening', which was itself the sub-title of 'I don't care'.

'Well I think I did pretty well.'

'What would your husband have thought?' Alistair droned. You did not have to be all that cunning to spin out a whole hour's session without having listened to a single word.

And so it went on. Mrs Wallace with her rapier thrust, which Alistair parried. He looked at his watch. Ten minutes to go. Ten minutes in which to think of something to say to her, a summing-up, a veiled suggestion or two, some parting-shot that would show

153

her the door. But he could think of nothing but Esau. And not in specifics. Just the person of him, and those new dimensions that he had brought into Alistair's own life and how desperately he would miss him. He noticed that Mrs Wallace had suddenly fallen silent. 'Well?' he said.

'Nothing more,' she said. 'I feel better now that I've got it all off my chest.'

He had a vague curiosity as to the nature of the burden she had carried, but that passed. He was glad that she had done herself some good, and he felt faintly guilty that he was taking her money. He consoled himself in the knowledge that at least he had provided the couch.

'You are learning about the futility of blame,' Alistair said. 'You are beginning to understand that the pursuit of blame stunts growth.'

It was a homily he could have issued to any one of his patients with a margin of applicability, but it would more than do for Mrs Wallace.

She rose from the couch, shod herself and smiled at him. Again he was curious as to the burden she had off-loaded. He tried to convince himself that it was his presence that had facilitated her release, and she confirmed it by telling him how much of a help he had been to her. He gave her a smile, the only positive offering he had made during the whole session. 'See you next week,' he said.

His next patient was a Mr Watson. Stephen Watson was a barrister, though he had not practised at the Bar for many years. Or indeed practised at anything. He simply could not function at all. His condition was one of acute depression. Some years ago, on a motoring-tour with his eight-year-old son, he'd had a collision and the child had been killed. He himself was unscathed. Since that time he had withdrawn into his grief and, for the first six months, had not uttered a single word. Such information had been passed to Alistair by the doctor who had referred him.

Even after a year's treatment with Alistair, Mr Watson had never mentioned the accident. He was not ready to accept that it had ever happened. Lately, however, he had been more talkative. But in general terms, as is the habit of those desperate to escape from the particular. He would dwell on the notion of collective guilt, that, were the concept of original sin taken to its logical conclusion, then everybody in the world was guilty of everything, including the death of his son. From his self-deluding deduction, Mr Watson drew great solace. He was simply one of culpable millions. 'That's why I cannot practise at the Bar any more,' he said. 'For I am as guilty as those I am accusing.'

Alistair was loath to talk him out of such a comforting rationale, for the alternative of self-confrontation could be catastrophic. Moreover, it would take time. Years perhaps. Even a whole lifetime to begin to understand that being a survivor does not render one guilty. Poor Mr Watson must reach even his deathbed before coming to such a conclusion, and then the concept of survival would be a pathetic irrelevancy. Once again, Alistair questioned the honesty of his profession. He listened as Mr Watson, meticulously and often with passion, outlined his theories. The consulting room became a courthouse, in which Mr Watson, as prosecutor, summed up the case in hand, accusing the whole world for all its grief. And pleading that that world be sentenced, not to death but to life, for life was far more punishing. When he had finished, he trembled, and Alistair sensed that no-one was more aware of the fallacy than Mr Watson himself, and that he lived in daily fear of losing confidence in his own cover.

'Why are you trembling?' Alistair asked.

155

'It's not because I'm afraid,' Mr Watson said quickly. And rose as quickly to go. He would not stay for Alistair's interpretation. He could not afford to. 'I'll see you next week,' he said, already at the door and in his gloves. And he was gone before Alistair could respond. Alistair slumped on his desk. Mr Waston had depressed him profoundly. He feared for him and for the madness to which his theories might lead.

He plodded through his patients with the occasional Doris-doodle in the intervals. In the course of the day, the body became line-perfect and he had hopes that soon, very soon, he would confront her.

He was wary of going home that night, wary of being with Esau. He phoned Virginia again. When Doris answered, he had an uncomfortable feeling of having been replaced.

'Are you coming to the concert, Daddy?' she said. 'I'm going to be a fairy.'

'I can't, darling. I have patients,' he said.

'What are patients?'

'They are people who have troubles and I help them.'

'You're a kind Daddy,' she said. 'Are you a big Daddy, or little? Are you fat or thin?'

Her questions struck him like a thunderbolt as he realised, as if for the first time, that she had no more idea of what he looked like than he of her. Except for her body, but his had been denied her. For his only child, he was a mystery man, a concept on which her imagination could feed, turning it into dreams or nightmares.

'Is Mummy there?' he said.

He suddenly felt evil, conscious of the injury he was doing Doris, with each passing invisible day, building up those terrible couch-hours that she would have to face as a grown-up woman, off-loading herself like Mrs Wallace on some threadbare divan in Harley Street. He was no better than Esau's father.

156

Virginia came to the phone. 'How are you Alistair?' she said.

He wished profoundly that he could tell her about Esau but, to understand his grief, she would have had to have known another Alistair, one who'd never shown his face during their marriage.

'I'm fine,' he said. It was a formal response which could have meant anything.

'Are you sure?' Virginia said.

'Yes, fine,' he protested, distancing yet again that truth that was unmentionable. I'm broken, he wanted to say. I have lost my best friend. But he said it to himself to erase the lie of his composure. Now he wanted to get off the phone. He wanted to talk to himself for only to himself could he tell the truth. 'I'll ring you tomorrow,' he said. He wanted to delay his return to Esau's house, but the thought of him lying there alone, unguarded, uncomforted, disturbed him. He would go back and sit with him a while. But first he needed a Doris-doodle.

He took out his portfolio. It was dense with his random ravings. Again he drew only her body. It was as if he had consigned her face to oblivion. As he drew, he felt an anger creep upon him, an anger against Doris, against Esau and most of all against himself. It was a comforting anger for it blunted the edge of his grief. He hoped he could hold on to it, nurture it, and finally break down in a fury that would overwhelm him and numb his pain.

When he arrived at Esau's house, he was relieved to see a light on in the hall. He opened the door and in automatic reflex he called Esau's name.

'Hello?' It was Margaret's voice. She came into the hall to greet him. 'I couldn't leave him alone,' she said. 'I'll stay here with you until Simon comes.'

He was abundantly grateful. 'Thank you,' he said.

'I've made your supper,' Margaret said.

He suddenly realised how very hungry he was and he was offended by his appetite. 'Will you eat too?' he said. 'I don't want to eat alone.'

'Of course. I've set it out in the kitchen.'

Despite the promise of company and food, his anger had not waned and he was glad to keep it by him. After supper he would sit with Esau, and he would feed it. He wanted to talk. He was sick of silences. His anger could wane in silence. Margaret had been with the family since Esau's birth and, no doubt, had he asked, she could have told him a thing or two about that destructive household. But, much as he wanted talk, Alistair was not curious about that topic. Esau's past was of academic interest only. His infancy, his adolescence and his reluctant adulthood were matters for the couch, and Alistair had done with that. The only past that interested him was Esau's yesterday, and on that subject Margaret knew no more than he did.

So it was a silent supper, and after it, Alistair excused himself and went to Esau's room. And, since he needed to talk to himself, he talked to Esau.

'Why did you do it to me?' was his first question. And in that question his anger exploded. It was now so sublime that it obliterated sorrow. The dead hairless face on the sheet was a mere receptacle for his rage. No pity now for that ape-like creature, no compassion for his years' long pain. All that Alistair had given, all that loving, and this now was his return. 'I did my best for you,' he wept. 'You had no right to treat me like this. I'll tell your father on you.' This last phrase stunned him, for he knew it as an echo from his own childhood, an echo of that constant threat from his mother. The equation only served to feed his fury, and he clenched his fists in fear that he might strike Esau in his hairless face. He sat and stared at him and itched for a Doris-doodle.

At ten o'clock Margaret called him down for cocoa. She offered him a nightcap, but that was Esau's territory and those days were over. He went to bed shortly afterwards, his anger still fermenting, and he was loath to sleep lest it abate. But in the morning he woke from a fitful night with his rage still intact. He breakfasted with Margaret and in the same silence as the night before.

Simon arrived shortly afterwards.

Alistair could decipher no family resemblance. He was cold, official and had the look of one who had come solely to put things in order. He shook hands formally with Alistair whom Margaret introduced as Esau's closest friend. His raised eyebrow was automatic and Alistair could not fail to miss it. He put down his suitcase and asked immediately to view the body.

'Where is he?' he asked.

'I'll take you to him,' Margaret said.

Alistair was glad that Simon would be accompanied. Somehow he didn't trust him. He felt it would be appropriate if he went to his consulting rooms leaving Margaret and Simon to sort out the dreary paraphernalia of funeral between them. He felt ousted and a deep resentment against Simon fuelled his ever-present anger. He waited for them to have done with the viewing. After a while they came down the stairs. Simon was clearly shaken.

'I'll make you some breakfast,' Margaret said. 'More coffee, Dr Crown?'

'No,' Alistair said. 'I'm off to work.'

'You'll be back this evening?' It seemed she was making it clear to Simon that Alistair was part of the household.

He was grateful. 'Yes,' he said. 'I'll be home. . . back early. Anything I can do?' he threw in Simon's direction. 'I shall make myself free to do it.'

'Perhaps tomorrow,' Simon said.

He actually gave a hint of a smile.

'And thank you for what you've done.'

Margaret had clearly given Simon an earful in the bedroom.

He was glad to have a full day of patients and throughout the whole day his anger did not abate. At the end of it, as he was Doris-doodling, Virginia phoned enquiring after his welfare and, for some reason or another, it needled him. He gave the statutory answer. Short and wanting in courtesy. 'I'm fine.'

But there was more to come. 'Won't you change your mind about tomorrow's concert?' she said. 'Doris keeps asking for you.'

Blackmail. No less. 'I can't,' he practically shouted at her. 'I've got a job to do. I've got patients.' He glanced at his diary. On the day of the school celebration he had no patients until 12.30. Except for himself and that self was broken and beyond healing.

'That's not the reason you're not coming.' Now Virginia was angry. 'It can't go on much longer like this,' she said. 'Do you realise what you're doing to her? You're the bloody psychiatrist,' she said with contempt.

She was right of course, and he knew very well what he was doing to Doris, but for the moment he was concerned with what had been done to himself.

'I'll ring you tomorrow,' he said brusquely. 'You can tell me about it then.'

'Swine,' she said, and put down the phone.

He put his head in his hands and rested it on the desk. From nowhere, the tears flowed and he didn't know whether he was weeping for Esau, Doris or for himself. I'll cry it all out, he thought, and afterwards I shall decipher why. After a while he raised his head and he noticed how the doodle had been blotted with his tears. Now even Doris's body was unviewable, blurred

160

as it was with his weeping. The angles of the limbs were out of joint. The torso was amoeba-like, without definition, and it seemed to Alistair that, even as a doodle, he had lost his daughter.

He put the portfolio back in the desk-drawer and made his way home.

Margaret had dinner prepared for the three of them. Simon had spent most of the day sleeping off his jet-lag, so little had been achieved in the direction of funeral arrangements. But he came to table with a list – he was clearly a list man – itemising all that needed to be done.

'I am free till noon tomorrow,' Alistair said.

'Thank you,' Simon said. 'There's a notice to be put in *The Times*. Perhaps we could word that after supper. But before that I shall have to fix the date of the funeral. Then there are catering arrangements for afterwards. And the cars.' He might have been talking about a wedding.

'When will you fix the date?' Alistair asked, hearing how he too had picked up the betrothal jargon.

'In the morning, I hope. I managed to make arrangements with the undertakers this morning. Before I flagged out with jet-lag. There's one not far from here. I found it in the yellow pages.'

Alistair suddenly wanted to laugh because he knew that Esau would have laughed, too. And not with that agonised scream of his, but with a guffaw of delight at the joke that had finally been pulled on on him. That, after all his pain, after all his stripping struggle, he had become a mere item in the yellow pages.

'They are coming early in the morning,' Simon said. 'Before 7.30. It's easier to find a parking-place at that hour.'

What is this Simon made of? Alistair wondered. What flesh? What, if any, blood? He was only a cousin, it was

161

true, but the unrelated policeman had been more moved than he.

'What job do you do, Simon?' Alistair was bound to ask.

'I run a computer-dating service in Sydney.'

Because it figured so accurately, it was a conversation-stopper.

Margaret felt it too, but felt also the need to keep the conversation alive. 'Are you busy?' she asked.

'Always,' he said. 'There are always people wanting to get married. It never goes out of fashion. Like death. Undertakers are always busy. Though my work is probably more seasonal. Spring, for instance, is a very busy time.'

There was no more mileage in that topic, so Alistair tried another tack. 'How are you related to Esau?' he asked. 'On whose side?'

'My father was his father's brother. But they were very different,' Simon said.

Alistair didn't probe. He didn't want to know the difference. Esau's past and lineage was suddenly irrelevant. Only the dead body lying upstairs had any pertinence.

But Simon was going to clarify in any case. 'My father was an unambitious man,' he said. 'That's why he went to Australia. You can be laid back there and nobody judges you. He never made any money, but I think in the long run he was much happier than his brother. I was happy, too. I don't think Esau fared so well. Margaret will tell you. She saw it all.'

'It doesn't matter now,' Margaret said. 'He is at peace.'

Simon clearly would have liked to pursue the subject. He was rather smug about his luck in having had such an undemanding father. He would have liked to have gloated a little, and gossiped perhaps, but Margaret would have none of it. 'What's past is past,' she said. 'Let it lie.' She spoke on Alistair's behalf as well. She rose and started to clear the table. It marked the end of the evening.

'A nightcap?' Simon asked.

'Let's have it in the kitchen,' Alistair said. 'I'd rather not go in the living room. We used to spend our evenings there, Esau and I. We would exchange our doings of the day.'

'You were very close?' Simon said, and again the raised eyebrow.

But Alistair didn't care what interpretation Simon, with his computer-dating mind, surmised. 'Yes,' he said. 'Very.'

Simon went to fetch the drinks. He poured Alistair a cognac and one for himself. Margaret refused.

'Let's drink to Esau,' Alistair persuaded her, for which reason she consented to a glass.

'To Esau,' Alistair said.

And they drank in silence.

'I think I'll go to bed,' Alistair said at last. He wasn't tired but he didn't want any more of Simon's company. 'What is it I should do in the morning?' he asked.

'Perhaps you should sort out his clothes,' Simon said. 'There must be an Oxfam around here.'

'I'll look in the yellow pages,' Alistair said, and he heard Esau's chuckle.

He went to Esau's room. He sat by his side and held his hand. And still he couldn't believe it. On the chair by the bed lay the neatly folded track-suit, his final signature, his last longing. He must be buried in it, Alistair decided. Else they would put him in a suit, with a cravat perhaps, to hide the tell-tale necklace of his quietus. He turned down the sheet. He saw that the body was still fairly stiff. Dressing him would be no easy task. He noticed that his member was erect, probably a reflex of the hanging. It looked so alive, so full of appetite, so pointlessly prepared. He crossed to

163

the chair for the track-suit and prepared the trousers first. Again he wondered where they had made their debut and what words or deeds had quenched Esau's spirit. He drew them gently over the ankles and thighs, then to the waist. The jacket was easier to fit, though he had to lift Esau slightly in order to adjust the back. He noticed that the hair had begun to grow on his chest, as futile now as his erection, and he prayed that he would be buried soon while he was still fit to meet his father. That he could strip for him and be sure that, hairless he would find him beautiful. He fastened the Velcro on the jacket, then ripped it open again with a flourish, as Esau would have done. Do you not find me beautiful? he would have said, as he had said to Alistair on their first meeting. He closed the jacket. 'Yes, you are beautiful,' he said.

He went to his room, but not to bed for he knew that he wouldn't sleep. He tried to foster his residual anger, for that at least had taken him through the day. But now that anger was on the wane and what had replaced it was an apathetic sorrow. His future was bleak. Tomorrow his daughter would make a debut of a kind, not track-suited, but pink-ginghammed and her audience would be as captive as Esau's. But with all the will in the world, he could not bring himself to be part of it. Moreover his parents' arrival was imminent and he still hadn't told them about their freak of a granddaughter. And on top of all that, he would have to find somewhere to live for there was now nothing to hold him to Esau's house. He sat on his bed and wondered what problem to dwell on first. But his grief overrode them all. So for most of the night he mourned his loss until sheer fatigue overcame him and he lay back on the bed and slept.

He was woken by a loud knocking sound. A wooden sound. In a state of oblivion he wondered where, why and who he was. Then, within seconds, he knew everything. He leapt out of bed. They were taking away his friend. He rushed to Esau's bedroom. On the floor lay the crumpled discarded track-suit, the two pieces unrelatedly apart. Esau was uncovered and naked once more. Two black-suited men were manhandling him into a coffin positioned by the side of the bed. Simon was watching them like a foreman in time and motion study.

'Why isn't he dressed?' Alistair said, his voice trembling.

'It's not necessary,' Simon said.

Had not Esau been degraded enough? Alistair thought. After a whole lifetime of vilification and reproach, did he not merit more than this further humiliation? His bile rose in anger. He looked at Simon's priggish face and he could have struck him. He moved over towards the body so that he could touch it in gentle apology. The men looked at him with pity, surmising a thing or two. Then they winked at each other, and finally settled Esau into the box. Alistair's fury was sublime, as was his helplessness. He stood on the landing and watched Esau's descent, orchestrated by Simon who led the cortège. At the foot of the stairs Margaret stood, weeping. Alistair joined her, seething with a rage equal to his grief. Simon opened the front door and went out into the street. He looked both ways, ascertaining that the coast was clear. He was ashamed to be in the company of death. He felt it cast doubt on his character. Then he signalled to the bearers that they could emerge. He stood in the middle of the porch and watched the men as they loaded their cargo. His position masked Alistair's last look at his friend. All Alistair could see was the car as it made its shamed take-off down the street.

Simon returned, rubbing his hands. 'Well that's done,' he said. 'Now, what about some breakfast?'

165

Margaret was already in the kitchen. She would be glad when Simon went back to Australia.

Simon slapped Alistair on the back. 'I've got a little list for you,' he laughed. 'I'll give it you over breakfast.'

'I'm not hungry,' Alistair said. 'Give it to me now.'

Simon took a sheet of paper out of his pocket. The chores were numbered neatly and each digit was circled. Ten trifles in all, headed by the impossible sorting of Esau's clothes. Alistair took the list and went upstairs. He did not trust himself to stay too long in Simon's company. He decided to take a bath and change. While he was dressing he heard Simon leave by the front door, no doubt about Esau's business and tangentially his own.

He joined Margaret in the kitchen and took some coffee.

'I have a list to attend to,' he said.

She smiled at him. 'You're a good man, Dr Crown,' she said.

Good? Would Doris have said that? Virginia? Only Margaret who knew only what she had seen. His anger fairly exploded. He looked at his watch. It was a little after eight o'clock. He had most of the morning to go about Simon's business. And to do what he had to do.

# Ten

A LISTAIR REACHED his consulting rooms shortly
before his first patient was due to arrive. He was
met on the stairs by his secretary.

'Dr Crown,' she said urgently. 'Your wife has phoned
so many times. She said you must phone Doris's school
immediately. I have the number.'

He faltered on the stairs. His knees melted in fear
and the dread of what further agony could be thrust
upon him. He snatched the number from his secretary's
hands and rushed to his rooms. He picked up the
phone immediately and started to dial. Then quickly
he replaced the receiver. He felt he should in some
way prepare himself for calamity. He breathed deeply
knowing that it would be of no help at all. He dialled
again. A man's voice answered. Expectant.

'This is Dr Crown,' Alistair said.

'Dr Crown,' the voice on the other end repeated.

'I was asked to call.'

'Yes,' the voice said. 'I think you had better come to
the school.'

'What's happened?' Alistair shouted. 'Is something
the matter with Doris?'

There was a pause.

'I really think you'd better come down.'

'What's happened?' Alistair screamed. 'I'm her father.
I'm entitled to know.'

'She's missing,' the voice said.

'Missing? What does that mean? And who is this

167

speaking?'

'This is Hugo Winters. I'm the administrator of the school. Doris disappeared from the playground. She's missing.'

'You mean kidnapped,' Alistair said.

'All we know is that she's missing.'

Alistair bristled. The difference between 'missing' and 'kidnapped' was only marginally more than that between 'Down's Syndrome' and 'Mongol'. 'Is my wife there?' he asked.

'She's out with the police. They're cruising the streets.'

'I'll come right away,' Alistair said.

He rushed to his secretary's office. 'Cancel my appointments,' he told her.

She stared at him. 'Are you all right, Dr Crown?'

'Cancel them all,' he said. 'Everything. And cancel my life too.'

He ran from the room and into the street, brushing past a patient on the stairs. His heels burned the pavement as he waited for a cab. When it drew up he was panting with fear. He gave the school's address and hunched himself on the edge of the back seat. He was shivering with terror. He prayed that nothing had happened to her, that she had wandered off, perhaps, and would be found and would wonder what all the fuss was about. In his anguish he slipped to the floor, and stayed huddled there in fear, until the cab pulled up outside the school. A police-car was parked outside. A small crowd was gathered round it although there was nothing to see. The playground was empty and still as death, but for one swing that idly creaked in the breeze. He paid off the cab and rushed into the school. Three or four policemen were gathered in the corridor.

'Dr Crown?' one of them said.

He nodded.

'Your wife's in there.' He pointed to a door.

'Thank you,' Alistair said, and wondered how, in his state, he could still remember his manners. He opened the door. A man sat behind the desk. Virginia was by his side, weeping.

'I'm Hugo Winters,' the man said. 'We spoke on the telephone.'

'What happened?' Alistair said. He addressed himself to Virginia. This was a private matter and he wished that Winters would leave.

'Doris came to school this. . .' Hugo started to explain.

'What happened, Virginia?' Alistair shouted.

'I'm trying to spare your wife,' Hugo said.

'Thank you, but I'd like to hear it from her.'

Hugo twiddled with a pen on his desk. What Virginia had told him about her husband was amply confirmed.

'I brought Doris to school this morning,' Virginia began. There were many intervals in her tale while she tried to control her sobbing. 'We were early. Doris was nagging to get to school. She was so excited about the concert. I left her in the playground with other children. There was a teacher there, and I came inside to talk to Hu . . . Mr Winters.'

With her faltering syllable she had told a whole story, a tale very different from the one she was trying to unfold. But Alistair was not interested in her unintentional tale except in so far as it served to intensify his dislike of the man at her side.

'Yes? And then?' he ordered.

'I had to talk to Mr Winters about Doris's future. I was only here a short while.'

'How long?'

'Less than ten minutes,' Hugo said.

'While I was here,' Virginia went on, 'it seemed that a child fell off the swing and the teacher brought him inside to look after him. So for a while there was no adult with the children. When I went back into the

169

playground, Doris wasn't there.' She broke down again, sobbing.

'We called the police straight away,' Hugo said, 'and your wife went with them to look for her. But . . . nothing, I'm afraid. We're waiting now for the Inspector. He will question the children.'

'But time is going by,' Alistair said frantically.

'There's nothing we can do for the moment,' Hugo said.

'The children will know,' Alistair said, suddenly full of hope. 'They have to know. They must have seen him take Doris away.'

'Or her,' Hugo said.

That possibility had not crossed Alistair's mind. He could not help but think of a sexual motive, and the suggestion that it might have been a woman gave him a measure of relief.

'It could have been a mother who had lost her own child,' Hugo said.

'But she wouldn't want a child like . . .'

Virginia looked at him in horror.

'But the children will know,' Alistair said. 'They're bound to have seen whoever it was. You can't walk into a playground and take a child away without leaving witnesses.'

'I wouldn't expect too much of these children, Dr Crown,' Hugo said. 'They're special in their own way, but they would not make reliable witnesses. But we shall see.'

There was a knock on the door. 'I think that will be the Inspector now,' he said. 'Come in,' he shouted.

A policeman announced that the Inspector had arrived and that they were ready to go into the hall.

'Come. Let's go,' Hugo said.

Alistair helped Virginia from her chair and he took her arm.

'Oh Alistair,' she wept. 'What shall I do?'

'What shall *we* do,' he corrected her. 'We'll find her. Don't worry. She can't have gone far.' He heard the hollowness of his hope. Doris had not gone anywhere. She had been taken. Kidnapped. He could think of no gentler word. He led her from the office. 'I'm coming home,' he said. 'If you'll have me.' It wasn't because the coast was now clear and that he could roam about the house without fear of confronting those terrible eyes which had gone missing. Neither was it because of Esau's death, a fact that for the last hour or so had entirely slipped his mind. It was because he simply wanted to go home. He was ready to start on reparation.

Virginia squeezed his arm with her acceptance. For her part she would be glad to have Alistair back, and not only to have someone beside her to share her fears, and God forbid, she prayed, her grief. But because, since that morning, she had grown a loathing for Hugo for a cause of which he was entirely innocent. She had gone to him that morning on no official business, but in pursuit of a little loving, and she was in his arms when a teacher streaked into his office to break the news. It was then that she had begun to hate him with a hate that turned into herself.

She squeezed Alistair's arm again as he led her to the platform. It was on this platform that Doris was due to make her singing debut in her pink gingham dress. The hall was decorated with streamers and balloons and its air of festivity was sadly at odds with the dire agenda of the meeting.

Alistair looked at the sea of expectant faces. Any of them could have been Doris. He only knew she was missing because they had told him. The absence of a pink gingham dress was the only confirmation that she was gone. Not all of them were Down's Syndrome children. Some of them looked quite normal, though they must have harboured some defect, some missing chromosome, to be in that company at all. Hugo called for their attention, though their attention had already been given and probably long before the police had entered the room when there was as yet no target of their scrutiny. Their silence was unnerving. Alistair found their obedience pathetically servile.

'Children,' the Inspector said. 'We can't find little Doris Crown. Do any of you know where she may be hiding?'

A shriek of giggles rose from the floor. This was a game. At last the children showed some animation. Virginia stifled her sobs.

'She's in the cupboard,' one little boy shouted.

Now Alistair understood what Hugo had meant by unreliable witnesses.

'We've looked in all the cupboards.' The Inspector played along with them. 'We think somebody took her away.'

'I saw him,' a little girl shouted. 'I saw him in the playground. He just took Doris away.'

The police took out their notebooks and the Inspector leaned forward hopefully.

'What did he look like, this man?'

There was no answer.

'Did he have a moustache?' the Inspector asked.

'Yes,' she obliged, and very quickly.

'What was he wearing? Did he have a coat?'

'Yes,' she laughed.

'What colour?'

'Black,' she joked.

'And a hat?'

'Yes. He had a policeman's hat.' This last response made the little girl convulse into giggles. Help was not coming from that quarter.

'It was a lady,' a little boy shouted. 'I seed'er. It was a lady wot took her away.' He said it with such loud protest that it appeared he was indignantly defending his gender. 'She didn't 'ave a coat on. Nor an 'at. She just picked up Doris and ran away. I saw 'er.'

'Did anyone else see anything?' The Inspector sounded desperate.

'I saw her,' a little girl said. One with illegal eyes like Doris, and Alistair had great hopes of her testimony for he felt that Doris never lied.

'What did she look like?' the Inspector asked.

'I didn't see her properly,' the little girl said. 'But she told me she was taking Doris away, and soon she would bring her back and she would be all pretty. I said I wanted to go with her too.'

Nothing more unreliable could follow that.

'All right children,' the Inspector said. 'Thank you very much. You've been very helpful.' He rose to signal that the meeting was at an end, then he asked Virginia and Alistair to come into Hugo's office.

Hugo remained outside. He wanted to be alone for a while. He was as anxious as Virginia. But less hopeful. He envisaged an ultimate tragedy. He went to his secretary's office to busy himself with the concert. That had to proceed for the sake of the other children. And the party that was to follow. He knew that reporters would come, and photographers, and he dreaded the invasion. Perhaps he could delay them until the concert was over.

Inside Hugo's office, the Inspector did not attempt to disguise his concern. 'We will find her,' he said in loud protest, trying to convince himself that recovery were possible. Though he knew from long experience in these matters that recovery more often than not applied to a body buried in a ditch somewhere.

'We need a photograph,' he said. 'Preferably one in the pink dress you said she was wearing.'

Virginia reached into her bag and Alistair turned his head away.

'We'll put it on television and in the newspapers. Somebody's bound to have seen something. I know it's silly to say "Don't worry", Mrs Crown. But no news is good news.' He knew he was lying. No news was terrible news, for no news was time-giving, time to abduct, conceal and take one's pleasure. About a year ago, he'd handled such a case. A five-year-old boy. There hadn't been news for months, and then there came news that the world could have done without hearing. He tried not to think about it and he prayed that this would not be a similar case.

'Isn't there anything we can *do*?' Alistair said. 'She's out there somewhere and we're here doing nothing.'

'All police have been alerted. They're looking for her. With a photograph, we can make door-to-door enquiries.'

'Here it is,' Virginia said. She looked at it carefully. 'It was taken only a few weeks ago,' she said. 'She loved that dress.' She heard the past tense that she had uttered and she shivered.

The Inspector examined the photograph. 'She's very pretty,' he said bringing Doris back into the land of the living. 'We'll find her,' he said, knowing that it was folly to make such a promise. 'You go home, both of you. You just have to sit it out, I'm afraid. We'll be in touch. And you can phone me any time. Here's my direct number.' He gave Virginia a card. 'Can I run you home?' he asked.

'No,' Alistair said. 'We have my wife's car.'

The Inspector shook their hands, anxious to get away. He couldn't bear other peoples' suffering. After years in the force, and seeing it almost daily, he was still touched by it, almost as if it were personal. God help them, he thought, in their sleepless nights to come.

Virginia made for the exit.

'Should we not talk to Mr Winters before we go?' Alistair said.

'What have we got to say to him?' she whispered. 'Oh, Alistair, what can we do?'

174

'We'll go home, and we'll take my car and then we'll go looking ourselves.'

So they drove home. When they reached the house, Alistair delayed her entry. 'Please, Virginia,' he said, 'if there are photographs of Doris around, could you put them away? Please?'

'What about the newspapers? The television?' she said. 'You won't be able to avoid looking at her.'

'I simply won't look,' he said angrily. 'It would be cheating. For five whole years I've not had the courage to face her. It would be a coward's way to look at photographs.' He started crying then, uncontrollably. 'We've got to find her,' he said. 'Then I shall look at her, and, after that, all the photographs you've ever taken.'

'Wait here,' she said. 'I'll remove them all.'

He waited outside and he could not stop crying. He felt twice bereaved, but Esau was no longer part of his loss. He was mourning Doris and weeping, too, for the daughter he had never seen.

Virginia called him into the house. 'I'll make some tea before we go,' she said.

They sat together silently. Then after a while Virginia said, 'Where shall we look?'

'We'll start round about the school,' Alistair said. 'She may have gone off and lost her way.'

'That's where I went with the police,' she said.

'You might have missed her. We'll try again. For God's sake, we have to do *something*. Is there a park? Did you ever take her to a park?'

'Yes, she likes the park.'

'Then we'll try there.' He hoped it wasn't the park. Parks overheard dark secrets and hid them there. No. They wouldn't go to the park. He was terrified of what he might find there. 'Let's go,' he said.

'What about you parents?' she said. 'I couldn't take them now. Not with all this.'

175

'They mustn't come,' Alistair aaid decisively. 'They simply must not come.'

'How will you stop them?'

'I'll tell them the whole story.'

'You'd better do it now,' she said.

He went into the hall to the phone and as he walked his erstwhile decisiveness evaporated. He very rarely phoned his parents and his letters to them were sparse. For in truth he was afraid of them. Always had been. Afraid of their judgement and their censure. They would blame him for this too. This thought fostered a small anger in him, enough to give him courage to dial their number. But when his mother answered the phone, he trembled once more. Even her 'Hello,' rang like an accusation.

'It's Alistair, Ma,' he said.

'What is it? What are you phoning for? What's the matter?'

In his mother's mind something always had to be the matter. Something always had to be wrong. And this time it was. So he gave it to her, fact by fact as he had been told it, and as he heard the tale from his own lips, he could hardly believe it himself. He heard her sighs of 'ohs,' on the other end, and her desperate calling of 'Father,' – she had never called her husband by his name – to get on the other line and to share the burden.

'Tell Father,' she said. 'Start from the beginning.'

So Alistair gave an encore and in its repetition found it even more incredible.

'D'you still want us to come, Son?' his father said.

Alistair was stunned by that appellation. He had never heard it before. It was the first time his father had actually expressed a hint of affection. He was glad that his father had given him an opening. 'That's what I'm ringing to tell you,' he said. 'We're so overwrought, Virginia and I. And it would be upsetting for you. It's better for you to come when it's all over.' He daren't think of what he meant by that.

'When she's found you mean,' his mother said.

'Yes, when she's found.'

'We'll cancel the trip then,' his father said. 'Don't worry, Son, it'll be all right.'

'But you must keep in touch,' his mother said. 'You must, you know.'

'I'll ring as soon as we have news,' Alistair said and he wondered when he would dial California again. He went back into the living room

'Supposing someone phones while we're out?' Virginia said. 'You never know. There may be news. It will be in tonight's paper and on television.'

'Would you rather I went alone?' Alistair said.

'Yes,' she said. 'I'd rather wait by the telephone.'

Then he kissed her and she held him close, desperate for protection.

'Have a drink,' he said. 'It'll help.'

'That's dangerous,' she said. 'This waiting can go on for ever.' She broke down again.

'We'll find her,' Alistair said. 'You must not give up hope.' He was almost shouting at her, but he was talking to himself too.


He was half-relieved that Virginia was not with him. She would have insisted on the park.

He drove back to the school and took his bearings from there. He stopped the car and stared into the empty playground. He heard the sound of singing float across the yard. Plaintive and painfully out of tune. It would have been a better sound with my Doris, he thought. He turned on the engine to drown the noise, then he cruised sadly around the block not knowing where he was going or what direction he should take. On his second block-round, he realised the absolute futility of his undertaking, and he was tempted to drive straight

177

home. On the one hand Virginia might be glad to have him there, but she might also think he was negligent in curtailing his search. So he drove around the streets a little longer. He was looking for a pink gingham dress, his only clue to his daughter of five years. He drove mindlessly, looking into doorways, idling on corners, conjuring up a fleeting flash of pink squares. How far could a five-year-old walk, he wondered, before she sat down to cry? He saw little point in looking beyond a mile radius of the school. Beyond that it was a car-ride abduction, and more he dared not think about. He decided to go back to Virginia. He needed her protection as much as she his.

He drove home quickly. As he put the key in the door, he called, 'Virginia,' and immediately thought of Esau whose name he had so often called from the threshold. But all that, all his Esau life, though curtailed only that morning, already seemed many years ago.

'Alistair?' Virginia called. 'Anything?'

'Nothing.' He joined her in the living room. She seemed soldered to the telephone. 'If you want to go out, to walk a bit,' he suggested 'I'll stay by the phone.'

'No,' she said, 'I've no patience to do anything but sit and wait. 'Oh, Alistair,' she said, 'if we don't hear anything today, it's bad. It's very bad.'

'We'll hear,' he said, then regretted it. He had no right to give her hope, when he himself was so lacking in faith. And he knew she was right. If Doris was found today, she could have been only 'missing'. After today it would be another, far more terrible story. Almost the whole day stretched before them. There was hope. But how were they to use that day except in the self-punishing pursuit of waiting for the telephone to ring?

And then it did. Sudden and shrill.

And though she had been waiting for it, Virginia could not respond. She paled, her hands refused, paralysed in fear on her lap.

Alistair picked up the receiver.

'Hello? Mr Winters here,' Hugo said. 'I'm just ringing to find out if you're all right. If I can do anything.'

'No,' Alistair said shortly. 'We're all right, given the circumstances, Mr Winters.' He added the name for Virginia's benefit so that she should know who was on the line. 'I'm here with my wife,' he added, 'and I shall be staying. Please don't phone again unless you have news. You understand. Every phone-call is an extra heartbeat.' He paused, then, 'Thank you,' he said and put down the phone.

He sat by her side. 'I'm going to have a drink. Please have one, Virginia. It will help.'

She nodded and he went to pour two martinis. He looked at his watch. It was 12.30. Far later than any alcoholic's time, but not too early for legal drinking. Virginia sipped. 'You mustn't let me resort to this, Alistair,' she said.

'Don't worry. I'll take care of you.'

'If you're staying here,' she said, 'don't you want to go and collect your things?' She seemed nervous in his company. She could only bear her own pain. To watch him suffering, and worse, his attempts to hide it, was more than she could bear.

He sensed her unease. 'Perhaps I should go now,' he said. 'I have to straighten things out at the office first, and then I'll get my suitcase. I'll be as quick as I can. Are you sure you'll be all right?' he said.

'Yes,' she said to her lap. 'If only there was something I could *do*. Doing nothing while Doris is . . . Oh I don't dare to think about it.'

He put his arms round her. There was nothing with any honesty that he could say.

He drove first to his consulting rooms. On the way his car radio chimed one o'clock and he dared to listen to the news. It was the first item. He had to pull the car into

179

the kerb, his knees were trembling so. He listened as the announcer described his daughter. Down's Syndrome. Pink gingham dress. A friendly little girl. Would talk to anybody. The announcer knew more about his daughter than he. He felt usurped. 'Missing since nine o'clock this morning,' the announcer went on. 'The police are very concerned.' For the first time he actually believed it had happened. Until then it had slipped in and out of nightmare from which he would eventually wake. The audience of half-eye-witnesses, the telephone-call to his parents, all had been episodes in a terrible dream. But now he knew he would not wake from it, that he would have to live with it for ever. And that today was the worst day. But also the best. For today they were entitled to hope. Tomorrow that hope would not be viable. And every day thereafter.

Word got round that he had reached his consulting rooms. Gerry came in to see him.

'What can I do?' he said. His concern seemed genuine enough. Any father would have envisaged it as a personal calamity. 'Is there a search?' he asked. 'Could I join it?'

'Search' was a word that belonged to the tomorrows. 'Search' was a forest and a long straight line of community care, armed with innocent sticks and fear of discovery.

'No,' Alistair said. 'But thanks all the same.'

'If there's anything I can do . . .' Gerry insisted. 'Or Janet. She could go and stay with Virginia.'

'I've gone back home,' Alistair said.

'Thank God for that,' was Gerry's comment. He sounded relieved, as if he himself had been let off the hook. 'We'll come over this evening anyway,' he said. 'And we'll bring supper.'

'Thank you,' Alistair said. He would be grateful for company. Even Gerry. Someone to share the burden of the silent phone.

'I'll go now and make arrangements with Janet,' Gerry said.

When he had gone, Alistair instructed his secretary to write letters to all his patients. She would offer an explanation, though no doubt they would be aware of it already through the media. She would tell them that Dr Crown's practice would be suspended until further notice. That way he could allow for both faith and despondency.

He gathered his papers together. He avoided the central drawer. He was deeply ashamed of his Doris-portfolio, that coward's path he had taken over the years. He wanted to destroy it, to remove all evidence of his faint-heartedness, but it would have been like burying her. In any case, he could never hide it from himself. So he locked the drawer and hid the key, hoping that in time he would forget its hiding-place. Then he realised that that was the most cowardly deed of all.

His secretary was solicitous. And embarrassed, too. She was childless and, unlike Gerry, could only understand the calamity in principle.

'D'you want me to sit with your wife?' she asked, dreading an affirmative response.

'Thank you,' he said. 'But I shall be with her. All the time.'

He saw his secretary suddenly Wellingtoned, and with a stick, treading softly over the minefield of a forest and he turned away.

'I'm going now,' he said. 'I'll be in touch.'

It was a relief to get away from that locked drawer but, as he drove to Esau's house, a great pall of depression shrouded him. He experienced a moment of total and absolute hopelessness. He wished it were all over, but he dared not define the 'it'. He put the key in the door, but there was no reflex call to Esau. Instead he called, 'Margaret,' who came to meet him in the hall.

'My little girl's disappeared.' 'Disappeared' was as ambivalent as 'missing'. 'Kidnapped' was too final. He would reserve that word for ever.

Margaret was crestfallen. She too had heard the news, but in her own troubles it had passed her by. In any case she had not connected it with Alistair. She would now make room for another sorrow. She took his arm. 'There's hope,' she said. 'You must hold on to hope.' She made him coffee. 'Are you hungry?' she asked.

He was, and ashamed of it.

'You'll have a light lunch,' she decided. 'You shall have it with me.' She started on her preparations.

'I'm going back to my wife, Margaret,' he said.

'Of course you must. This experience will bring you closer together.' She was careful in her choice of word. 'Experience' could be of joy or of sorrow. All options open.

'Is Simon here?' Alistair asked.

'He's in Esau's room. And he's in a very foul mood.'

'What happened?'

'He's been going through Esau's papers and he found a copy of his Will.'

'He didn't lose much time,' Alistair said with disdain. 'It's probably the only reason he came. Does the Will disappoint him?' he asked.

'He's been left nothing.'

'Whom did Esau leave it to?' Alistair asked. It was none of his business and he was barely curious to know, but he felt that Margaret wished to tell him.

'He left it all to the Dental Association. For research. For the life of me I cannot imagine why.'

But Alistair understood. That Will was Esau's final revenge on his father.

'Everything?' he asked.

'Yes,' Margaret said. 'The house as well, and all that was left of his inheritance.'

'Was there no personal beneficiary?' Alistair wondered whether Esau had any friends at all.

'Just myself,' Margaret said shyly. 'He left me a very generous pension. But you must not mention that I have told you,' she said, suddenly feeling guilty that she had spoken about it at all. But her motive had only been to grasp at some topic of conversation that would for a moment take Alistair's mind off his catastrophe.

'Whatever it is, you deserve it, Margaret,' he said.

'I shall call Simon for lunch,' she said. 'But we will have ours first.' She set his dish before him. 'You dressed Esau so beautifully,' she said. 'I shall never forgive Simon for sending him naked to his grave.' She started to cry. 'It was like discarding him.'

They were silent while they ate. Alistair was ravenous. And ashamed. It was as if he needed to consume his sorrow and he ate with speed as if there would never be time enough to consume it all.

'Has the day been arranged for the funeral?' he asked.

'The day after tomorrow. The crematorium.'

'That's rather quick, isn't it?'

'I think Simon wants to get back to Sydney.' She put her arm on Alistair's shoulder. 'You don't have to come, Dr Crown,' she said. 'Esau would understand. You have troubles enough of your own.'

'I'll be there,' Alistair said. 'I want to come.' He was sad that Esau had died, but his death no longer churned his heart. He was grateful that he had been privileged to know him and he was aware that that strange friendship had given him the strength to endure his present torture. He took another cup of coffee. Then, 'I'll go and pack my things,' he said.

He tiptoed past Esau's room. He didn't want to encounter Simon. As he packed his clothes and papers, he recalled how, a lifetime ago, he had unpacked them

183

with Esau's meticulous help. Now he simply threw them into the case and he was glad Esau was not around to see him. He said goodbye to Margaret and left the house that he had once considered his home. He would never want to enter it again. He had found happiness there and also sorrow, but he had been given no time to dwell on either.

He drove quickly, desperate to know if there had been a call. He would have telephoned from Esau's house, but he was afraid the ring might give Virginia hope, a hope only to be shattered by his own voice. He pulled up to his house and rushed to the door.

'Virginia,' he called. He went straight to the living room. She sat immobile, exactly as he had left her, the dead telephone within her frightened reach. Her face told him there had been no calls.

'I'll unpack my things,' he said.

'Mother phoned,' she said. 'They heard it on the news. They're frantic. They wanted to come over. I told them we wanted to be alone. I felt badly about it, but I can't take on their agony too.'

'They want to be with you, Virginia. They're entitled.'

'You ring them then, will you? Tell them to come tomorrow.'

He rang them before unpacking. He expected hostility, but they were kind and he felt ashamed. 'Come tomorrow,' he told them. 'Virginia's in shock. Please don't lose hope,' he added. 'We'll find her. We must.'

He unpacked in the guest room. He felt it would be impolitic to return to the marital bed so soon. Unless Virginia wanted it for comfort. He thought he might ask her what she wished.

The house seemed dead and hollow, a space in which no sound, not even that of the telephone, would reverberate. It had lost its life, its throbbing pulse. It was a shell despairing of live tenancy. He dawdled with his unpacking, for in truth he was loath to re-join

Virginia and to share her silent paralysis. This was the worst day and the best day, he kept telling himself, and he daren't wish it to be over.

He heard the telephone ring and he streaked down the stairs. Virginia looked at him as he lifted the receiver. He recognised his father's voice.

'Any news, Son?' he said.

'No. Nothing yet. It's my father,' he whispered an aside to Virginia.

'How's Virginia taking it?' his mother said on the other line. It was the first time she had called Virginia by name. 'Your wife' was the furthest she could go.

'Bearing up,' Alistair said. 'But I have to ring off now. We absolutely must keep the line clear. I'll ring you as soon as we have news.'

'Keep your chin up, Son,' his father said.

The 'Son' was beginning to get him down. His father had come to affection late in life, and now it seemed that he was making up for lost time. Even his mother seemed to be unbending a little, and God knows what vocabulary she would detonate once affection had struck her. He sat down. Was it too soon for another drink?

'Shall I refill your glass?' he asked Virginia.

'Why not?' she said apathetically. It was as if she had surrendered, having lost all hope, seeing a blurred future in an alcoholic anaesthetic haze.

He refilled her glass and his own.

'Gerry and Janet are coming over tonight,' he said. 'They're bringing supper.'

'That's kind.'

'We're going to need company, Virginia,' he said.

'I just want silence,' she said helplessly. 'The telephone bell is the only sound that I could stand, and I'm not sure that I could stomach that.'

'But you can't spend your life soldered to the phone.' He wished he hadn't said it. It was a surrender of a kind.

185

'My life?' she said listlessly. 'Without Doris, my life is nothing.'

'She'll come back,' he said, helplessly.

There were not many hours left of the day, this day that was the best and the worst. 'D'you want me to phone the Inspector?' he asked.

'What's the point? He would have phoned us if he had news.'

'He's probably out looking for her,' he said.

She didn't answer. He held her hand. 'It's terrible,' he said. 'It's all so terrible,' he cried.

He was able to cry and she envied him. But perhaps she was keeping her tears for the real mourning that might well come. She would save them for that. She would not waste them while she was still entitled to hope. Alistair was as broken as she, and she pitied him, for he could not recall the image of what had gone. He could only guess at what his tears were for.

He wanted to pace the room, but such an activity could only be pursued in private. It would get on Virginia's nerves. The silence oppressed him, and he wondered how long they could endure it. He wondered whether he should tell her about Esau. If nothing else it would help to pass the time.

'I've been staying with a friend the last few weeks,' he began. 'D'you want to hear about it?'

'If you want to tell me,' she said.

It was little enough encouragement, but he had to fill in the silence somehow. So he told her how Esau had come to him and of his cabaret in his consulting rooms. He watched Virginia's face for some response, but it was blank. She wasn't listening. But he plodded on. He needed to tell the story if only for his own sake, for he felt that the figure of Esau and the part he had played in his life was slipping into dark unfathomable shadows, and there might come a time when he would forget about him altogether. He told her about the chance meeting in the street and how Esau had invited him to stay in his house. There was still no reaction from Virginia and, by the time he was telling her about Esau's influence on his own life, it was clear that he was talking to himself. It was by way of a memorial. He hesitated before recounting Esau's last moments. Was it not sensation-mongering to tell that to somebody else? He was glad that Virginia was not listening. So, in tender whispers, he told himself of Esau's dying. How he had found the legacy of hair, the folded track-suit and the necklace of rope.

Virginia heard his voice as a drone, and the silence again when he stopped speaking. She looked up and saw his tearful face. 'I'm sorry,' she said, not knowing what she was sorry for, but it would do, for she was sorry for everything.

She had emptied her glass and held it out to Alistair for a refill. He hesitated, but it was, after all, the best of days and the worst. As he reached for the bottle, the front door-bell rang. He rushed to open it, dreading what he would find. He was relieved to see benign neighbours. The two Miss Gibsons who lived next door and pretended to be sisters.

'We heard it on the news,' they said. 'Her picture was on television. We're so sorry. Is there anything that we can do?' They shared the words between them, clearly having rehearsed them well beforehand.

'No. Nothing,' Alistair said. 'But thank you. We're just waiting for information.'

'Anything at all,' one of them said. 'Just knock on the door.'

'Thank you,' Alistair said again. He returned to the living room.

'That was nice of them,' Virginia said, having over-heard the conversation. She was beginning to respond again. She deserved a drink for that. He refilled her glass and his own. They drank. The silence in the room was now less oppressive. Sedated with alcohol, it now appeared unremarkable. And when the telephone rang, Virginia picked it up as if it were any phone-call in the course of any other day.

Another neighbour. Another's words of sympathy. Another's offer of help.

'No thank you. Please get off the phone. We're waiting for a call. No, there's nothing you can do. But thank you anyway.'

And so on. Virginia and Alistair shared the calls between them, and, when the phone rang again with a similar enquiry, they chorused their thanks together. For the first time that day Virginia rose, but only to refill her glass. She tottered over to Alistair and did the same for him. By the time Gerry and Janet arrived, laden with supper, their hosts were numbed against their pain. Though both knew that their best and their worst day was perilously close to its end.

# Eleven

SURRENDER is not abrupt. It takes shape in a passing thought that all is not well. In time, that thought assumes a greater probability. Then there comes a time when it ceases altogether to be a notion at all. It creeps to the heart, losing all logic on the way. And there, in the pain of despair, it declares itself. For Virginia and Alistair, that declaration came on the second day.

They had slept fitfully, their ears cocked for the phone. They had shared a bed for each other's protection and in the morning they had clutched each other against the coming day. The Inspector had not phoned and Alistair suggested he go to the police-station to ascertain what, if anything, the police were doing.

'Where could she have slept last night?' Virginia whispered. Then broke down completely in heaving sobs. Alistair let her cry it out, though he knew she could never exhaust her sorrow. He went to the kitchen and made breakfast for both of them. He put it on a tray and took it upstairs. Neither of them had any appetite, but they forced it down because this was what was meant by 'life goes on'. He dressed. 'What are you going to do today?' he dared to ask her.

'What can I do?' she said, 'except wait for the phone to ring? Perhaps we should stop hoping, Alistair,' she said.

'No. Never,' he shouted. 'It's only been a day. She'll come back.'

'How can she come back if she was taken?' Virginia

said. The word 'missing' was no longer viable.

'I'll go to the station,' Alistair said.

'Don't be long. Please don't be long.'

'Would you rather I stayed?' he asked.

'No. I need to know what's happening. What they're doing.'

He hoped he could come back with some report, but he feared that all he would bring back with him was their concern.

He drove to the station. 'I'm Dr Crown,' he announced at the desk. 'Doris's father. Could I please see the Inspector?'

'One moment, Sir,' the desk clerk said. He was deferential and solemn and Alistair feared there had been news. Shortly he returned and led Alistair through a corridor to the end door. He opened it for him with infinite pity.

'I don't want to disturb you,' Alistair said at once. 'But . . . has anything happened? Are there any leads?'

'We have nothing I'm afraid,' the Inspector said. 'I have to be honest with you, Dr Crown. We have nothing. No witnesses, no possibility of an identikit.'

'What are we going to do?' Then, after a while, 'Must we give up hope?'

'No,' the Inspector said quickly. 'There's a possibility she was taken by a woman. If that is so, we will eventually find her. And she will not be harmed. We have started door-to-door enquiries with Doris's photograph. It's not easy to hide a new child in a neighbourhood especially if that child is handicapped. This is one small advantage we can reap from the situation.'

'How long will you give that line of enquiry?' Alistair asked.

'Until it's exhausted.'

'What can I tell my wife?'

'Nothing, I'm afraid. Just not to give up hope.

190

Children have gone missing for weeks and have been found safe and well.' The Inspector still insisted on 'missing'.

'But you're concerned, aren't you?' Alistair said. He had to take something back to Virginia.

'Of course I'm concerned,' the Inspector said. 'We're doing everything. I promise you.' He showed Alistair to the door. 'I'll phone as soon as I have news,' he said.

'Could you phone in any case?' Alistair said. 'Just contact of a kind is helpful. It's this terrible not knowing. Not knowing,' he said.

'I'll drop in this evening,' the Inspector said.

Alistair made his way through the corridors and the policemen he met gave deferential room for him to pass. He wondered if they had surrendered.

At home, Virginia had taken up her phone-stand once more. He repeated what he had heard, stressing the hope that she should hold on to. He did not mention their concern. The door-bell rang shortly after his return. Virginia's parents were on the door-step. He'd forgotten he'd asked them to come. But he was glad to see them.

'We didn't like to phone you,' they said timidly.

'That was wise,' he said. 'The phone is a nightmare.'

They were already in the living room with Virginia in their arms. There was nothing any of them could say. Alistair stood on the sidelines feeling very much the outsider. Having played so little part in his daughter's growth, they felt he was not entitled to their measure of grief. So he could only mutter, 'We mustn't lose hope,' and listen to the echo of his silly platitude.

'What can we do,' Virginia said. But it was no question. It was simply a statement of their helplessness.

'What are *they* doing?' her mother asked.

191

'Door-to-door questioning,' Alistair said. He knew Virginia would have difficulty with reply. 'A woman might have taken her away,' Alistair said. 'A woman who's lost her own child. Somebody would notice a new child in a street especially if . . .' But he held his tongue.

'Have you eaten?' Virginia's mother asked.

'I'm not hungry,' Virginia said.

'But you must eat,' her father said. 'You must keep up your strength. Mother,' he said. 'You've brought lunch. Get it ready, dear.'

Mrs Warner was glad to have something to do. She busied herself in the kitchen while her husband fumbled with his cuffs and shrugged his shoulders.

'Would you like a drink?' Alistair asked.

'That would do nicely,' Mr Warner said.

Alistair would give one to Virginia without asking her. That would save her embarrassment. He crossed to the drinks cabinet and noticed that the martini bottle was almost empty. 'I'll have to replenish,' he said. 'But there's some whisky. Would you like that?'

'That's my tipple,' Mr Warner said, as if Alistair should have known.

He poured him a glass and offered it to him. 'I must go to the off-licence,' he said. 'I won't be long.'

He was glad to get out. Virginia's parents were suffocating at the best of times. He stocked up with drink.

'Any news?' the man behind the counter asked.

'No. Nothing.'

'I saw it on television last night,' he said. He had a mind to get chatty. 'I'm very sorry. The police are very good in these matters. They'll find her. Don't worry.' He did not add in what state. 'Your poor wife.' There were customers waiting but he would have happily let them wait.

'I must get back,' Alistair said. 'My wife is waiting.'

192

The man packed the bottles reluctantly. 'I can bring them over if you like,' he offered. He would have relished a glimpse of the mourning mother.

'No thank you. I have the car,' Alistair said. He drove home saddened. Doris had become an item of gossip.

Lunch was set and Mrs Warner stood at the head of the table clearly having taken over. There were no glasses on the table, an omission that Alistair quickly rectified. Mrs Warner made no attempt to hide her disapproval. 'What are we celebrating?' she said as Alistair uncorked ther wine.

'Hope,' he said coldly. It was a masterful silencer, and his mother-in-law served the meal suitably chastened.

'If there was only something we could *do*,' Mr Warner said.

'That's the worst of it,' Alistair told him. 'The waiting and the doing nothing.'

'You're not eating Virginia,' Mrs Warner said.

Virginia was drinking wine. It would be her food until Doris was found. It would balance her on the edge of oblivion with just enough consciousness to hear the telephone ring.

It should have been a silent meal. Alistair and Virginia had grown comfortable within that silence, for they knew that the alternative was speculation, and that would lead to tears. But, for Mr and Mrs Warner, it was by way of being their first day, one that could be eaten away with words until darkness fell and consumed the words themselves. So Alistair and Virginia heard them talk without listening, as they gently gave words to each other, syllable by syllable of their stifled screams. The day wore on, at a snail's pace but that didn't matter for there was nothing at the end of it. If there was Doris news, it could come at any time, and neither the minute nor the second hand on the clock would determine its telling. Doris's disappearance and her

193

possible recovery no longer hinged on time. It was too late, and they all knew it. Each one of them at that table. In their syllables and silences they knew it, and soon one of them was going to say it, and it would be a relief for them all. But until that time, they would make do with make-believe and fantasy.

The wine-bottle was empty. Alistair uncorked another. He knew that an overall silence was not far away.

Early evening, when the door-bell rang, it shattered a silence that had long since settled. Alistair rushed to open it. He had forgotten about the Inspector and he was relieved to find him at the door. Virginia was many martinis gone. She sat in her usual place but did not trust herself to rise. Mr and Mrs Warner managed to stand and to blurt out together, 'Is there any news?'

'These are my parents-in-law,' Alistair said by way of introduction.

'No news, I'm afraid,' the Inspector said. 'I just came to see how you were.'

'Would you take a drink?' Alistair asked. 'I'm afraid this is how we're coping.'

'It helps,' the Inspector said. 'Certainly I'll have one with you. I'm off duty, so a little whisky will suit me nicely.'

'Who's looking for Doris then?' Mrs Warner almost whispered.

'Half the police force of London,' the Inspector said.

'It's good of you to come,' Alistair said, handing him a glass.

'Well, what are they doing?' Mrs Warner insisted.

'Quiet, Mother,' Mr Warner said gently. 'I'm sure they're doing all they can.'

'It's mainly a house-to-house,' the Inspector said. 'It's amazing how much information we can glean from such an investigation. We are hampered by having

194

no witnesses. At least, none that is reliable. We've questioned everybody in the area. Nobody was seen loitering about the playground area in the days before Doris went missing. Which leads us to believe it was an impetuous act, one that was not premeditated. This is hopeful, for impetuosity is found more often in women than in men. Which is why we're looking for the sudden appearance of a new child in the neighbourhoods. Hence the door-to-door enquiries.' As he spoke, he began to believe in it himself, but when he had finished, he heard the echo of failure in such a search. And so did they all, and once more they sought refuge in silence.

'It's important not to be alone,' the Inspector said. 'It's good to have family at such a time.'

'Isn't there anything we can *do*?' Mr Warner said, talking to himself.

'We just have to wait,' the Inspector said.

'And after the door-to-door investigation, what then?' Mr Warner insisted.

'It depends on what information we gather,' the Inspector said. He didn't want to mention woodland searches or the dragging of lakes. He wanted to get back to his family, but he knew that this was part of the job. Tomorrow evening, he would send his deputy.

So he joined in their silence, while he sipped his drink, taking it slowly to give him something to do.

Outside it grew dark. The worst of times. The thought of Doris in darkness, wherever and however she was, was unbearable. Alistair walked over to the window. Normally he would switch on the lamp, but that would make a production of the darkness that they all feared. It was Mr Warner who eventually switched on the light. The Inspector rose. It had not been easy to take his leave in the dark. 'I'll be going now,' he said awkwardly. 'I'll be in touch tomorrow. I'll see myself out,' he said quickly. He didn't want any private pleading or speculation on the door-step. But Alistair saw him out. And without a word.

He couldn't go back into that silent room. He needed sound of a kind, if only of his own weeping. He leaned his head against the wall and drenched, aloud and yielding, his broken heart.

As night drew in, the Warners were loath to leave and, had they been asked, they would have stayed.

'Come in the morning,' Virginia said.

'Of course. We'll be here first thing.'

'I have to go out in the morning,' Alistair said, 'so it will be good if you come.'

'Are you going to work?' Mr Warner asked.

'Just one patient,' Alistair said. He would not add that that patient was dead.

He helped Virginia to her feet. 'We must try and sleep,' he said. 'We will need all our strength.' It was the closest he could come to telling her that it was all over. For one did not need strength to rejoice. One needed it to weather catastrophe.

In the middle of the night he woke sweating in the tail-end of a nightmare. He was relieved that Virginia was sleeping. He crept out of bed and went to Doris's room. As was his wont, he did not turn on the light. He felt his way towards the bed and knelt beside it. Then he drew back the sheet, and with his fingers he lovingly outlined the contours of her last impression. He knew them by heart; the curl of the knee, and the lean of the thigh, the arms crossed over the chest, and the hands loosely woven. Slowly he fingered her neck, and dared the ascent to her face on the pillow, that unknown mine-riddled territory. He caressed the outline of her mouth, her cheek and her nose. In its bridge he lingered before the final assault and then fearfully treading Outer Mongolia, he touched her eyes. He let his fingers rest there a while until they cramped with the pain of loss. Then he turned back the sheet and left the room.

The Warners arrived early in the morning, laden with the day's food. Alistair noted a bottle of whisky in their hamper. They had joined the survivors.

He was glad to leave the silent house even though he was making for a greater silence. He turned on the car-radio in time for the news, and listened all the way through. There was no mention of Doris. She had become yesterday's news. By the time the bulletin was finished, he had reached the crematorium. He was early so he sat in the car, watching the hearses come and go. There were a number of chapels in the complex and, as one emptied, another filled up. One grief queuing after another and the echoes of sundry sermons and the final hymned farewell. Then the fire. And, after that, the sandwiches. And, after the sandwiches, the silence. The only people he would recognise for Esau's send-off were Margaret and Simon. He would have to find them because he was not sure which chapel to attend. So he went into the courtyard and looked around him. They were a singularly unmournful crowd and, in general, very well-dressed. He noticed a number of long-last greetings, between people who clearly had not seen each other in years, and he could guess at the dialogue that ensued. 'It had to come to this before we met again.' And, once that was over, reverence given, they could catch up on their separate news. He recognised no-one, then moved into a smaller courtyard clearly reserved for the friendless deceased. And there he saw Margaret, standing alone, and a scattering of people, no more than half-a-dozen, wallflowering the edges. He went across and greeted her. She was glad to see him. And surprised too. 'How good of you to come, Dr Crown,' she said. 'And with all your own troubles. Is there anything new?'

197

'Nothing. Nothing at all.'

'I'm so sorry for you. And your poor wife,' she said. 'How she must be suffering.'

'It's a terrible time,' Alistair said. Then after a pause, 'Where's Simon?'

'He's coming with the funeral car,' she said. 'He should be here soon.'

And as she said it, it drew into the courtyard. It was not like the other hearses. It was almost bare. One single wreath lay on the coffin. Simon sat beside the driver looking suitably solemn. The chapel door was opened as a sign that the mourners should enter and they straggled in, all eight of them, as Alistair counted them, one by one. They could have been, and probably were, a rent-a-crowd, or rather, a rent-a-handful, so conscientiously did they perform their role. A slow march into the chapel with handkerchiefs at the ready.

'Is this all we are?' Alistair whispered to Margaret.

'I'm afraid so,' she said. 'We told everybody who knew him. There weren't very many. Come and sit with me,' she said.

He followed her into the front pew, and shortly afterwards the canned music accompanied the coffin to the stand. Simon brought up the rear, then took his seat next to Margaret. Alistair tried to picture Esau in the box, but his image escaped him. In its stead was a headless body in a pink gingham dress.

The minister took his stand, shuffling the few notes he had hastily scribbled beforehand. He ascertained that they did not apply to the last soul he had sent to the fire or to the one after this one. Having assured himself that he was reading about the current unknown, he asked the small gathering to stand. The music faded out as he started on his hired peroration.

'We are gathered here to celebrate the life of William Waterson.' At first Alistair thought that the man had picked the wrong notes after all. Then he realised that he had never known Esau's real name. Esau was what William saw himself to be. Esau was what he called himself to spite his father. But it was in the name of William, that name that his father had given him, that Esau would go to meet that time-honoured target of his rage. It was Esau, the hairy one, the stripping showman, who plied his daily nemesis from surgery to hostile surgery; but it was William, the hairless, who would go to the forgiving fire exactly as his father would have wished. The preacher droned on, not knowing what he was talking about, much less about whom; and nobody was listening for he was talking about someone none of them could recognise. Simon shuffled his feet impatiently. According to Margaret he was taking the night-plane to Sydney, legacy-less, and of a temper very sour. There would be drinks at the house afterwards, she had whispered to Alistair during the William-recital. 'For Esau,' she had stressed. 'To remember him.'

The music had started again, this time in accompaniment to a hymn. The preacher led bravely, but was little helped by the sparse congregation so it was more by way of a solo rendering. His cheeks gathered colour as he sang, both from the strain and sheer embarrassment. He was staring at the coffin, willing it on its fiery way, and at last, to his sublime relief, it moved, its single wreath quivering. By the end of the hymn it was out of sight. The preacher opened the end doors of the chapel and the congregation moved into the sunlight, where it was appropriate for mourners to greet the next-of-kin and to view the flowers. But, since Simon was the only relative and there were no flowers to view, that part of the ceremony was over very quickly. The rent-a-gathering dispersed and Margaret and Alistair shuffled on the flagstones. Through the still open doors of the chapel, Alistair could see that the next grief was already filing into the pews and he noticed that the

199

preacher was once more shuffling his notes. Then the doors were closed.

'I have hired a car,' Simon said. 'We could go back to the house now.'

'I'll follow,' Alistair said. 'I have my own.'

He drove behind Simon, once again tuning into the news. But there was nothing. He was anxious to get home. There could be news there.

There were just the three of them in Esau's living room. It was a dead room now, its stuffed animals on the wall staring vacantly into space. The tiger rug on the floor seemed suddenly moulted and the black piano lid was coffin-closed. Simon poured the champagne, then handed it around.

Then, raising his glass, 'To William,' he said.

'To Esau,' Margaret and Alistair chanted together.

So, outnumbered, it was to Esau to whom they drank and whom they sped on his way.

Simon downed his glass. 'Now I must pack,' he said. All duty done, and with precious little reward, he saw no reason in entertaining further. 'I'm glad to have met you, Dr Crown,' he said. 'Might as well stay and finish the bottle. Pity to waste it.' Then he was gone.

Alistair filled Margaret's glass.

'I shall be going home, too,' she said.

'What about this house?' Alistair asked.

'I shall come in from time to time and keep it tidy until it is sold. But we will keep in touch, won't we?' she said.

'Gladly,' Alistair said, handing her his card.

'I shall keep my ears open for news of your daughter,' she said. She wrote her address on a piece of paper. 'If there's anything you need, any help I can give, please be in touch,' she said.

He kissed her and wished her well. Then he gave a last look at the room where he and Esau had spent such happy hours of music and talk exchange. But he had to admit that his heart, what was left of it, was not, on Esau's account, broken.

He drove home. There was no news on the radio and he had to make do with 'Gardeners' Question Time'. The expert was talking about compost. Alistair switched him off. Considering where he had left and where he was going to, the subject was far from his taste. He drove home in silence as a rehearsal for that which was to come. As he opened his front door he heard voices and saw, through the open living room, the back of a policeman's uniform. His heart fluttered. He rushed into the room. 'What is it?' he shouted. 'Is there news?' he heard his voice falter.

'We've had some information,' the Inspector said. 'As a result of our door-to-door investigation, a woman in Wandsworth said that she saw a little girl answering to Doris's description on the Common, the morning she was reported missing. About eleven o'clock, she said. She was holding a man's hand. She could only see the back of them. But we're going to follow it up,' he said. 'It may come to nothing.'

Either way, he knew it was bad news.

'When will you start?' Mr Warner was the only one with voice to speak.

'It's already started. I'm going there now,' the Inspector said. 'I shall keep you in touch with our every move.'

Alistair saw him out and returned to the living room. He noticed that they were all drinking and he poured himself a whisky. Now it was a different calibre of waiting, though the silence was the same. They drank through the afternoon waiting for the telephone to ring or the door-bell to sound. Either noise would have paralysed them. For now there was something positive to wait for, the possibility of a find, and they were all praying that the search would be fruitless and that they could all go back to the old kind of waiting in which the heartbeat was numb but regular.

They drank away the time until the six o'clock news when Mr Warner turned on the television. Alistair discreetly left the room. Since Doris's disappearance his source of news had been the radio, that sightless informer. He had avoided newspapers and television in fear of Doris's picture. He would not allow himself that. But outside the room he listened to the sound and heard that a search had been undertaken on Wandsworth Common in response to a sighting of Doris Crown, the little four-year-old who had been missing for three days. There followed a short silence no doubt depicting the searchers at work. 'The search will continue till nightfall,' the announcer was saying, 'and if necessary resume at first light.' He wondered what was meant by 'if necessary'. Presumably they were hoping to find some clues before nightfall. Or perhaps some final clue that would call off the search for good and all. The news-announcer had now moved onto other things, and he went back into the living room and joined in that other kind of waiting.

It was supper-time and Mrs Warner went about her preparations, glad to busy herself. Mr Warner set the table. He, too, needed something to do. But Virginia stayed rooted to her post, her one hand clutching her glass, and the other in terrified reach of the phone.

Shortly before nine o'clock, Alistair made to leave the room in anticipation of another news bulletin but, on his way into the hall, the door-bell rang. He dashed back into the living room for shelter. They all looked at one another. No-one was willing to answer the door. The bell rang again. Suddenly Virginia rose, as if over the last few days her strength had been gathered for such a moment. She made her unsteady way towards the door. Half-way there, Alistair caught up with her, and together they prepared for the worst.

202

It was the Inspector. His face was no more solemn than usual. It was his everyday face which carried everyday news. In short, nothing.

'I've come to tell you about our progress,' he said. 'No progress in fact, for we have found nothing. But we will continue in the morning.'

'Won't you come in?' Alistair said.

'They found nothing,' Virginia said to her parents. She was almost smiling.

Alistair poured the Inspector a whisky.

The Inspector had exhausted all his news on the door-step. Now he scratched in his mind for something to say. 'We're lucky with the weather,' he thought of at last.

'Yes,' Mrs Warner said, not knowing why, for their grief was grief, come rain or shine.

'If it's bright tomorrow, we'll start early in the morning.'

'Should one of us come along?' Mr Warner asked. He desperately wanted to do something.

'We don't encourage that,' the Inspector said gently. 'There would be nothing for you to do there. Except wait. And you are better off waiting here. I'll be in touch, don't worry.'

'We appreciate your consideration,' Mr Warner said formally.

'It's the least I can do,' the Inspector said. He felt he'd stayed long enough. He rose. 'I hope you're getting some sleep,' he said, 'I know it's hard, but you need your strength.'

The phrase tolled like a passing-bell, but they let it lie, listening to its echo.

'Thank you for the drink,' the Inspector said. He looked at Alistair and gave an almost imperceptible nod of the head. In that gesture, Alistair read that he wished to be taken to the door. So he showed him out, shutting the living-room door behind him.

On the threshold, the Inspector touched his arm. 'It doesn't look good, Dr Crown,' he said. 'She has been missing for too long. Our best chance was a bereaved mother. We have enquired into recent deaths of Down's Syndrome children and we have checked on all their parents. No leads. We mustn't give up hope, but the longer she is missing, the less chance we have of finding her alive.'

Virginia slept till eleven o'clock and, on waking, saw Alistair by the bed. She sat bolt upright and said, 'Is there any news?'

'No. Nothing,' Alistair said. I was just watching you sleeping. Your parents are downstairs.'

'Another day,' she said. 'Another waiting day.'

'Breakfast is ready,' he said.

'You know something,' Virginia said. 'I'm hungry. In fact, I'm starving.' She had admitted last night to fatigue and now, shamefacedly, to hunger. Perhaps it was a turning-point. Perhaps she had begun to give up hope. But the Warners were armed still with clichés. 'It's all part of life's rich tapestry,' Mr Warner was consoling himself as he fed the toaster, and as Mrs Warner brought in the coffee she said, 'We have to keep our health and strength.' In times of crisis, a man's only resort is to clichés. A man will grasp for dear life at any floating truism, for in pain, platitude is permissible and beyond judgement.

Alistair would have preferred the silences, but he understood that everybody was talking to themselves. So it was a silence of a kind.

Virginia gravitated to her chair and her ever-full martini. No friend rang nor neighbour called. The Crown family in their troubles had become an embarrassment. In the evening when the front door-bell rang, Alistair prepared the Inspector's whisky. But it was not the Inspector. This time he had sent his deputy. He had loaded another pair of shoulders with the burden of no news. He shuffled into the living room. 'The Inspector couldn't come,' he said. 'He's tied up at the station. He told me to tell you that the search has been called off. We found nothing.'

'Have a drink anyway,' Alistair said, handing him the Inspector's whisky.

'Thank you,' he said, 'but I'm still on duty.' He wasn't, but he wanted to get away.

'Thank you for coming,' Alistair said.

'What happens now?' Virginia whispered from her chair.

'We carry on with our investigations,' he said. He backed towards the door. Alistair understood his discomfort and showed him out.

'Thank you again for coming,' he said.

'There's still hope,' Mrs Warner said when he returned to the living room.

He couldn't answer her.

'While there's life there's hope,' she persisted, unwilling to accept that there was no evidence of life to hope for. But her proverbs kept her going and Alistair could not deny her.

Eventually they left. Another day had been consumed.

'Shall we go to bed?' Alistair asked.

'I'm not tired,' Virginia said. 'And I'm not hungry either.' She had started waiting and hoping all over again.

# *Twelve*

O N THE fifth day, Alistair decided to go back to
work. He had given the Inspector his private
telephone number in the office in case there was any
news. Nevertheless, he phoned him throughout the day,
and, though the Inspector was polite and even friendly,
Alistair sensed that his every phone-call was a nuisance.
Sometimes the Inspector was out but Alistair never
believed it, though he had to make do with his deputy.
But there was never any news. 'Investigations are under
way,' was the standard response. So he phoned his
parents and off-loaded on them the same answer. His
father kept calling him 'Son', and his mother kept asking
after Virginia. Both expressed a wish to visit, but rather
as a formality, and, in between the syllables, Alistair
heard their hope that such a visit would be discouraged.

'Come when it's all over,' he said, shipping the dire
ambiguity over the wire.

'Thank you for calling, Son,' his father said.

As Alistair put down the phone, he understood with
overwhelming sadness that affection could come too
late.


The following day was Doris's fifth birthday. So poign-
ant was that day, so despairing, that it was not even
mentioned at the breakfast table. Both Alistair and
Virginia stifled the announcement for, given an airing,
her birthday might have been her death-day too. He
placed Virginia in her telephone-chair before leaving.

A safety move. She would guard the fort during what he feared would be an ominous day.

On reaching his consulting rooms, his first act was to ring the Inspector. Again he was out and again his deputy gave his standard response. Alistair gave his first patient scant attention. His heart was breaking. Another birthday which, with all his cunning, he would have been at pains to avoid, but one which this year had, in any case, been denied him. He shuffled through his patients till lunchtime. And then his phone rang. It was his private phone. Only Virginia knew that number. And now the Inspector. He let it ring, terrified, for either caller would have news. Perhaps it was Virginia. Perhaps she felt no longer able to stifle Doris's coming-of-school age. To silence it would have been a kind of betrayal. Her five little years had to be acknowledged, whether in celebration or memorial. He picked up the phone. It was a man's voice. The Inspector's.

'Have you a moment, Dr Crown?' he asked.

'Of course.' Alistair heard his voice quivering.

'We've had some new information,' the Inspector said. 'A woman was horse-riding in Hyde Park on the morning of Doris's disappearance. She went away for the weekend and has only just returned. She heard that Doris was missing' – that euphemism again – 'and she has just been in touch. She recalls that she saw Doris. She vividly remembers the pink gingham dress. Doris was holding hands with a gentleman. Alas, she saw only the back of them. They were walking towards the Serpentine. I have been to see her and she seems to me to be a reliable witness. We're going to make a search, Dr Crown,' he said. 'First of the park, which has already begun, and then, if necessary, we will drag the lake. I would like to keep this search as quiet as possible, though of course that won't be easy in such a public central place, but I would prefer it if your wife did not know. Not for the time being anyway.'

Alistair's mouth was dry. He opened it to speak but nothing, not even a croak, emerged.

'Are you still there, Dr Crown?' the Inspector said.

'Yes,' he mouthed and again into silence. He coughed confirming his presence at the end of the line.

'Are you all right Dr Crown?'

Alistair wet his lips. 'It's her birthday today,' he said, and heard it loud and clear. It was a relief to make the announcement. 'She is five today.' He kept her in the present.

'This must be a very hard day for you,' the Inspector said.

'Five-years-old,' Alistair said. 'It's not much, is it, Inspector? Hardly a lifetime.'

There was a silence then. After a while, 'I'll be in touch,' the Inspector said. 'Until what time are you at this number?'

Alistair looked at his appointments book. 'Until seven o'clock,' he said.

'Good. If I have any news before then I shall phone you. In any case, I will call on you this evening.'

'Thank you,' Alistair said. His voice had gone again. He put the phone down, trembling. Then his hand reached for the key to his desk-drawer. The portfolio drawer, that he had not opened since Esau's death. He reached for the handle slowly, not, as hitherto, with an addict's itch, but with a calm necessity to put things in order. He could not stop his trembling. He clenched his fists as he turned the key in the lock. He took out the portfolio, handling it gently as if it were a holy script. He took a new sheet of paper and started, as was his wont, with a circle, that earth's circumference that would embrace the earthquake within. But he did not draw Doris. Not even those viewable parts of her. He found himself drawing trees, their trunks and branches in finest detail. He gnarled the oak-bark like a doodle and he veined each leaf with a surgeon's precision. It was a time-consuming task, but he performed it like a purge and its effect was indeed as liberating. He filled the circle with trees and a few untidy clumps of grass. At last, after diligent labouring, the circle was almost full, except for a small space beyond the trees. In this vacuum he drew a horse, and on its back, a rider. His hand trembled as he drew, but he forced himself to complete the picture. Then, when it was finished, he shut the folder quickly and replaced it in the drawer, for he dared not look at what he had done.

He was suddenly hungry. It was certainly past his lunch-hour. But he dared not leave his private line. He had become hooked, like Virginia, on appalling probability. He buzzed his secretary and asked her to bring him a sandwich and a coffee. Meanwhile he drank from a bottle of whisky he kept in his medicine chest. As Virginia was probably tippling at the same time. He thought of phoning her, of ignoring the Inspector's advice. Virginia had as much right to know about the new information as he himself. But he refrained. He would tell her face to face when he reached home, so that he would be there to comfort her. When his secretary brought his lunch, he ate with ravenous appetite.

He ploughed through his patients until the end of the day. His last was Mr Watson, he who believed that everybody in the world was guilty of everything. But in the last few weeks Mr Watson had changed, and Alistair wondered whether it was for the better or worse. For no longer was everybody to blame for the world's sins. He had let the world off the hook. Only one was to blame, he himself, Stephen Watson, who had taken upon himself the guilt of all. In certain ways, Alistair thought, it was an improvement. To move with such painful logic, from the general to the particular, was progress of a kind. It was to set oneself, however reluctantly, on the road to self-confrontation. But, in that same direction, madness lay, depending on the speed of one's progress. If slow, one could monitor each stage of the route, whittling away the peripheries, until the single event of his son's death could be isolated and dealt with. But if progress was frenetic, and Mr Watson's manner was far from calm, that same road could lead to Bedlam.

'Give me an example of what you're guilty of,' Alistair said.

'I've told you.' Mr Watson was impatient. 'I'm guilty of everything.'

The only way he could atone was to become the vehicle of atonement itself. The collective scapegoat. It was a terrifying role to play.

For the rest of the session Mr Watson remained silent, studying his gloves the while.

'What will you do when you leave here?' Alistair asked.

'I shall go home and have supper with my wife,' Mr Watson said. Normal. Benign. But, for some reason, Alistair was not reassured.

'Goodbye,' Mr Watson said. At the door he turned. 'I am truly sorry about your little girl,' he said, and somehow that parting-shot disturbed Alistair most of all.

It was well after seven o'clock but there had been no telephone call. He drove home but he did not turn on his car radio. There would be no news that he didn't already know. When he reached his house he found them all drinking. Drinking and waiting. He poured himself a whisky. Mrs Warner raised her glass. 'It's Doris's birthday today,' she said. 'Let's drink to her.'

Now it was out. And more than out. It was bandied about for all the world as if it were cause for celebration. It was a desperate measure to keep her alive, though Alistair knew that the puff sleeves on that gingham dress had wilted like plucked poppies, that the flounces and frills of the skirt were shamefully deflated like wrinkled balloons.

They raised their glasses.

'To Doris,' they all said.

'There's been some news,' Alistair whispered.

Virginia dropped her glass and the crystal shattered in disbelief.

'The Inspector phoned me this morning,' he said.

They stared at him. They did not want to listen to his news. For days they had managed without information, drowning their ignorance and their impotence in the ether of alcohol.

'I don't want to know.' Mrs Warner had reached for a chair.

'What is it, Alistair?' Virginia said.

He went over to her and put his arm round her shoulder. And he told them. Exactly as the Inspector had spelt it out to him. The lone horse-rider, the reason for the delay, the pink gingham dress, the trees, the Serpentine, the search. He itemised the whole story, careful not to dignify his tale with an adjective or ornament of any kind. He told it bare, for, bare, it was clothed enough.

They received the news in silence, and put their glasses down. Now the hollowness of their toast echoed like a funeral bell.

'They may not find anything,' Mr Warner said helplessly. 'Then we can go back to waiting.'

Waiting had now become a career, almost, and one that would forever postpone promotion.

'He said he would call this evening,' Alistair finished.

'I'll prepare supper,' Mrs Warner said. 'Father, you lay the table and clear up that broken glass.' She wanted everything normal. It was eight o'clock and that, in any civilised household, was supper-time, whatever was happening on the outside.

'When is he going to come?' Virginia asked.

'Sometime this evening.'

She looked at him. 'It's over, Alistair. I know it.'

He took her in his arms in token of his own confirmation.

Mrs Warner insisted that they ate. And between each reluctant mouthful they listened for the front door-bell. When it came, shortly after nine o'clock, it paralysed them. They stared at each other.

'I'll go,' Alistair said after a while, half-longing for the relief of knowing that the ordeal was over. And when he saw the Inspector's face, he knew that the waiting was done.

'We have found her,' the Inspector whispered in the hall. 'Her body was buried under a tree. Such a shallow, hurried grave,' he said sadly. 'But she was not hurt.' He raised his voice. 'She was most definitely not hurt.'

Alistair steadied himself against the wall. Sweat singed his skin. 'I must tell my wife first,' he said. 'Please wait here.'

He went back into the living room. They looked at him and they knew.

'She wasn't hurt,' Alistair said. 'She most positively wasn't hurt.'

Then he fell into the nearest chair, shivering.

Virginia rose, pushing her telephone-chair behind her, as if she would never sit in it again. For the vigil was over. She went and held Alistair's hand, but she could say nothing. None of them was interested in where or how Doris had been found. Doris was dead and unhurt in her dying. That was enough for them. They sat in silence and sobbing for a while. The Inspector's feet were heard shuffling in the hall. Mr Warner went to fetch him inside. He stood at the door of the living room and joined in the silence. Then after a while, 'I'm very very sorry,' he said.

'Would you like a drink, Inspector?' Mr Warner asked.

He shook his head. The drinking was over. Together with the waiting.

'Can we see her?' Virginia asked.

'There are tests to be done, Mrs Crown. We'll bring her home as soon as we can. I promise you,' the Inspector said, and his voice rose in painful protest, 'I promise you on my own daughter's life, that, whoever it was, we will find him.'

'It won't bring her back though,' Mrs Warner said, and though no-one would have voiced it, she was speaking for them all.

'A word with you, Dr Crown, if I may,' the Inspector said.

Alistair followed him into the hall. His gait was that of a drunken man whose balance had been eroded by grief.

'I need you to identify her,' the Inspector whispered. 'Could you come with me now?'

Alistair nodded. 'I'll tell them,' he said. He went back to the room. 'I have to go with the Inspector. Papers to sign,' he invented. 'I won't be long.'

But Mr Warner, who had guessed his errand, asked if he should accompany him. Alistair declined the offer, though he knew that his father-in-law was in a far better position to identify Doris than he himself. For, in truth, Alistair had no notion of what she looked like. But he knew the gingham dress. There must be something left of that. And, more important, he knew Doris' body with a greater accuracy than anyone else on earth. He had explored it often enough and he knew its contours by heart.

'We'll go in my car,' the Inspector said. 'I'll bring you home afterwards.'

Alistair couldn't stop trembling. And he didn't know whether he was trembling at the news of Doris's death or the thought of the ordeal that awaited him. He would be looking at his daughter's five-year-old face for the first time and he knew that, with all his doodling, nothing had prepared him for this encounter. He felt a fraud. What right had he, amongst all of those who

213

had known her and loved her and forgiven those illegal eyes, what right had he to be chosen to name her? All he had done was to love her as an absent father, for only in her invisibility could he envisage paternity. He had not identified her at her birth and he had no right to do so at her death. He would never forgive himself.

The Inspector said nothing during the drive. He dreaded their arrival at the morgue. He had seen Doris's face and it was not pretty. Strangulation is the devil's tool. It uglifies, disfigures, sullies any trace of former beauty. Stranger as he was, he had turned away from the little body with a heaving stomach and an explosive rage. That little face had never left his mind and he saw it now as Alistair trembled by his side, and he broke the long silence of the drive.

'She wasn't interfered with,' he said, as if that were a bonus of a kind.

'Interfered with?' Alistair asked. Was murder not interference enough?

'She was not sexually assaulted.'

'Please stop the car,' Alistair said. 'I have to get out.'

The Inspector pulled up quickly and Alistair rushed to the side of the road. There he threw his heart up. Then sat on the verge, his head on his knee, weeping. The Inspector was at his side. Passers-by assumed that they were witnessing the apprehension of a drunk and they idled to view the outcome. They were surprised by the affectionate arm of the law on the man's shoulder. More surprised when the policeman squatted down beside him and took the man's hand, offering him what seemed words of consolation. Which indeed they were. 'Would you prefer to leave it till tomorrow, Dr Crown?' the Inspector said.

'No.' Alistair made to rise. 'It must be done,' he said. 'Let's do it now.' He breathed deeply for a while. The nausea had gone but he couldn't stop trembling. He felt he would tremble for the rest of his life.

They got back into the car. When they reached the central station, the Inspector drove into the underground car-park. 'This will save a lot of walking. And avoid a lot of people,' he said. 'There's a door that leads straight to the morgue.' He'd often wished there were another word for that terrible place, for that cold ungiving terminus at the sad end of waiting. It was a joke word used by those who had possibly never been inside one. It was an offensive word, the Inspector thought, but he knew that its monosyllabic stolidity rightly translated that death-chamber without echo. He took Alistair's arm. He himself was loath to look at the body again, but he would do so in support, then lead him away from the horror of it all.

They came to a door at the end of the corridor. The Inspector knocked and a soft 'Come in,' was heard from inside. The Inspector led the way, holding on to Alistair's arm. The room was large and empty. A few trestle-tables stood at the sides, scattered with instruments that would find no other purpose except in a place such as this. In the middle of the room was a trolley, covered with a sheet. Alistair faltered but found himself being led towards it. On one side stood a morgue official in a spotlessly white coat. His rimless glasses gave him a sinister look which seemed to befit his trade.

'This is Dr Trude,' the Inspector said.

The man gave Alistair his hand. 'I'm very sorry,' he said. 'This won't take long. All we need is confirmation. So just nod your head.' He put his hand on the sheet. 'Are you ready?' he said softly.

Alistair nodded. The doctor lowered the sheet down the face and held it just short of the neck. He wanted to spare the father the scar of his child's murder. Alistair looked at Doris's face and suddenly stopped trembling. He raised his hand to touch her, and Dr Trude made to cover her once more.

'No,' Alistair said, 'let me look at her for a while.'

He caressed her cheeks, those cheeks that he had so often stroked with his crayon. Then her nose, her lips and her chin, those 'mentionables' of old. And then, with all his love, her eyes, those knowing signposts to her handicap. He bent over and kissed her, tousling her hair with his fingers. He wanted to look at her for ever and never to lose sight of her again and he shuddered with the shame of seeing her not only for the last time but also the first. He saw that the eyes were bruised, the cheeks swollen, and the lips blue. He looked up at the doctor, 'She was beautiful, you know,' he said. Then, 'I want to see the whole of her.' Dr Trude removed the sheet entire. Alistair caressed her feet and re-journeyed inch by inch that territory that he knew so well. Then he noticed her neck and the stain of appalling assault. He held his breath as surely as his little girl had done. But she, with little option, had held it for ever. He looked up at the Inspector, barely seeing him through his blur of tears. 'This is my little girl, Inspector,' he said. Dr Trude recovered the body with the sheet. The Inspector took Alistair's arm. 'Come,' he said. 'We'll get a cup of tea.' Alistair remembered how Sister Thomas had made the same offer after Doris's birth. Her little life was rounded with cups of tea.

'What happened to the pink gingham dress?' Alistair asked.

'It's being cleaned,' the Inspector said. 'When it's ready, she will go home in it.'

So Doris came back to the house as she had left it, so many years of waiting ago, pink-ginghamed, but with puffs deflated and flounces shrunk. Virginia laid her on her bed and sat with her alone for a long time. The phone had begun to ring again, and callers came with flowers and condolences. Virginia had cried herself out.

216

She knew that Doris, once a sorrow, inconsolable, had now become a grief that time would heal.

Mr and Mrs Warner crumpled suddenly into age, bewildered by the unfairness of it all. And Alistair stood aside and trembled.

The funeral was arranged for the end of the week.

Alistair phoned his parents. 'What is it, Son?' his father asked, and in the same breath, 'Mother, pick up the phone. It's Alistair.'

'It's Doris,' Alistair said. 'Her body was found. She'd been strangled.'

And for the first time, hearing his every word, he believed it. His daughter had been kidnapped and murdered.

'Oh,' his mother said, with an 'oh' that lengthened to part-chant, part-prayer, and, all of it, heartbreak. Then his father added a descant of another 'oh' and cadenced it with 'Son'. Then a silence.

'What can we do?' his mother said at last.

'Would you like to come?' he asked. Suddenly he wanted to see them. He wanted their protection, that service that they now seemed ready at last to offer him.

'Mother?' his father said.

'Yes, we'll come. We'll come after the funeral,' she said. 'It's terrible.'

'Terrible, Son,' his father echoed, and with their joint love to Virginia, they signed off the call.

He was glad they would come. He needed their protection, and that they could provide. But he needed forgiveness, too. But he was not sure that such forgiveness lay within any human gift.

# Thirteen

THERE WERE five days until the funeral. Alistair busied himself with all the arrangements. But he still made time to see his patients. He wanted to go to his consulting rooms not so much for their therapy as for his need to augment his portfolio. He brought it out between each patient and added to his archive. Always he started with a circle as in his Doris-days. But now that he had seen Doris, there was no longer any remedial purge in drawing her. He was with trees again, and in meticulous detail, and always he left that treacherous space for the rider on her horse. In one drawing, he gave her a pig-tail. He was sure she had a pig-tail, and he insisted on it in every subsequent portrait. Daily he drew, so that, by the time of the funeral, he had achieved a dossier of memorial. In his last drawing, he noticed that he had left a positive gap between the trees and he wondered what it was for.

Doris was to be buried. For the second time. But this time with ceremony and love. The coffin was strewn with flowers and the hearse bedecked with wreaths. As the family car drove through the cemetery gates, Alistair recalled how, just five years ago, he had purloined a gift from this same holy ground. A gift for that child who now returned to lie in its peace. He shuddered to think that the one might be a consequence of the other.

The area around the little grave was dense with people. As the pall-bearers approached, they made way for the chief mourners. Virginia held on to Alistair's arm. But he felt no pressure. His flesh, like hers, was numb. As he stood by the grave, he sensed a growing feeling of detachment as if he were an onlooker of a spectacle that only marginally had to do with him. In the same category as those others who littered the churchyard, their neighbours, friends, Doris's teachers, a sprinkling of ghouls and press, and the plain-clothes men on the periphery. The Inspector had come in his uniform, leaving the detective work to others. It was a common assumption as part of a murder investigation that the perpetrator of the crime could not resist the final curtain, that he could well be amongst the mourners, posing as a neighbour perhaps, come to pay his detached respects. Alistair shivered and, pressing Virginia's arm, he tried to insinuate himself into family mourning, to become part of that core of sadness. But, though his heart was heavy, he could not help but feel an outsider. He heard the priest's words, but he did not listen. He saw the little coffin lowered, but he did not look. He donated his small shovelful of earth and had a shivering sense of déjà-vu. But without audience. Except for a pig-tailed pony-rider with a sharp eye and a telltale tongue.

The chief mourners were moving away and, though Alistair moved with them, he still felt a spectator. And continued to do so throughout the tea and sandwiches and, later, the wine. And even when they were all gone, and night was falling, and there was no more waiting to be done.

The following day he left early for his consulting rooms. Not for a patient but for his portfolio. He took it out of the drawer and viewed his latest entry. What struck him was the space he had left, that clearing under the trees. It stared at him, an accusing vacuum and he knew that to fill it was an imperative part of his waiting. He took his pencil and started to draw. From its black head drooped Esau, his hairless naked body hanging from a branch of a tree. Alistair did not wonder why he had drawn Esau. The connection was painfully clear. It was that spectacle and the dire rage that it had engendered, the outrageous sense of loss, that had led him to the clearing in the first place. He quickly shut the portfolio. He knew that there were more drawings to come, that he would have to return to his dossier, until the confession was complete. For he could not speak it aloud any more than in the past he could have looked at Doris's face. He had to draw. His crayon was his only means to the truth.

The weeks passed and life returned offensively to normal. Virginia went back to her teaching job, each day making a detour to avoid the site of Doris's abduction. The Inspector kept in touch, visiting occasionally, but he confessed to having no leads. Virginia was indifferent to his helplessness. It no longer mattered to her whether the murderer was found or not. Every day Alistair went to his consulting rooms, and every day he opened his portfolio. But he found it more and more difficult to add to it in any way, and his drawings were but repetitions of each other. One day, he found himself drawing a circle, a circle larger than any he'd drawn before. And that was all. An empty circle, that his crayon refused.

Since Doris's death, he had taken on patients with a vengeance. His indifference to his profession was in no way diluted, and he suspected he was probably a better therapist because of that indifference. It kept his emotions in strict neutral gear. No longer was he tempted to touch a patient with kindness. Esau's death had robbed him of that need. Neither was his heart moved by their pain, for Doris's death had numbed it entire. He knew that, after all that had happened, his life would never change, and that it would run its offensive course until the day he died. He felt close to Virginia, closer than he had ever felt before. But that closeness was a translation of his desperate need for protection. Whether he wanted to or not, he could never leave her again. His parents had not arrived. He sensed that they were not coming, and when, one night, they phoned to say that they would postpone their visit, he was not as disappointed as he had anticipated. His father still cadenced his every sentence with 'Son', and his mother sent her best, whatever that meant, to Virginia. Reconciliations and forgiveness are manageable commodities over telephone wires unthreatened by face-to-face confrontation, but they do not travel well, and it was possible that his parents had decided not to take the risk of encounter.

Virginia was relieved too. She, like Alistair, had gone back to her work with a vengeance, and she wanted nothing in her life that required leisure. Even the occasional visits from the Inspector irritated her for their demands on her social behaviour.

The Inspector, for his part, found himself calling more often than courtesy required. His visits were by way of keeping his hand in the case, for he still had absolutely no clues. Then, one day, his visits stopped, and Virginia surmised that he had better things to do. And indeed, something had come his way, and through no investigation of his own.

Shortly after his last visit to the Crowns, he'd gone to his desk as usual and wearily he had gone through the details of those cases that bore the slightest resemblance to Doris's kidnap. Then the phone call came from the front office. A gentleman wished to see the Inspector on urgent business.

221

'Send him in,' the Inspector said, glad of a diversion.

A policeman knocked on his door and showed the visitor into his office. The Inspector gave his caller the professional once-over. Very well-dressed, elegant almost, and probably well-schooled and spoken. Not by any means a criminal type. Nor an informer. Perhaps an eye-witness of some crime as yet unsolved.

'Sit down,' the Inspector said, slightly rising from his own chair in a faint gesture of respect that he thought his visitor might merit.

'My name is Stephen Watson,' the man said. He was indeed well-spoken. 'I won't keep you very long.'

'What can I do for you?' the Inspector asked.

'I have a confession to make,' he said. 'I have kept it in for over three months and I can keep it to myself no longer.'

'I'm listening,' the Inspector said.

The man took a deep breath and crossed himself. 'On Wednesday, the twenty-third of June, I kidnapped Doris Crown, and I took her to Hyde Park, and there I strangled her.'

The Inspector tried to hide his astonishment. And indeed his joy. For the man did not look like a crank. He was too calm for that. Neither was he compulsive. There was a terrible ring of truth in his words.

'Tell me about it,' the Inspector said. 'Tell me exactly what you did on that day.'

'I have said enough,' the man said. 'You know the details. You know them as well as I.'

'You don't have to say anything,' the Inspector said, 'until, if and when, you are charged, that is. And even then you can remain silent.'

'Which I choose to do in any case,' the man said.

'Perhaps you should contact a lawyer,' the Inspector said.

'I am a lawyer, and have been for many years. I am well-acquainted with the law and the rights it affords me. You know what you have to do, Inspector. I have given you a confession, one that I am prepared to write and sign. Then on the basis of that confession, it is your duty to charge me, and then give me all that rubbish about my rights.'

The Inspector had a moment of doubt. Perhaps, contrary to appearance, he needed a place to sleep?

'May I ask you where you live?' the Inspector said.

'Certainly.' Mr Watson gave an address in Belgravia.

'Have you any proof of that?' The Inspector was almost too ashamed to ask.

Mr Watson felt the inside pocket of his jacket and took out an envelope addressed to his name and the address he had given.

'Do you have a wife?' the Inspector asked.

'Yes, I have a wife. And I will answer no more questions, because they are irrelevant. All I ask is for a piece of official paper on which I may write down my confession and give it my signature.'

The Inspector couldn't make up his mind about this man. There was nothing cranky about him except his desire to be charged forthwith. But he didn't seem frenetic. His manner was calm and measured and he spoke with a certain authority. On the other hand, all the information that he had volunteered had long been in the public domain.

He handed him a printed statement paper. There was no harm in that. 'Do you need any guidance?' he asked. Mr Watson gave a hint of a smile. 'I have handled many of these papers in my time,' he said. 'I understand the procedure.' Which he clearly did, as he filled in all the required data without hesitation. When he had given his name, address, age and profession, he started on his statement. The Inspector watched him carefully. He wrote in a practised hand, in a script just short of illegibility that marked him as a professional. His confession was short and precise and amounted to no more than he had already verbally pronounced. He handed it to the Inspector. It took little time to read.

'I need more than that to charge you,' the Inspector said.

'What more d'you want, Inspector? You have a full confession.'

'Mr Watson,' the Inspector said patiently. 'You know the law as well as I. And probably much more. You are aware that after every murder someone arrives at the station with a confession. All bogus. I don't understand this need of theirs. It's a sickness I suppose. I have to tell you, Mr Watson, you have given me no reason to suppose that you are not one of them.'

Mr Watson smiled again. 'What more do you want from me?' he said.

'I want you to give me details. I want you to tell me things that are not already known through newspapers and television. There are other facts in this case, which only I and a few of my force are privy to. I would like some confirmation of those details from *you*, before I can make a charge. As you may surmise, Mr Watson,' he went on, 'this is a terrible crime, and we are desperate to apprehend the killer. But we are not so desperate that we will arrest just anybody.'

'I have told you all that I am prepared to tell.'

'What holds you back?' the Inspector asked.

'It's too horrible to repeat all that I did.'

There was a sudden silence between them. The Inspector saw tears start in the visitor's eyes, and he watched as he made a manly effort to send them back where they came from. Again the Inspector was disturbed. The man seemed genuine enough. But the police needed more. Much more.

The Inspector thought for a while then made a decision. He picked up the man's statement and put it in his briefcase.

'I'm going to leave you for a while,' he said. 'I want you to think deeply about what you've told me. I won't charge you. I need far greater detail. Here are more sheets,' he said. 'Take your time. I want to know exactly what you did when you got her to the park. My constable will bring you a cup of tea.'

'I'll try,' Mr Watson said. 'But I don't think I have the courage to tell you more.'

'But I need to know,' the Inspector said. 'I shan't be long.'

On his way out, he had a word with his deputy and filled him in briefly. 'Give him tea, coffee. Whatever he wants. But don't let him leave,' the Inspector said. 'I have an errand to do.'

He got into his car and checked on the address. A house off Knightsbridge, an address befitting the accent and the clothes. As he drove, he hummed softly to himself. He thought he might be happy. What he was about to do was possibly beyond the call of duty, and perhaps even outside its legal limits. But it was a chance he had to take. The man's confession rang perilously close to the truth. He checked once more on the address, and soon pulled up outside the house. Georgian, in a crescent of similar style. A carriage-lamp on each side of the door, window-boxes of dazzling colour and a plain pink awning over the porch. It was the sort of threshold on which one wiped one's feet and minded one's manners. He rang the bell. A uniformed maid answered the door.

'I'd like a word with Mrs Watson,' he said.

'Lady Judith Watson,' she corrected him. 'Whom shall I say is calling?'

'Inspector Braithwaite,' he said.

She called him in and motioned that he should wait in the hall. Then she disappeared into the further reaches of the house while he admired the Persian scatter rugs on the marbled floor. Shortly the maid reappeared.

'Lady Judith will see you now,' she said. She led him into the drawing room.

Lady Judith Watson was seated at a small desk. She looked up at the Inspector and smiled. She seemed in no way fazed by his job description. She rose slightly and asked him to sit down.

'I'll stand if you don't mind,' he said. This was not a social call.

'What can I do for you, Inspector?' she said.

'This may come as a shock to you, Lady Judith. I don't want to upset you, for it may be nothing at all. Your husband came to see me this morning.' He watched her carefully and he noticed how she paled.

'Whatever for?' she asked.

'He wanted to make a confession.'

Her pallor deepened and she clutched the edge of her desk with her hand. 'A confession?' she whispered. 'A confession to what?'

'Perhaps I should sit down,' the Inspector said. He took a chair. 'It's quite a long story,' he said.

'I'm listening.' She swivelled her chair away from the desk, but kept her hand there, possibly for support.

He told her briefly about the Doris case. She had read it in the papers, she said. 'A terrible tragedy. Those poor parents.'

'Yes,' he said. Then he gave it to her straight. 'Your husband has confessed to the murder,' he said.

'Oh my God,' Lady Judith said quickly, covering her face with her hands. 'I knew that one day it would come to this,' she said.

The Inspector leaned forward. He could hardly believe what he had heard. Mr Watson had been telling the truth after all.

She rose, 'I must see him. At once.'

'I will take you, Lady Judith,' he said gently. 'But first what did you mean by "I knew one day it would come to this"?'

'It's a long story,' she said. 'I'll tell you in the car.'

'Your husband doesn't know that I have come to see you.' He thought he'd better tell her that. 'It's not the orthodox procedure, but I didn't know whether or not to believe him.'

'I'll get my coat,' she said.

All the poise was gone. She was trembling and the Inspector felt deeply sorry for her. He waited in the hall. Shortly she joined him. She had thrown an agitated coat over her shoulders. 'Shall we go?' she said.

They drove out of the crescent. There was much traffic and the Inspector was glad of it, for the journey would give her time to tell her whole story. He said nothing. He would wait for her to begin. They were idling at the traffic-lights when she said, 'My husband is not very well, you know.'

He didn't interrupt her. He felt she needed no encouragement. The lights turned green, and he inched the car forward. It was her cue to continue.

'He has times of deep depression,' she said, 'and these are followed by periods of violence.'

He had to stop her there. He needed to know the nature of that violence.

'He smashes things,' she said. 'Once he destroyed a whole kitchen. Another time, he attacked me. He's been in hospital, you know. A number of times.'

'Do you have any children?' he asked.

She was silent. Out of the corner of his eye, he watched her. She was wiping away tears. 'We had a son,' she said. 'Eight-years-old. He was killed in a car-crash four years ago. My husband was driving at the time. His illness started shortly afterwards.'

The Inspector felt very uncomfortable. More and more Stephen Watson's confession echoed with the ring of truth. Yet he wasn't happy any more. 'I'm very sorry,' he said. 'You know what it is to lose a child. The greatest of griefs.'

The traffic thinned a little and they were nearing the station.

'Tell me, Lady Judith,' he said, 'do you think your husband is capable of murder?'

She started to cry openly. 'He's been so terribly depressed,' she said.

He drew up at the station. 'He has confessed to it,' he said, 'but I don't know whether or not to believe him. What you have told me leans me towards its credibility. If that is the case, Lady Judith, I want to assure you that there are mitigating circumstances.' Phrases like 'not responsible for his actions', 'unfit to plead', or 'of unsound mind', skidded across his memory, echoing from numerous trials in numerous courts. 'But he won't tell me the whole story. He refuses to give any details of what, if anything, he has done. I need those details Lady Judith, for all our sakes. Perhaps you could talk to him.'

'I'll try,' she said.

He ushered her through the reception area. His deputy nodded as he passed, assuring him that all was in order. 'Would you wait here, Lady Judith?' he said, showing her into an adjacent room. 'I think I'd better tell your husband that you're here.' As he reached the door he turned, 'You have been very co-operative, Lady Judith,' he said. 'I appreciate that very much.' Then he went to his office . . . .

Mr Watson sat in the same position as he had left him. He did not even turn when the Inspector entered. An untouched cup of tea cooled on the desk with a sandwich beside it, still in its cellophane wrapping. In front of him lay empty sheets of paper.

The Inspector sat down facing him. 'Have you decided to tell the whole story?' he asked.

'I want to. I really want to,' Mr Watson said. 'But I cannot do it.'

'I've been to see your wife,' the Inspector said.

'Mr Watson was surprised. 'Was that necessary?' he asked.

'I thought she might persuade you to help me. And to help yourself. I think you need her support at this time. So does she. And she's waiting to see you.'

'Judy? Here?' Mr Watson asked.

The Inspector nodded. 'Shall I bring her in?'

'I'd like to see her,' Mr Watson said.

The Inspector left the room. He would leave them alone for a while, he decided. He showed Lady Judith to his door and went into an adjacent office. He decided he had every reason to be optimistic. So sure was he now of an imminent arrest, that he picked up the phone and dialled Alistair's number.

'Dr Crown?' he said. 'Do you have a moment?'

Alistair was between patients and portfolio-tempted. But he had refrained. He was glad of a call to distract him.

'I'm ringing to let you know of a new development. It may amount to nothing,' the Inspector said. 'But I am hopeful.'

'What's happened?' Alistair asked, glad that the Inspector could not see his trembling.

'A man has volunteered a confession. He does not appear to me to be a crank. I am holding him. His wife is with him at the moment. I may well have news for you shortly.'

'Thank you for being in touch,' Alistair said, and put the phone down quickly in case his voice betrayed him.

The Inspector thought that perhaps it had not been politic to ring Dr Crown at this juncture. But he had made the phone-call less to inform him of the new development than to prove to him he was still very much on the case. For the last time he had visited the Crowns, he had formed a distinct impression that they had lost all confidence in him. He was impatient now to get back to his room, if for nothing else than to justify his phone-call. He would give the Watsons another five minutes, he decided.

Then he heard his name called. He went to the door and saw Lady Judith. 'He is ready for you now,' she said. She held her head high, as if with a sense of achievement. She had broken him. Of that the Inspector was sure. But he did not relish it. Lady Judith had suffered enough in her time. He followed her into his office.

'Your wife tells me you wish to talk,' the Inspector said.

'I can't write it down,' Mr Watson said.

'But you can tell it to me.'

'I'll try.'

'You put Doris into your car and drove to Hyde Park. And then?'

'I parked the car and we walked around a bit. I was looking for a place that was quiet. Where nobody was about. Then I found a place under a tree. I looked around and I saw nobody. The ground was soft and I was glad because it would make burying her easy. You see, I had to do it with my hands. I did not come prepared, you see. But I was wearing gloves. Even though it was hot. I always wear gloves. Isn't that so, my dear?' He looked to his wife for confirmation. She nodded, sadly. His glove-wearing, winter or summer, was his protection against any form of dirt to which he had a manic aversion.

'Go on,' the Inspector said.

'I put her on the ground.' His voice began to tremble. 'And she started to cry. It was a whimper and it did not worry me. But her face became unbearable. She looked as if she had been strangled already.' He paused. 'I couldn't bear her crying,' he went on. 'So I put my hands around her neck, I pressed my thumbs against her larynx. It was all over very quickly. I made sure that she was dead before burying her. Then I dug the soft earth with my hands. She was quite small so she didn't need a lot of space. When I'd finished, I drove away. It was all over in a few minutes.'

It was all over for the Inspector, too. The man was deranged. And violent, perhaps. And, no doubt, entertained murderous thoughts. But he had not killed little Doris Crown.

'Thank you, Mr Watson,' he said. 'You can go now. Take him home, Lady Judith,' he said. 'He is innocent. But he needs help.'

She took her husband's arm. He looked totally deflated. 'I thought I *might* have done it, my dear,' he said.

The Inspector watched them go. His pity for them both took the edge off his frustration. He had had high hopes of Mr Watson. But he was not displeased when they were shattered. Whatever he had needed to confess to, it was not to little Doris's murder. For the Inspector had information that he was keeping very close to his chest. Doris Crown had been strangled from behind.

# Fourteen

W HEN ALISTAIR put the phone down after the Inspector's call, he panicked and quickly reached for his portfolio. He had a sudden recollection of his last entry and he recalled the fear that that vast empty circle had evoked. The Inspector had told him that someone had confessed. Alistair now knew that the time had come, to rid his soul of all its secrets, to leave no gaps under the trees, or by the lake, or in the shadows of the horse's hoofs. And to give the pig-tailed ribbon its real colour, for he could not pretend that he hadn't seen it. No, he must leave no spaces, no hints that there was a single secret untold. He must choose different colours for his anger, his hesitation, horror, scruple, yes, and his love, and finally a colour for his sheer and consummate insanity. Yes, he would tell it all. He could not speak it aloud and certainly he could not tell it to himself, but he could doodle it with a stream of murky consciousness from the end of his crayons.

He did not need a circle. A circle was a cheat. Its orbit was a boundary, a containment. He needed no circumference, no limit, for his sin was boundless, uncircumscribed and without shore. Beyond space, beyond time, it could find no resting-place for atonement. Yes. He would doodle it. His death-doodle, rattling without echo.

He took a clean sheet of paper and started on the trees. But this time without detail. He did not vein the leaves nor crenellate the trunks. He doodled a mere impression of forestry in shades of green and brown.

232

Trees for shelter, shade and concealment. He sketched in a riding path and again without detail, and on it he doodled a horse with its pig-tailed rider. He drew quickly and in growing frenzy as if his hands itched with confession. Next he doodled the lake and, though it was not part of his sin and had never been envisaged as such, it was still part of the landscape of his crime and he had sworn to himself to omit nothing. He baulked at the next stage of the doodle, for the figure he drew under the tree was himself. The back of him. Strictly the back of him. For, even in this full-blooded confession, he could not bear a self-portrait. He was bending down, and at his feet was a hint of pink gingham. Alongside it, as in a strip-cartoon, he doodled its sequel. This time, his figure was half-turned. His courage was getting the better of his shame. And, in the third strip, it triumphed. Himself in full-frontal, masked slightly by the shadow of Esau hanging from a bough of the tree. He knew that the next cartoon was the penultimate one, and he steeled himself back into detail. In front of his crouched figure lay Doris, the gingham dress delineated square by perfect square. His own face was now firmly averted, and Doris's fair hair fell over his lethal fingers. He took her from behind and pressed his fingers deeply into the cavity of the neck, slightly above a mother-of-pearl button that secured the bodice. All these items he drew in the minutest detail, the angry veins of his murderous fingers, the freckled nacre of the mother-of-pearl. And, for pity's sake, he doodled his eyes closed.

For his last cartoon he could not help but draw a circle to circumscribe his own pain. And in that circle, his face averted, he buried her beneath the leaves.

Then he dared to look at the drawing in its entirety. His confession was told. Or rather, doodled. He had omitted nothing. As a last gesture, he drew an orange sun, high in the sky.

And that should have been the end of it, he thought. A confession draws a curtain on an event and gives that event finality. It relegates it to the past in which tense it can be forgotten or accommodated.

Yet, as the weeks passed and turned into months, the memory did not fade. Indeed it intensified, its image more acute, its outline more defined. The final doodle was etched on Alistair's retina, acid-grooved, registered for all eternity. The horror of the park greeted his every waking and elbowed his fitful sleep. But one morning he woke and thought of Christmas, and he trembled with gratitude, until he realised that he was still asleep and that a rogue and pleasant dream had gatecrashed the deserved darkness of his soul. He went about his daily business like an automaton, and in a mood of abject despair. Virginia did her best to comfort him, ascribing his sadness to their common loss. And this deception sickened him even more than the loss itself, for Virginia would never know the core of his guilt-laden grief. Each day in his consulting rooms, he considered opening his doodle-drawer, with intent to destroy his deed in the hope, perhaps, that shredding it would consign the murder to a non-event, a bad recurrent dream, the colours of which would fade together with the screaming. But he had already buried his daughter twice over, and neither burial could erase the face he had never seen. Except, he reminded himself, in the still bewildered rigor of death. So the doodle-drawer remained locked, and sometimes, in his nightmares, he heard the childish whimpering from within. He knew that he was being driven to the brink of madness. He did not fear a breakdown. A breakdown could be ascribed to his loss. Another deception. He would merit people's sympathy, whereas all he deserved was Esau's rope. Sometimes he was tempted to go to the Inspector and tell him the whole story. That way perhaps lay absolution.

234

And absolution was what he needed. A self-confession, which was all his doodling had achieved, would never lead to forgiveness. But the thought of telling the Inspector filled him with terror. He understood that he could never forget what he had done and that there was no point in trying to erase its memory. So he would dwell on it. With utmost concentration. He would go over that terrible day. Over and over again. He would try to understand *why* he had killed his daughter for, in his confused state, he was never sure. He would force himself to fathom his motives. If he could discover the 'why', it would perhaps lead to a self-understanding. Self-forgiveness would be too much to ask. But he would make do with an explanation. That would enable him to lead a life of sorts. Not a good life – he could not expect that – but one in which he could atone and pay his dues.

So, every day, he re-capped on the events that led to the park. It all started with Esau, that askew ray of sunlight that pierced his long-darkened spirit with a promise of friendship and perhaps even love. He dwelt on their early days together, over-dwelt on them in fact, for they were comfortable and full of pleasure. His homecomings, and the greetings in the hall, the sherry and the Schubert. In its time he knew it for happiness, so the joy of hindsight was not misplaced. He thought of Esau's forays, the harmless ones, those that had won approval, and his satisfaction. But he had to think of the dentist, too, and of the dubious masseur. He forced himself to dwell on those and, as he did so, he re-kindled that compassion, so alien to his nature hitherto. Their Paris journey came next, one of mixed recall. He lingered outside Notre Dame, loath to leave, for in hindsight he knew its wretched aftermath. Over and over again in his daily recall, he sat in that hotel dining room, coffee after coffee, waiting for Esau's return. And then the phone-call from the Préfecture. He winced at the shame of what followed. He was loath to enter the gendarme's office, for that was the site of his betrayal.

'He is deeply disturbed, officer.' That phrase echoed in his head, its sub-title, 'My friend's a lunatic. So let him go.' For that's how Esau had read it. Esau had then questioned their friendship. Did it all start with that betrayal? Alistair wondered. Did Esau's rope ravel itself out of that treachery, and did that rope lead to the park? Day after day, Alistair thrashed himself with these questions. He was desperate to find a link, but he suspected that what he really sought was a target for blame. He wanted to believe that he had killed his little girl *because* of Esau. But he knew in his heart that, in the moment of the killing, Esau was an irrelevancy.

Then there was Simon. Simon with his computer-dating service. A man of straw and yellow pages. Alistair recalled Simon's funeral arrangements and the list of duties that he had presented for cold execution. He remembered that he had omitted some of the orders. For he had had other things to do. He recalled his anger then, so sublime, that it propelled him to other business.

It was at this point in his recollections that Alistair called a halt and it was not until many weeks after Doris's death that he could bring himself to go further. To examine minutely what were those 'other things' that he had to do. He took it slowly, step by painful step. He remembered looking at his watch, that day. It was 8.30. He would be in time, but for what purpose he had no idea. He knew he was going to drive to Doris's school. He couldn't remember why. Perhaps he intended to go to the school concert. Perhaps he thought he was ready to look on Doris's face for the first time. He didn't know and he couldn't remember. And he would not try. His total concentration centred on the steering wheel and the occasional change of gear. He recalled arriving at the school and parking outside the railings. He saw the pink gingham dress mercifully facing the wall. And, looking around the playground, he was astonished to find nobody in charge. He was filled with a sudden rage that such children should be left unattended. Why, anybody could just walk into that playground and take his little Doris by the hand and out into the street and into a car and God knows what else! Which was exactly what he intended to do. That he remembered. That intent. But as yet, no purpose.

He dashed across the playground, praying that she would not turn round. Then he scooped her in his one arm and carried her back to his car. Nobody seemed to notice the abduction. And Doris made no sound. She was probably too startled to cry. He'd bundled her into the back of the car and driven off, turning down his driving-mirror as he did so, so that there would be no danger of catching sight of her. And then the sobbing began. And then the screams. He revved the car to drown the noise, but by now they were in the midst of traffic, crawling down Park Lane with early morning lorries on each side. Eventually the screams faded to a defeated whimper.

'Where are we going?' he heard.

'To the park. For a walk,' he said.

'Why?'

'I don't know.' It was the most honest statement he had made in his entire life.

There was a silence then as they idled at the traffic-lights. Then, as they took off once more, Doris whispered, 'Who are you?'

'I'm. . . .' His paternity simmered on his tongue. He did not know what he was going to do to her. He would kiss her or kill her. Either way, she had a right to know who he was. Either way she was young enough to enter heaven and the knowledge of paternity would lighten her path.

'I'm your father,' he said.

She sprang on his back and he was glad that the mirror was turned. He wondered at that magic trust that children placed in their parents and how rarely it was merited and how sorely it was abused.

'Daddy,' she cried, her arms about his neck. Her relief and her joy were unbearable.

I shall kill her, Alistair decided.

He pulled the car into a side street and parked. 'We're going for a walk,' he said.

He took her hand, his face averted. They crossed the road into the park, Doris skipping at his side. They paused at Rotten Row to give way to a woman rider. She had a pony-tail, he noticed, tied with a red ribbon. He did not mind her presence. Witnesses were irrelevant. He was simply going to do what he had to do. It was not a private thing. It required no secrecy. It was as natural as shielding one's eyes from the sun. In fact, he was doing exactly that, for the sun was particularly bright that morning, a cold orange blood-spot in the sky. He knew he had to do it quickly. He had patients waiting, and Simon's commissions to do. He dragged her across the grass to a tree. There were many trees, he noticed, but one would do as well as another. He looked around and saw that the rider had gone. Then he placed Doris in front of himself and put his hands around her throat.

'Is this a game, Daddy?' he heard her say.

'You would have liked Esau,' he said. Then he tightened his grip. It was all over very quickly with hardly a sound. She limped in his grasp. He felt her pulse and it was still. He laid her face-down on the grass and, with his hands, he dug beneath the tree. He remembered feeling strangely calm, elated even, that he had managed the whole procedure without once looking at her. Now it would be easy and all over. Just face-down in the earth. Covered and forgotten. The earth was soft and in a while he had carved out a grave of sorts. He dragged her body to the rim, and ascertained once more that her pulse was still. Then, very carefully, he lifted her into the grave. He thought the back of her head was beautiful. He filled up the hole and gently patted the earth that covered her. Then he went back to the car. He was relieved that there was no parking-ticket on the windscreen, and experienced a small thrill of pleasure in having cheated the Law.

Thus Alistair dwelt on his recall. Over and over again. And still he did not know the 'why' of it. He simply knew that it had to be done. That he never in his life would have been able to look at her and that she had to be put down so that she would not be a problem any more. So that nothing in his life would exist that he couldn't bear to view. It should have been a relief. But his heart curdled in its misery. He recalled that, at times, during the investigations, he had entirely forgotten what he had done, and had awaited news as eagerly and as painfully as the others. In fact, when the Inspector had told him about the park, he had thought it a strangely stupid site for a murder. So public, so open to view. Even now, he waited for the murderer to be found. But there were moments when he knew. Moments of terror and of self-questioning.

'I don't know why I did it,' he said to his desk. 'I simply don't know. Evil does not require a cause, and that's the whole truth of it.'

The file on little Doris Crown was never closed. It was neither forgotten nor remembered. It lay gathering dust in that space between oblivion and recall, where occasionally one is nudged by scruple.

Virginia and Alistair were bound. The past compelled them. Time, given time, is a healer. A healer of grief. Grief is loss, and can eventually, somehow or another, be accommodated. Virginia could share that loss with Alistair. But his was a solitary grief. Unsharable. A grief compounded by guilt, a guilt that would prolong his

239

mourning. Time would never heal it. Neither would confession. Death was the only latitude in which healing no longer mattered.

When, a year's grief later, Virginia found Alistair hanging from a rope in the garage, she put it down to his inconsolability. The Inspector, who'd witnessed such dénouements before, commiserated with her, and for a moment considered that he might justifiably close the file on little Doris Crown.